THE PHENOMENON TRILOGY

Annie Steinbach,

Best wishes!

Chris Raabe

THE PHENOMENON TRILOGY

CHRIS RAABE

LUNKER
PRODUCTIONS

Omaha, NE

Paperback: 978-0-9884740-3-1
Kindle: 978-0-9884740-4-8
ePub: 978-0-9884740-5-5
LCCN: 2013941177

Lunker Productions LLC
PO Box 391251
Omaha, NE 68139

The Phenomenon Trilogy
www.phenomenontrilogy.com

Printed in the USA
10 9 8 7 6 5 4 3 2

This novel is dedicated to
Emma, Reagan, and Olivia.

PROLOGUE

THE COMING STORM

Lightning flashed in the distance as Christian glanced at his cousin and his grandfather. The three fishermen plowed through whitecaps on Lake Albert in South Dakota. The fishing had been great, but the wind picked up now as a storm front moved in from the west. Christian's cousin, Joel, perched on the lid of the live well on one side of the boat, while Christian took his position on an overturned five-gallon bucket on the other. Grandpa manned the twenty-five horsepower Evinrude motor behind them.

They moved to the rear of the sixteen-foot Alumacraft to allow the front of the boat to lift higher into the air. It helped a little with the water in front of them, but as they came down the back side of each wave, the boat collided with the foaming front end of another. The boat bounced forward, tipped high, and then crashed down again. On each forward lurch, all three of them saw the white and orange buoys that marked the bay protecting their boat ramp from the wind. Those buoys would disappear again as the boat bounded up another whitecapped roller. The wind whipped needles of spray into Christian's face as the boat crushed through foaming wave after foaming wave. The end-of-July water warmed him, but the wind chilled Christian as it blew through his water-soaked shirt.

The dock came closer with each downward slap of the boat on the lake, and the clouds grew more ominous. As Christian squinted in the spray, he sensed the coming rain. The temperature dropped sharply and the wind grew stronger. Grandpa hollered over the roar of the engine and the wind, staring past the two boys toward the bay as he bellowed.

"Christian! When we hit the calm water of the bay, you jump up front and get ready to hop onto the dock. Tie us down and sprint to the truck. We'll need to load the boat onto the trailer before the storm strikes."

Christian nodded and looked to the front of the Alumacraft. The rope coiled like a lasso nestled against the trolling motor *battery. He looked at it a second time to make double sure it was securely fastened to the boat.*

Grandpa turned his voice away from Christian and said, "Joel, when he backs that truck into the water, get that cable hooked to the front of the boat as fast as you can!"

Grandpa's steel stare never wavered from the waves. Joel nodded, and the two boys looked at each other and smiled, excitement shimmering in their eyes.

The world changed in an instant when they reached the bay. The foreboding whitecaps calmed as the wind ceased to blow. The protected bay lay between a set of rolling hills and rows of thick trees, mostly pines. The trees formed a horseshoe-shaped windbreak around the bay. Grandpa had referred to it as a shelter belt when the trio arrived at the lake in the early hours of the morning. Christian raced to the front, grabbing the rope as he climbed past the trolling motor mount and crouched like a panther on the bow.

Grandpa slowed a little as he neared the dock, and then the motor shuddered into reverse. Christian timed the leap just right and landed on the front edge of the dock with the rope coil in his hand. He moored the boat like a calf-roper trying to beat a record time before he scurried off the dock up the hill to the truck.

Christian stumbled once before his sea legs adjusted to dry ground. He pulled the keys from his pocket as he reached his grandpa's blue Chevy Silverado. He felt sorry for the owners of the two trailers sitting in the parking stalls adjacent to Grandpa's truck. They were going to have a wild time on the water in the approaching storm.

The engine of the aged Silverado roared to life, and Christian looked out the windshield over the edge of the hill above the belt of trees. Even the lush greenery cowered from the coming storm as decades-old pines near the top of the hill bowed to the winds. The ominous clouds told him that they did not have long. Gravel spit out from the tires as he rounded the curve to the ramp. He backed the trailer in easily, even though he did not have a license to drive. Christian's grandpa always let him drive the farm tractors and the pickup when he came to visit.

As the boat trailer sank into the water, Joel jumped on and pulled the cable from the winch to the front of the boat. The winch whined as the Alumacraft lurched up the rollers. Joel locked the front of the boat into place, and Christian pulled the trailer from the water. Grandpa grabbed the tarp from the back of the pickup, and Joel connected the last bungee cord to the trailer frame just as the rain came. A crack of thunder announced the storm's arrival. All three jerked their heads toward the sky. The wispy white and blue above them had transformed into a roiling mass of charcoal thunderheads.

A blast of wind exploded straight down on them before the deluge hit. The freezing rain showered them with giant drops. Despite his sixty years, Grandpa moved like a cat when the rain hit him. He jumped into the driver's side, while Joel and Christian leapt in on the passenger's side. The windows fogged up as the men panted, trying to catch their breath.

"Wow! Would ya look at that rain!" Grandpa gasped in a farmer's drawl.

Joel reached over to hit the defrost button on the panel by the steering wheel while Grandpa turned on the wipers. The torrential downpour overpowered the low setting, so Grandpa switched the wipers' speed to high. The A/C cranked freezing air into the cab, and the fog on the windshield of the old truck lifted slowly, like a specter disappearing into thin air.

Grandpa gunned the accelerator, and the two boys were jolted back into the seat as he hollered, "Buckle up, boys!"

Christian heard a plink on the roof as he fumbled with the buckle of his seatbelt. That first note was followed by a chorus of many more tinks and plinks. Hail!

Christian recalled his father talking about hail in a severe thunderstorm. Christian would sit out on the porch during severe weather and his father would teach him all kinds of things about storms and how they formed. Christian knew that his father had always wanted to be a storm chaser, but had to work in the summer because their family needed the money. His father explained to him once that hail indicated a possible tornado. It had something to do with a hail core in a storm and the updraft and downdraft mixing into a twister, but Christian didn't recall all the details.

The plinking hail grew in size as a thunderous roar rattled the roof of the pickup. Little white golf balls of ice bounced off the turf like someone pitched them continuously onto the practice green of a golf course.

No one breathed a word as the truck swung out of the parking lot, through the barrage of hailstones and onto the paved road that would take them to the exit of Lake Albert State Park. Here, the road curved gently to the east before realigning to the north again, dissecting a grassy meadow. In a few minutes, they would be turning east and passing through another meadow before crossing the length of the dam of Lake Albert. The once distant black clouds overtook the lake. Sinister darkness surrounded the pickup on all sides, and Christian's grandpa switched on the headlights. They traveled about a mile down the west side of the lake, but still had a ways to go to reach the dam.

The truck raced through the gradual curve leading to a stop sign marking the connection to the exit road. Grandpa Pearson let off the accelerator but turned without coming to a complete stop as they headed toward the dam. The pickup passed through the meadow, and the hail subsided. The truck slowed as they neared a slight curve marking the threshold of the dam. Water crashed onto the rocks outside Christian's window. Since the hail stopped, he rolled the window down for a better look. Even with the A/C cranked up, a rush of cold air waylaid Christian, and he could hear the high-pitched whine of a tornado siren warning them of immediate danger.

"Do you hear that?" Joel asked through chattering teeth as he reached to turn down the fan for the A/C.

"Tornado sirens," Grandpa said calmly. "You boys buckled up tight?"

"Yes," the two teens answered.

The grins in the boat earlier were now replaced with nervous looks at one another.

"Good! Now, whatever happens… you two stay calm," Grandpa ordered. "If you lose your wits, you got nothin' when things go bad."

Christian noticed his grandpa's attention strayed from the road straight ahead of them. His grandfather glanced in the mirror on the driver-side door reached out his window to wipe off the rain water, and then rolled the window back up. Hail rang out a second *chorus on the roof of the pickup as smaller pea-sized hail blanketed the road in front of them.*

"When things go bad?" Christian whispered to himself.

He paused.

"Why isn't Grandpa focusing on the road?" he thought.

He stopped in mid-thought and slowly turned around to look out the back window. Through the hail he could see what had drawn his grandpa's attention from the road. There was at least 1000 feet to go before they were off the top of the dam. They had no escape from the road here because the water flanked the pickup to the right, and a steep drop down the face of the dam to a spillway blocked any attempt to go left. Grandpa could not stop or turn around, because the tail touched down in the field behind them.

Joel turned in his seat to see what Christian was gawking at.

The breath left Joel like a punch in the gut as he whispered, "Tornado."

"It's a tornado," Joel managed to utter a second time, even though terror gripped his body.

"I know," Grandpa said, nervously. "I saw it drop as we turned the corner to the dam, we're going to have to outrun it, if we can."

Christian's grandfather gripped the steering wheel with such force that his whitened knuckles looked as if they were going to crush the wheel or pop his fingers off while trying. His muscles tensed. For a man in his sixties, he still possessed the strength of an ox, and Christian's physique mirrored that of his grandfather's.

Even though only a couple of years separated Christian from his cousin, Joel's light, lanky middle-school frame paled in comparison to Christian's. Both were athletic, but Christian was built for power, while Joel's body was more suited for distance running.

The pickup traveled dangerously fast. The hail stopped, so Christian rolled his window down a second time for a better look at the road. Ice pellets covered the pavement and their options were limited. They had to get to the other side of the dam before they could turn out of the path of the twister. The last time Christian had looked back, the tornado was only about the length of a football field away from them. He turned again, expecting to see the twister losing ground, but the funnel had grown closer and intensified and pickup had lost ground on the slick road.

"Can't this thing go any faster?" Christian yelled over the howling wind.

"Not with that boat hitched on back," Grandpa stated.

Christian's ears popped as the air pressure changed and an indescribable roar consumed the air. The danger no longer lingered behind them. The tornado caught them three-hundred feet from the end of the dam.

When catastrophic events take place in people's lives, they often talk about time standing still or things moving in slow motion. Christian experienced that phenomenon. The wind stole the breath from his lungs, and he struggled for air. Pieces of rock stung his face and arms as he attempted to roll up the window. The truck fishtailed toward the water, and Christian glanced back in horror to see the boat lifting off the road behind them, pulling the truck with it. The deafening roar was pierced with their screams, and Christian distinctly heard someone yell, "Look out!"

He turned toward his door to see an uprooted oak tree slam into the passenger side of the pickup. The metal crunched, and a branch stabbed at the window. A second thump and broken glass and bark covered Christian. The world turned upside down as the truck flipped backward in mid-air. The steel frames of the truck and trailer groaned during the twisting, and the view of black sky out of the windshield morphed into a scene of water and sharp-edged rock.

Christian thought aloud, "This is going to hurt."

He heard Grandpa say, "Hold on, boys!" as the truck landed with a sideways roll into the water.

The whole world went black for a moment. When he came to, Christian found his right arm submerged in water. He pulled his arm from the water and breathed a sigh of relief, because they had missed the rocks which extended at least thirty feet from the shore.

"Everyone all right?" Grandpa asked.

Joel groaned and Christian echoed the sentiment. Water trickled through the door on his grandpa's side of the truck, but water did not rush in through Christian's broken window. The right-side of Christian's body was pressed against his door, and Joel's weight was leaning against him.

Christian stuck his arm through the open window into the water that should have been rushing into the cab of the pickup. He could see only murky black beyond his hand. Christian turned to look past Joel toward his grandfather. He saw flashes of lightning out the driver's window, and he could see the undulation of the waves just above the corner of the windshield on his grandpa's side of the truck.

"Boys, are you okay?" Grandpa questioned.

"I'm okay," Joel winced, "Christian's bleeding."

"Well, I caught some of that glass with my face, but I'm not bleeding too badly," Christian responded. "Why isn't the water rushing in on us?"

"I guess your side must be down and my side up, so we're kind of sittin' in an air bubble," his grandpa replied.

Christian remembered the truck rolling sideways on impact. Fortunately, the open window was down in the water, so the air was trapped in the cab of the pickup. Had they landed the other way, gravity would have won out, and the water would have rushed in on them instantly.

"So are we just floating like a bobber?" Joel asked.

"I would guess the trailer caught on the rocks somehow. We probably aren't far from the shore," Christian answered.

"Hey, can you two get your belts off?" Grandpa asked.

"Yes," Christian and Joel responded simultaneously.

"Let Joel out first. He's skinny enough to fit through that window. I'm going to need you to help me get out of here, since I ain't as young as I used to be, and Joel isn't strong enough to help me by himself," Grandpa said.

Joel unhitched first and wriggled past Christian. After crushing Christian's left shoulder to align himself with the door, Joel slowly slid into the water through the window. He stopped his descent when the water reached his waist. The truck lurched a little bit downward, and they all paused with baited breath. Water swept in on Christian's right side as Joel hung on to his seatbelt.

"It's cold isn't it?" Joel said, before he ducked his head under. His outline swam up across the front of the windshield, and Christian watched as Joel slowly faded into the haze of the storm-churned water. Then Christian unbuckled his seatbelt.

"Now, I don't want to fall when I unbuckle my seatbelt, so I'm gonna try to hang my weight on this steering wheel and keep my balance by using the transmission housing," Grandpa said, referring to the big hump that ran down the middle of the floor of the pickup.

For his age, Grandpa was in good shape, but it would be tough for a man with two bad knees to get out of the truck by himself, so Grandpa would go first. Christian knew that he would be the last one to exit the pickup.

Christian nodded as his grandfather continued, "I'm not sure if I can fit through that window, so try to unlatch the door before you unhook my seatbelt."

Christian tried pushing on the door.

"It barely budged, but if you put your weight on it, I think it'll go," Christian told him.

"Okay, you ready?" his grandfather asked.

"Here goes nothing," Christian responded, hoping the two of them working together would keep Grandpa from falling.

Christian unhitched the seatbelt, and his grandfather did not fall. Grandpa slipped a little as he tried to right himself and Christian grabbed his grandpa's legs in an effort to take some of the weight. Grandpa Pearson lowered his feet, in order to stand on the door without knocking Christian down. The muscles in Grandpa's biceps pulsed from the weight they held up, and Christian hoped the steering wheel would hold.

His grandpa placed his full weight on the door. It popped open a little further almost causing his grandfather to slip and fall. The water came up over their knees as they stood there laughing nervously, relieved that they would be escaping this underwater prison. Lake water continued to trickle through the driver's side door. It reminded Christian of someone leaving a faucet running in an upstairs bathroom of a house until it overflowed and leaked through the ceiling of the room below. Fear held them for a moment, but they knew they were going to be okay.

"I'm going to pop the door open a little wider for us," his grandpa said.

Grandpa Pearson shifted his weight a little too much, and the door swung wide. His grandpa's whole body slipped through the opening and into the water, but he managed to grab hold of the door frame. Christian barely spied him in the growing darkness as he pulled his body even with the truck. His grandpa tapped on the glass of the windshield, giving Christian a thumbs-up, before he pushed off the glass to propel himself toward the surface. Metal groaned, and a popping sound sent chills down Christian's spine.

The force of Grandpa's weight had snapped the only connection between the trailer and the pickup, the ball hitch.

When the pickup entered the water, the upside-down boat caught on a huge, jagged piece of rock. This kept the truck from descending to the bottom of the drop-off in front of the dam. Since they had fished this water only a couple of hours earlier, Christian knew a sixty-foot drop-off started at the edge of the rocks.

When the ball joint snapped, the trailer released its grip from the pickup. The truck rolled to let out the air bubble and Christian fell head-first toward the driver's side of the pickup. He saw the steering wheel, and the world went black as the truck slowly descended to the bottom of Lake Albert.

Christian woke up in complete darkness with a foul taste in his mouth. His eyes were open, but pitch black surrounded him. A floating sensation had hold of his body, and an unexplained shiver shook him. He could hear a dull, distant rumbling sound, but it slowly faded.

"Am I in some dream?" Christian thought.

Another muffled rumble slipped into his ears as images trickled back into his mind. A tree smashed into the side of the truck… glass exploded… the truck flipped through the air. Christian's memory rushed back in a flurry. His grandfather had rocked the truck, while making his escape to the surface, and Christian had fallen. He must have blacked out.

"Where am I now? Am I dead?" he thought.

Was this death? Weightless blackness and cold. He tried to move and realized he floated in an enclosed space. His back and his right arm rubbed against a rough surface that had a cushioning quality to it.

"Is this what a cloud really feels like?" he thought.

The softness cushioned his back but abrasively rubbed the skin raw on his arm as he moved. His head throbbed.

"Can you get headaches when you're dead?" he thought.

He heard the rumble again, and Christian listened more intently, trying to pinpoint its location.

He lay there for what seemed like an eternity, straining to hear the rumble. Up to his right, a yellow glow appeared, but it disappeared in an instant. Christian tried to sit up, and he could, but it was laborious, like some force fought the simple movement. The subtle rumble returned, reclaiming his attention in the quiet stillness that surrounded him. He held his breath, sensing something wrong.

Christian could not tell the exact location, but the rumble came from somewhere above him. A rough-textured wall impeded him to his right, but he could feel nothing to his left, just open space.

"*Where in the world am I?*" he thought.

Confusion clouded his mind.

He reached his arm out straight in front of him and moved it in an arcing sweep to his left.

"*So this is what death feels like,*" he thought.

Christian sighed.

The back side of his left hand bumped something hard.

Christian reacted quickly by jerking his hand back to his body. The force working against him doubled its effort to slow his movements. The faster he tried to move, the greater the force worked to resist him. His heart pounded and his breath raced out of his lungs. His breath came even more rapidly, nearing hyperventilation.

"*Breath? Dead men don't breathe,* " he thought.

He was alive.

Christian reached out a second time to the object he had touched before. With his hand moving cautiously, he located the object with the tips of his fingers. It felt smooth as he ran his hand across it. The small rectangular shape allowed him to clamp his fingers onto it. Holding it, he leaned a little that way.

The unseen object shifted slightly.

Christian jerked back too quickly, thinking he might slip into the abyss below the ledge he sat perched on. The back of his head smacked a hard, flat surface, and he recoiled forward.

Christian grabbed for the object, hoping it would keep him from going over the edge, but he failed to hold onto it. As he fell forward, he stretched his arms out in front of him. His hands smacked something hard and his feet landed on what felt like solid ground just below him. He reached into the darkness and found the steering wheel. Christian realized he was sitting in the middle seat of Grandpa's pickup.

His breathing slowed as he held the steering wheel in his hand. Christian recounted the events in his mind: the race across the dam, the truck flipping and twisting into the water, the air pocket allowing his grandpa and Joel to escape. His grandpa jolted the truck as he made his escape and that jolt shook the pickup enough to dislodge the truck and send it to the bottom of the lake. Christian came to the conclusion that he was sitting on the bottom of Lake Albert, but he was breathing like he was on the surface.

"How is that possible?" he thought.

The rumble returned again, and Christian remembered the broken window. He moved toward it, finding that the door stood wide open now. As he leaned out, he looked up to see a yellow glow flash across his view again. A few seconds later, the low rumble followed. Thunder followed lightning.

He knew the bottom of the lake reached a depth of sixty feet along the face of the dam, almost the same distance from the pitcher's rubber to home plate on a regulation baseball field. It really was not that far of a swim from the truck to the surface, but the blind swim through the murk worried him. Christian waited for another flash before he hesitantly pushed off from the truck and began the ascent to the surface.

As he propelled himself upward, the yellow glow of the lightning grew into a brighter intensity and the rumble of thunder became stronger. As he neared the surface, another flash filled the sky. The light brought detail to the rippling waves and he broke through to the open air and a symphony of low rumbles.

Flashing red and white lights swept the landscape in front of him and distant voices shouted. The faint crackles of static over CB radios croaked like bullfrogs from the road across the dam. Nighttime had descended on Lake Albert.

"How long have I been down there?" he thought.

Christian decided he needed to find out how long he was missing before swimming directly to shore to questions about where he had been and what happened. He could breathe under water, but he did not plan to tell that to the authorities. Christian cheated death, and he had no idea how or why.

Instead of swimming straight ahead toward the flashing lights of what looked to be a South Dakota State Trooper's car, Christian swam parallel to the shoreline. The road exited the dam by way of a T-intersection. A right turn took a driver over a bridge across the water of an inlet Christian fished that morning. A left turn took the driver away from Lake Albert. The bridge offered Christian a safe hiding place to gather his thoughts and decide what to do next.

He could see the outline of the bridge extending across the lake, and he set his course for the first column rising from the water. Two hundred feet lay between him and his hiding spot. When Christian remembered he could breathe under the water, he tried to increase his speed and stay hidden as he swam without coming up for air. Somehow, Christian had the ability to pull oxygen from the water, but the odd sensation of breathing water and the taste of lake in his mouth forced him to swim on the surface. This strange ability was going to take some getting used to.

As Christian neared the columns of concrete supporting the structure of the bridge, he slowed his pace and treaded water until he found the slope of the rocks on the bottom with his feet. Being careful not to injure himself on the jagged edges, he waded the rest of the way to shore. A car thundered onto the bridge above him as he collapsed onto the rocks. He started talking through things to himself.

"Okay, I should be dead, but I'm not. How long was I down there?" Christian whispered to himself.

His waterlogged watch was no help at all.

"It was six o'clock when we came off the water," Christian said, talking through things aloud. "The sun doesn't completely set until after nine o'clock this time of year. That's at least three hours, and we aren't anywhere near sunset. I could have been down there for at least four hours or more."

The thunderstorms moved off to the east and thousands of stars sparkled in the clearing sky. In the distance, he could hear the outboard motor of a good-sized boat. The water of the lake calmed to minor undulations of the surface. A spotlight appeared as a boat moved off shore, scanning the water with a powerful beam.

"They're looking for me," he said in a whisper. "I can't tell them I spent four plus hours on the bottom of Lake Albert breathing underwater like a fish. They'll lock me up and send me off to some institution, or they'll turn me into some science experiment, a bunch of guys in white lab coats dissecting the strange fish-boy."

Christian worried about Grandpa and Joel. They made it out of the truck, but had they made it to shore? What if they were sitting on the shore thinking Christian was dead?

Christian cried, and it was not the watery-eyed, slow crying like when a sad movie touches a boy, and he holds it in because he doesn't want his girlfriend to see it affecting him.

Christian bawled.

He cheated death, but his body had turned into some scientific oddity in order to survive. He needed to come up with an explanation for being in the water so long. He was not going to enter his freshman year of high school as the new freak show in town. He shuddered as another car rocked the footings of the bridge.

Then, Christian had an idea.

Calmly, he rose to his feet and felt his way from the darkness of the bridge. Once he escaped the shadows, the moon illuminated the rocks of the shore, so he moved more easily across the uneven shoreline. He crawled up the steep slope toward the road and scrambled the last ten feet on all fours. Jagged rock nipped at his hands. Finally, he found solid footing on the asphalt of the road and walked a short distance. Then he took a deep breath before turning up the road toward the flashing lights on the dam.

"Well, here goes," Christian said to himself.

The boat swept the water with its spotlight, but it scanned farther out from shore than before. The state trooper vehicle he saw earlier sat cockeyed in the roadway. The driver's door stood open and the radio inside the cruiser hissed.

A voice coughed out from the static, "We have found the boat, but no one is on board. I repeat. No one is on board the vessel."

Another hiss of static scratched the air.

"Any visual on bodies?" a man answered.

A click and white noise followed.

"No, we haven't seen any sign of those two, Jim."

"Keep sweeping," the voice responded.

As Christian listened to the voices on the radio, he wondered if the two missing people were Joel and his grandfather. He assumed they were okay, because they escaped the truck, but he remembered when they escaped that a storm still swirled above the water. The searchboat floated half way across the lake from where Christian stood on the dam, and its search light continued to scan the water.

Static clicked again a while later, and a voice said morosely, "Jim, we found them."

"What is their condition?" a stern voice responded.

"Jim, they're both dead."

"Damn!" came the reply, followed by more static and clicks. "Collect the bodies and meet us at the boat dock. We'll have the coroner's office send a truck."

"Will do, Jim. Hey, anyone found the kid?"

"No, but it's been six hours now, so it doesn't look good."

"How is his grandpa taking it?"

Those words exploded in Christian's ears. Grandpa Pearson had survived, and Christian took off on a sprint from the cruiser and hollered for his grandpa into the flashing lights. He searched for anyone with a uniform who could give him more information.

"Grandpa! Where are you? Grandpa!" Christian shouted as he raced past another state trooper's car.

A man stood next to a South Dakota Game, Fish, and Parks truck with a CB in his hand.

Christian ran to him and shouted, "My grandpa, where is he?"

Bewildered, the man asked with unbelieving eyes, "Are *you* Christian Pearson?"

"Yes!" Christian shouted, "Yes! Where is my grandpa?"

The man wore a South Dakota State Trooper uniform. He stared down at Christian, his mouth gaping as he lifted his left arm and pointed to an ambulance down the road.

As Christian raced around the truck, he could hear the man speaking into the radio, "Tommy, you can call off the search. The boy is up here on the dam."

Christian did not hear Tommy's response. He raced past another state trooper, closing the distance to the ambulance with each stride. The back door of the emergency vehicle stood open. Christian skidded, breaking down and lowering his center of gravity to keep from falling. Grabbing the door, he excitedly hollered for his grandpa, but the ambulance was empty.

"Is that you, Christian?" a voice trembled from behind the other door.

Christian darted around to the other side and smashed into Grandpa. No give came from his grandfather's end of the collision, and Christian crumpled into Grandpa's huge hug. His grandfather squeezed him so tightly that Christian thought his own head might pop off. A boy appeared from behind Grandpa Pearson.

Christian recognized Joel's big, toothy grin once he got his head free from Grandpa's bear hug. Joel's brown hair stuck up from a bandage that was wrapped around his head. His dark brown eyes flickered, when he realized Christian noticed his new headwear. Grandpa Pearson let go of Christian and stared. His grandfather must have had a dozen questions running through his mind, but he did not say a single word. He just looked at Christian in what appeared to be disbelief, his eyes watering with tears.

"It's me, Grandpa. I'm okay," Christian reassured his grandfather, hugging him again. "I'm glad you two are okay, but what's with the headband?" Christian pointed to Joel as he let go of Grandpa a second time.

His grandpa continued to stare, and Christian felt a little uneasy as the old man scrutinized him with an eerie gaze.

"I took some shrapnel when I got out of that pickup," Joel said, running his hand across the right side of the bandage. "The chicks are gonna totally dig it. It was a real mess when I got to the surface. I was clinging to the boat, watching that twister move away from me to the east, when a bolt of lightning hit that bridge over there and I thought the worst place to be was clinging to a metal boat. I made a dash for the shore, but I didn't look where I was swimmin'. I swam head first into a big log that was partially under the water. Grandpa came up just as I hit that thing. He grabbed me and pulled me to shore. It turned out that the water I was going to swim through was only four feet deep, so I head butted that log for the fun of it, I guess. I think I'll leave that part out when the girls ask me. I'll have to make up a better story. Should I tell them I saved you, Grandpa?"

Joel turned toward Grandpa Pearson, who continued to stare at Christian. Grandpa's deep, blue-green eyes were penetrating and intense, and he gripped Christian's wrist, like he did not want to let go.

"I'm okay," Christian said, reassuringly, as he pulled his wrist free from his grandfather's tight hold. Christian felt a little woozy from all the excitement, but the dizzy spell quickly faded.

Grandpa Pearson's eyes dulled as a look of concern swept over his weathered face.

"Are you all right, Grandpa?" Christian asked.

"Boy, are we glad to see you," his grandpa responded, breaking into a warm smile. "When I broke the surface, Joel was tangled up in that tree. I found my footing and pulled him away from it. He was bleedin' like a stuck hog. Shoot, I pulled him to shore and turned to wait for you. I figured you came up on the other side of the boat, which was upside down with the trailer wheels sticking out of the water. It caught on a big boulder. I waded out to it and hollered for you, but you didn't answer."

Joel joined the story, "When I heard Grandpa yell for you, I waded back out into the water, too. When the ledge got too deep, I swam to the front of the trailer, but the truck was gone. It just disappeared."

His grandpa continued the story, "We figured the ball had worked itself loose from the truck."

"I can see underwater, so I swam down five or ten feet," Joel said, "but in that dirty water, with little daylight to help, I couldn't see how far down it went. Grandpa kept yelling your name, but you never popped your head above water. What happened to you?"

A serious look replaced Joel's grin, consuming his face as he relived those moments. Christian failed to keep eye contact with Joel. Averting the question, Christian turned toward the water, trying to gain his composure as his head swirled.

"Son," an unfamiliar voice said from behind Christian, startling him.

An intimidating man with chiseled features strode past Grandpa Pearson.

"I am Sergeant Jim Thompson of the South Dakota Highway Patrol. You have had quite a night. Let's get you checked out."

"I'm fine," Christian said. "I'm just a little tired."

"You may not realize this," the trooper said, "but you have quite a bruise on your forehead, and that hand of yours needs to be tended to."

Christian looked at his left hand and used his finger to trace a gash across the back of it. He had not noticed the bleeding in the water and darkness. The cut went from the base of his thumb diagonally to the base of his little finger on the backside of his hand, but it didn't look deep. The wound oozed a little blood as he pushed on it.

"Okay," Christian responded.

"Donna, come take a look at his hand," Jim said.

"So, what happened?" Joel asked.

Christian's eyes caught his grandpa's gaze, and Christian did not answer Joel.

A woman in a paramedic uniform grabbed his hand to inspect it carefully. She pushed on a couple spots and asked him if it hurt. Christian shook his head even though his hand throbbed with each poke and tug. He continued to look into Grandpa's eyes, compelled to keep the visual contact with his grandfather.

"Nothing appears to be broken. Let's go to the back of the ambulance and take a better look at that cut," she said. "The light is better over there."

"Don't forget to check that bruise on his head," Joel said. "He already has brain damage, so you probably don't have to worry about that."

Donna led Christian around the door. He felt Grandpa's swirling pools of blue-green searching for answers until he passed behind the vehicle and out of his grandfather's line of vision. The paramedic wiped up the blood with gauze and took another look.

"Let's bandage it tight and have someone take a look at it in Brookings," she stated.

"Is it going to need stitches?" Christian asked.

He was used to getting stitches. He cracked his head on more things in his almost fifteen years of existence than most people do in a lifetime. Three headboards, concrete twice, and a baseball bat in third grade all required a little knitting to be done on his head. That did not include a box cutter to his left thumb last year and the collision with the mailbox while doing some trick on his bicycle two summers ago. Yeah, Christian knew the drill when it came to stitches.

"Are you playing any sports right now?" Donna asked.

"Nope, but football practice starts next week," Christian replied.

"My recommendation would be stitches, but they'll make the call in Brookings at the hospital," she said. "Now, what do you think smacked you in the head hard enough to get that bruise?"

Christian moved both hands to his forehead, which throbbed a little bit with the reminder. He sat on the edge of the ambulance staring at the ground and wondered if the truth was the best answer.

"The steering wheel," he answered her, hesitantly, as he looked up.

Christian's eyes met his grandpa's stare again, but this time the lack of light made them look softer, calming Christian's anxiety.

"I fell in the truck and smashed my head into the steering wheel," Christian explained.

"You're lucky that didn't knock you out," she replied.

Christian nodded, and his grandfather appeared to wince at her words.

"If you only knew," Christian thought.

"I am glad to see you are okay," Jim Thompson interrupted.

Christian got a better look at the state trooper, whose chiseled features were enhanced without the shadows that obscured Mr. Thompson's face when Christian first met him. The officer's skin was worn from years of service. Hundreds of indentations riddled his rough textured face, and beady black eyes peered at Christian from behind bushy eyebrows. Officer Thompson resembled an eagle standing over its prey.

"Can you tell me what happened?" the officer asked.

An awkward silence hung in the night air as Christian tried to remember his explanation.

"No, I can't," Christian said awkwardly.

"You mean to tell me that you go missing for six hours after the truck you're in goes to the bottom of the lake, and you aren't going to tell me what happened?" Jim Thompson said sharply, agitated by Christian's answer.

Yellowed teeth from years of smoking protruded in irregular angles from the state trooper's gums.

"Maybe, he means he can't remember what happened," Grandpa Pearson stated coldly.

Christian looked from the trooper to his grandpa and then back to the trooper.

"Yeah, I can't remember," Christian said. "I was climbing out of the truck and swimming through the water. I remember getting to the surface. Then the next thing I know, I woke up on the shore by that bridge."

Christian pointed to the bridge he hid under after coming out of the water.

"Donna, you may want to have him checked for a concussion in Brookings," the trooper said.

"Let's get him to the hospital," Grandpa stated. "Joel, why don't you ride up front? Can I sit in back with him?"

"You sure can," Donna answered.

Joel climbed up front and Christian helped his grandpa into the back of the ambulance. Donna climbed in and someone shut the door behind her. Christian and Grandpa heard Joel ask the driver to turn on the sirens for him. The driver must have shook his head or told him "no" because they heard Joel pleading with him. Joel just turned thirteen, almost two years younger than Christian, and he still acted like a kid at times.

"I'll bet you a million dollars Joel gets him to turn on that siren before we get to Brookings," Grandpa Pearson said with a grin.

Christian smiled back.

"How far is Brookings?" Christian asked Donna.

"About thirty-five miles," she replied.

"I bet you a million dollars Joel gets him to turn it on before we leave the dam," Christian countered.

They felt the ambulance back up and turn around. Christian looked out the back window to see the open door of the first cruiser he came across after leaving the hiding place under the bridge. The siren wailed for a split second and Christian smiled.

"I guess your Grandpa owes you a million dollars, Christian," Donna said with a laugh, her voice reminding him of the nurse at his old school in Omaha.

"Double or nothing, he gets him to run that siren longer before we get to Brookings," Christian said.

His grandfather did not answer. He had his hands wrapped around Christian's bandaged hand, and Christian looked up into the cool pools below Grandpa's corn seed cap. A silver tear ran down his grandfather's cheek.

"You really have had a rough night," his grandpa said.

"Yeah," Christian said groggily, as his body relaxed for the first time all evening.

"I sure am glad you had that guardian angel lookin' out for you," Grandpa Pearson said.

"Grandpa, you wouldn't believe the kind of night I've had," Christian responded.

"It sure is a good thing you can't remember," Grandpa said with a smile.

But Christian could remember, and he wanted to tell his grandfather everything. Christian knew exactly what happened, and he wanted to share his secret. It killed him to keep it pent up inside, but he knew this secret was going to have to stay hidden for a long time, maybe forever.

The siren on the ambulance cycled through one time.

"I guess I owe you two million dollars now," Grandpa chuckled, letting go of Christian's hand.

"Joel sure can be a pest," Christian commented affectionately as he attempted to stifle a yawn.

The three sat in silence for a while. On occasion, part of the conversation drifted from the front of the rig, or the siren wailed for a couple of seconds. Christian switched seats with Grandpa, so his grandfather would be more comfortable, and soon, Grandpa dozed on the stretcher. Grandpa Pearson seemed so much younger when he slept. The hard lines from years of working the land relaxed, and his round nose snorted a bit, as his mouth opened slightly. Christian's grandma used to tease his grandpa about all the flies he caught while he slept. She used to joke about how many fewer flies buzzed in the farmhouse after Grandpa took a nap. Christian decided he needed to make sure he called his grandmother when they got to Brookings, since she was probably worried that they had not arrived home yet.

Grandpa Pearson decided to take Joel and Christian on a fishing trip a few weeks before school started. The two boys were both old enough, so Grandma and Christian's father did not have to come with them this time. His dad couldn't take a trip anyway, with his new job in Red Oak, and Grandma Pearson did not want to bother them during what she called, "Male Bonding Time."

For three days, they had a blast. Joel caught his first Northern Pike on day one. On day two, Christian caught a twenty-pound carp. Grandpa kidded about how hard it was to catch Walleyes, when his grandsons kept catching Northern and Carp. Joel and Christian always fired back with, "Huh, whadya say?" Their grandpa needed a hearing aid, and they were relentless in letting him know about it. The trip ended on a sour note, but at least they were all okay.

The ambulance pulled into the hospital in Brookings, and Christian shook Grandpa to wake him up.

"Have you called Grandma?" Christian asked.

"Nope," Grandpa Pearson replied groggily.

"Make sure you call Grandma when we get inside," he told his grandpa. "Grandma would be pretty upset if you didn't call her right away about tonight's excitement. My cell phone was in the pickup, so you'll have to use a phone here."

Christian wished he had not brought the cell phone with him on the trip, since there was no service at Lake Albert, anyway. He had no idea if his parents would ever get him a new one.

"Whadya say?" Grandpa answered with half open eyelids.

Christian smiled and repeated it louder and much slower, "Call Grandma to let her know we'll be a little late. Tell her we're okay, but we won't be home tonight as planned. She's going to be expecting us to arrive at the farm, but we need to tell her we won't make it until at least tomorrow."

"Why tomorrow?" his grandfather asked.

"Because we won't be able to walk all the way there tonight," Joel piped from the cab.

"Are you still with us, Joe?" Grandpa said.

Whenever Grandpa Pearson wanted to tease Joel, he called him "Joe."

"Huh, whadya say?" Joel responded with his best farmer's drawl impersonation of Grandpa.

All three were in pretty good spirits, considering they had no vehicle to drive home and Grandpa's boat and trailer were totaled. At least they were all in one piece. As they climbed out of the back of the ambulance, Joel came alongside and they walked through the doors marked "Emergency."

"We'll have to rent a car in the morning," Grandpa said.

When Christian's head hit the pillow at the Super 8 Motel in Brookings, South Dakota, he was beat. The red numbers on the digital clock were blinking "12:00."

"I guess it's still midnight," Joel joked in reference to the clock's time.

"Who cares?" Christian said groggily.

They all slept in the same clothes, since their clean ones accompanied Christian's cell phone to the bottom of Lake Albert. Even though they mostly dried out, the aromas of lake water and body odor filled the room, but they had no concern about showering. The soft bed enticed Christian to stay put, regardless of how badly he smelled. He was exhausted, but the events of the evening replayed in his mind as he tried to fall asleep. He tossed and turned while reliving every moment. It was only when he remembered the image of his grandfather's blue-green eyes that Christian's mind relaxed, and he calmly drifted off to sleep.

CHAPTER 3

Christian climbed out of the car and headed to the front door of his house. His muscles ached because two-a-day football practices had taken a toll on him. He could take the conditioning, and he enjoyed the contact, but breathing the humid August air made exercising more difficult.

"Don't forget to check the mail on the way in," his mother hollered as she pulled the car around to the back of the house.

The Pearson's new home in Red Oak differed from any house Christian had ever seen. Of course, his life spanned only fourteen-and-a-half years. The ranch-style house looked small from the front and appeared to have no garage. A narrow one-lane driveway of concrete ran from the street to the back door alongside the north side of the house, where it seemed to end in the back yard. Actually, it curved sharply to the right, past the backdoor, angling downward to a level slab that was twenty feet wide and fifty feet long. A three-foot high brick retaining wall boxed in this lower portion of the driveway on the south and east sides. On the west side, a two car garage rested beneath the house. Parking the cars was like doing a giant U-turn around the back porch to get into the garage. A basketball backboard with a slightly bent rim towered atop the south wall and a row of hedges stood tall behind the hoop, keeping the basketball from traveling into the neighbor's yard. Christian had drawn a three-point line all the way around the basketball hoop on the first day in the new house.

In the front, two massive oak trees stood as sentries to the sidewalk that ran up the middle of the yard, and a little black mailbox hung nailed to the wood siding below the house number. Christian marveled at the oddity of a street with no mailboxes on the edges of the yards, which was the opposite of the suburban neighborhood where he used to live. Every house in Red Oak had the mailboxes in the same location: right next to the front door.

The lid creaked open and Christian pulled out a stack of mail. Every piece of mail except one had yellow forwarding address labels reminding his family to notify the sender of their new address at 500 Highland Street in Red Oak, Iowa, and not 15318 Wycliffe Drive in Omaha, Nebraska. Christian pulled out the one with the new address on it that Grandpa and Grandma sent.

The name on the envelope said "Christian," so he opened it.

Dear Christian,
Thank you for taking good care of Grandpa on the trip to South Dakota. From what he tells me, you had quite an experience. You know how I love to send you clippings. Well, I clipped this article from the paper in Brookings. I thought you might want to read it.
In Christ,
Grandma

His grandma always sent clippings from the newspaper when any of her grandchildren made news. In fact, she typed up stories of their successes on the field or in school and sent them to the paper in Wisner, Nebraska. Christian guessed a small town did not have much news, so they took what they could get, even if it was from a biased grandparent. Christian pitched his first no hitter in seventh grade, and that made the newspaper in Wisner. His cousin, Amy, won a Most Valuable Player award for a volleyball tournament in Chariton, Iowa, and that was published as well. In fact, almost every grandchild in the family proudly received recognition in the Wisner paper. This time, Christian did not want to be reminded of the event three plus weeks ago, but he reluctantly unfolded the article. At the top was a picture of Grandpa Pearson's boat lying upside down with the trailer wheels sticking in the air. The title and the article appeared under the picture.

Tornado Claims Two Lives, Sparing Nebraska Man and His Family
Lake Albert, SD
Mother Nature took two lives and gave a Nebraska man and his two grandsons a wild outdoor adventure on the night of July 31, 2009. The three fishermen were on a three-day trip on Lake Albert, which lies ten miles north of Arlington, South Dakota. After a

successful day on the lake catching walleye, the trio attempted to get off the water before severe weather hit.

Jim Thompson of the South Dakota State Patrol was the first responder to the lake after a tornado touched down on the southwest side of the Lake Albert Recreation Area. Thompson contacted South Dakota Game, Fish, and Parks officers and paramedics from Brookings.

"We are very fortunate that only two people were killed tonight," stated Thompson. "The way that storm popped up out of nowhere, the numbers could have been much higher."

The Fujita Scale is a system used to measure the intensity of tornadoes. This scale scores tornadoes from F0 (little damage) to F5 (catastrophic damage to buildings). John Kisner of the National Weather Service estimated the twister to be in the F3 to F4 range on the Fujita Scale. "Reports of destroyed outbuildings and vehicles blown off the road mean this tornado was pretty strong. Until we can get to the affected areas, we are only speculating at this time," said Kisner.

A Nebraska man and his two grandsons experienced the full force of the tornado. While driving east across the dam, their pickup was thrown from the roadway and into the water. The three were treated for minor injuries at the hospital in Brookings and released.

"Those three are extremely fortunate to be walking among the living," said Thomas Brooks of the South Dakota Game, Fish and Parks. "When I arrived, one grandson was still missing. We searched the water for hours before he crawled out from underneath a bridge. The truck they were driving is about 60 feet down in the water. They were lucky to survive."

The names of the Nebraska man and his grandsons have not been released.

Charlie Townsend and Buck Stone rode out the storm on the north side of the lake. The two men from Castlewood realized they were not going to make it to the dock in time. They pulled the boat to shore in a little bay and waited the storm out in a ditch.

"Those thunderheads built quickly," said Stone. "We knew we weren't going to make it in, so we watched the fireworks from shore. We tied up to a tree and found cover. That wind almost yanked that tree up by the roots."

As of last night, officials had not released the names of the two men who drowned, when their boat capsized during the storm. Damage to state property at the lake included a dock and cabins in the Eastridge Campground.

Christian folded up the paper and put it back in the envelope. The screen door slammed behind him as he walked into the house. To the right, two carpeted steps led up to three bedrooms. One belonged to his parents and the other two were his sisters'. The first door up the stairs led to his sisters' bathroom, while another bathroom adjoined the master bedroom for his mom and dad. Christian tried not to venture into this upstairs portion of the house too often, but he had to share the bathroom with his sisters. It was the closest one to his room, which happened to be on the opposite side of the house and in the basement.

To get to his bedroom from the front door, Christian walked through the living room, the dining room, and the kitchen. He took a right turn before reaching the back door. The stairs were pretty narrow, so he ducked on the last three steps to avoid hitting his head. He averaged about four headaches a day due to the low clearance, either on the way up from his room or on the way down. His bedroom took up about half of the basement, and the only downside to his room, besides the low ceiling at the entrance, revolved around the high volume of traffic that passed through it. To get to the laundry room, storage area, or garage, his family walked through his basement home, making privacy an everyday issue.

On the flip side, he did have the biggest bedroom in the house. Ugly, dark wood paneling covered every wall. The wood paneling was removed from an eight-foot section where Christian and his father built some closets when they first moved into the house. These closets were painted white, which helped brighten up an extremely dreary bedroom.

"Don't get too comfy," his father called from the kitchen. "We need to go over and help the Matthews move into their new house today."

Christian groaned.

Like Christian, the Red Oak Community School District was going through huge changes. The district hired four new school administrators for the upcoming school year. Robert Matthews was hired as the new athletic director at the high school. His son, Brad, was in the same boat as Christian this school year, since they each had fathers who were new administrators in Red Oak. At least Brad would only bump into his dad at athletic events. Christian's father, on the other hand, was the new principal in the same building where Brad and Christian were to attend school. Red Oak did things a little backwards. Instead of freshmen going to the high school, like any *normal* school district, ninth grade was held in the junior high. The high school contained only sophomores, juniors, and seniors.

This meant that Christian's dad would keep tabs on the boys while they were in class, and Mr. Matthews would be there when they went to football practice. Christian only had to deal with his dad in the same building for one year. Next year, Brad would start a three-year sentence with his father at the high school.

"Let me change clothes," Christian said from his bedroom.

"Mom made you a sandwich," his dad said. "Why don't you eat it on the way up to the Matthews'splace?"

Christian threw on an old baseball shirt, slid into a clean pair of shorts, and grabbed a baseball hat. He smashed his head on the ceiling as he walked up the stairs. Rubbing his head with one hand, he grabbed the sandwich off the plate on the counter and headed out the back door.

"You have to remember to duck," his mother reminded him as the screen door slammed behind him.

"Thanks for the sandwich, Mom," he called as he walked up the driveway to the street. He massaged the sore spot atop his head before pulling the ball cap down tight.

"Thanks for helping the Matthews," she said from the kitchen window that peeked out from above the driveway running alongside the house. "I'll see you over there in a while."

His father waited in the front yard next to one of the big oak trees. On the day the Pearsons moved in, Christian tried to put his arms around the rotund trunk of the oak. His youngest sister, Kat, even pulled on each of his arms to help him reach, but the tree's girth proved to be too much.

"We are going to need to cut down a couple of dead branches before winter," Christian's father commented, looking up into the expanse of the foliage.

"Add that to the list," Christian responded.

Moving into a new house excited Christian, but it created a lot of work for him, too. Christian and his dad already built closets for the basement bedroom, and a toilet sat in the laundry room, wrapped in plastic, waiting for Christian and his father to complete the plumbing in the non-bedroom half of the basement. The toilet would give Christian his own bathroom. In addition, the screen door on the front of the house needed to be replaced, while the deck on the back of the house needed to be covered with a clear coat of weatherproof sealant. Other small repairs required attention, but today, they would not get to them.

Christian and his father walked up Highland Street to Corning Street. The hot August wind rattled the leaves of the oaks and maples that lined the street. When they turned the corner, Christian saw the white and orange of a U-haul sitting on the slope of the narrow brick driveway that ran along the right side of a light green, two-story home. The Victorian structure sat much higher than the street, and a huge screened-in porch covered the entire expanse of the front of the house. Mr. Matthews stood next to the truck, leaning with his back against the hood. He waved when he saw Christian and his father. Since Brad Matthews was in the same grade and also out for football, Christian had already been introduced to Mr. Matthews. In fact, Mr. Matthews was one of the few people in town who Christian knew.

Mr. Matthews insisted that Christian call him Bob.

"Unless you are up at the high school," Christian's father added when Mr. Matthews first told Christian that they were on a first-name basis.

"Nonsense," Mr. Matthews replied, but Christian had always been brought up to address adults as Mister or Miss.

Mr. Matthews was a slender man with a full beard of black that was well kempt. He smiled ear to ear, which made it impossible not to smile back. The dark brown eyes behind a pointed nose were a requirement for the family. Everyone in the Matthews household had them. Mr. Matthews was a lot like Christian's father. Both of them were teachers at heart.

Bob's son, Brad, appeared from behind the truck and smiled, because he was glad to have help. He stood about five inches shorter than Christian, who towered over him at six feet even. Brad's dark brown hair was cut short on top, with the sides buzzed even shorter. A little rat-tail of hair protruded from the back and clung to his neck. His crooked smile gave the appearance that Brad knew something that no one else knew. One of his front teeth was yellowed because it was a fake. When they first met, Brad swore that the tooth was knocked out in a bike wreck a couple years ago, but Christian thought the tooth was discolored because Brad smoked.

Brad and Christian had become friends rather quickly, even though they were quite different. Christian's world revolved around sports, and he worked hard at them. In contrast, Brad played football, basketball, and baseball just because everyone else did. He enjoyed the camaraderie a lot more than the game itself, and Brad seemed to be well-liked by his teammates. He quickly pulled out jokes and one-liners, but most importantly, no one felt threatened by Brad. It didn't hurt that his father was the athletic director.

Brad easily fit in when he moved to Red Oak from another Iowa town, because he understood the dynamics of a small school. Christian, on the other hand, had no idea what his parents were getting him into by moving to Red Oak. He assumed he would be accepted because he was smart and good at athletics. If someone moved into his school in Omaha, and that person could help the team, Christian would have welcomed the new classmate with open arms, but the first week of football practice in Red Oak was a real eye-opener for Christian.

"It's a daunting task to haul anything heavy up into the house," Mr. Matthews warned them with a white-toothed smile. "Be careful going through that front door."

From the truck on the street end of the driveway to the house, they hiked up a pretty steep incline that reminded Christian of a hill he used to climb to go sledding in the winter. Every time Christian returned to the truck for more boxes to carry, the house seemed farther away, and that hill kept getting steeper. A cascading waterfall of concrete stairs led up to the front door of the house. The lower steps were wide and rounded, but they gradually narrowed as he approached the door. Creaking floorboards made him aware that he crossed the threshold into the sunroom porch. Another three strides and he entered the linoleum foyer leading to the living room. Christian's mother arrived to the house littered with boxes and furniture pieces stacked three or four deep. While Mrs. Matthews and Christian's mom, Lynette, worked hard to unpack and organize the kitchen, the men continued to haul box after box into the house.

Their mothers struck up a friendship immediately, and the sound of those two chattering warned the men that they were close to the front door of the house with every haul. They emptied the final items from the truck in the early afternoon, before they crowded around a small table in the kitchen. Christian piled four ham sandwiches and a mound of potato chips on a plate and snuck out the back door, down four squeaky, wooden steps. He walked out to a picnic table on a brick patio in the backyard, and Brad followed on his heels.

"You wanna soda?" Brad asked.

"What have you got?" Christian replied.

He produced a Pepsi and a Dr. Pepper. Even though Christian loved Dr. Pepper, he told him that he would drink whatever Brad did not want. Brad took the Pepsi.

They finished up the sandwiches before raiding the kitchen for some cookies. Both moms chided their sons for eating the family out of house and home, but the barrage of pesky nagging failed to dent the boys' resolve.

"Hey, we're in training. We have to keep our weight up for football," Christian claimed.

The two boys decided to leave the unpacking to the adults and walked back to Christian's house.

"Man, coach was really impressed with you today," Brad commented as they turned the corner onto Highland Street.

"Great," Christian muttered, a little sarcastically. "The more congrats I get from the coaches, the less I'm liked by the team. Honestly, I don't get it. I'm not cocky, I don't say anything mean, and I play hard. What's their problem?"

"You scare 'em," Brad answered. "This is a small town, and the social status has been set. It was like that in Washington. I guess all small towns run about the same."

Brad moved from Washington, Iowa, to Red Oak, and the two towns had similar demographics.

Brad continued, "The pecking order has been set here, and the social elites have their places. All students in this school know exactly what their places are, and then you come along. You are through-the-roof smart, and that is strike one."

"Come on," Christian said. "Why would they care about my grades?"

"It isn't your grades that they are afraid of," Brad replied. "They don't like the fact that it doesn't stop at brains."

"What do you mean?" Christian asked, puzzled.

The two stopped walking.

"Well, if you were some kid with thick glasses and a high IQ, they could handle that. You'd be controllable. They could poke fun at you and not worry about the consequences, but you aren't some geeky whiz kid. You are a good athlete, too, and that is strike two."

Christian followed Brad's logic, but he had not bought into it.

"So what's strike three?" Christian asked.

"The chicks dig you, man," Brad said like a California surfer.

"What chicks?" Christian responded.

"Come on, Christian. Are you blind?" Brad asked. "Don't you notice the girls giggling and talking when you go by them after practice is over? This morning, three cheerleaders asked me about you while I was waiting for you to finish up in the locker room. They thought you were hot. You also need to throw into the mix that you don't say anything to your teammates. You don't joke around with them. It's all business at practice, so face it, they just don't like you."

"What do they want me to do, shake hands and kiss babies?" Christian responded, irritated. "I sat out a week of practice because of my stupid hand. They didn't seem to mind me, then. I even talked to some of them, but as soon as I put the pads on, no one wanted to even stand by me. It's like I contracted the plague or something."

"Easy, bud," Brad said. "Don't take it out on me."

"I'm sorry," Christian replied.

Brad told Christian what he already realized. He was smart, athletic, and the girls noticed, and he stepped into a small town high school onto someone else's turf. In Omaha, no one noticed a new student at the beginning of the year because a new student blended in as another face in the crowd. In Omaha, Christian did not know everyone in his own grade, let alone the entire school, but in Red Oak, everyone knew Christian before he arrived.

"So why don't they bother you?" Christian asked.

"I'm not a threat," Brad said, casually. "At least, not yet."

They walked the rest of the way to Christian's house. Neither of them said a word, until they reached the back door.

"You up for shootin' some hoops?" Christian asked.

"Dude, can't we just watch some television? We have practice tonight," Brad complained.

"Come on, a little shoot around, then we can vegetate," Christian pleaded.

Brad caved, so Christian grabbed a ball from the basement, as they passed through his bedroom to the garage. The garage door groaned as it lifted. Christian dribbled the ball twice and laid it in off the backboard.

"Are you up for a little game of horse or do you just want to shoot around?" Christian asked.

"Tell you what. You shoot around, and I will watch from the cheap seats," Brad said.

Brad walked over to the far side of the driveway and collapsed onto the stone wall by the giant oak. The tree shaded the entire slab of concrete, its massive, twisted branches extending quite a ways past the roofline of Christian's house. Christian shot free throws, and Brad watched.

After a couple of minutes, a face appeared from behind the hedge while Christian attempted to make his tenth free throw in a row. The slender face belonged to Calvin Robinson. A short, light brown tuft of hair lay glued to Calvin's forehead beneath a black baseball hat with an orange bill. Two hazel eyes peeked from behind a narrow nose and a brazen smile of pointy teeth. Christian's shot clanked off the back of the rim.

"Nice shot, Pearson," Calvin commented sarcastically.

Calvin lived next door to the Pearsons. He was a freshman, like Christian, but he was a member of the top step of the social ladder in Red Oak. Calvin was a good athlete, and Christian thoroughly disliked him, but not because of his athleticism.

When Christian's parents told him that a freshman boy lived next door to the house they bought, he was pumped. He met Calvin the day they moved in and thought Calvin and he were cut from the same cloth. They both liked sports, and they both rooted for the Nebraska Cornhuskers. The following day, Christian took that fateful trip to South Dakota.

When Christian returned, Calvin introduced him to a couple of his friends. Christian seemed to fit in, although he couldn't shoot baskets or throw the football well, due to his injuries from the accident. He even watched a pickup game of basketball in his own backyard. They included Christian in the discussion after football practice, but he had not been cleared to play, yet.

The day he was allowed to participate in full pads for football practice, Christian knocked Calvin on his butt during a tackling drill. By the end of the week, the coaches moved Christian to strong-side cornerback, which was Calvin's position, and they switched Calvin to weak-side corner, the position Christian played before. Calvin saw it as a demotion with Christian responsible for the change.

Things went downhill from there, as Christian's teammates, except for Brad, quit talking to him. As a freshman, the upperclassmen already disliked Christian. The first team did not mind Calvin spending his days on the starting defense, but Christian was the "new kid," so he was ostracized from the group.

Calvin's slender, athletic frame jumped gracefully from the stone wall as he grabbed the carom of Christian's errant shot. Calvin chucked the ball as hard as he could at Christian's gut. The sudden action caught him off guard, and Christian jammed his finger as the ball deflected off his hands toward Brad. He tossed the ball back to Christian, who wanted to fire the basketball into Calvin's face and maybe knock out a couple of Calvin's teeth. Instead of channeling his anger into hurting Calvin, Christian steadied his nerves and drained a free throw.

"What are you two girls doing out here?" Calvin laughed. "Shouldn't you be resting up for practice tonight or inside watching soaps?"

"We were just heading inside," Christian responded.

"Amen to that," Brad said. "I could use a nap before watching practice tonight. I mean, I get awful tired sitting on my helmet on the sidelines, while you guys hug each other on the field. I know, I know, it's called tackling, but you guys both tackle like girls."

Christian chuckled because he knew Brad was kidding. Calvin's face reddened, and his clenched teeth turned his smile into a razor sharp sneer. The breeze ruffled the leaves above as Brad stopped, realizing that Calvin was not laughing.

"You better change out of your skirts before practice," Calvin snorted before leaping up the stone wall and disappearing through the hedge into his own backyard.

Brad and Christian walked through the garage and into the downstairs bedroom. Christian laid the ball on the chair and collapsed onto his bed as Brad flopped down on the bean bag chair.

"Of all the people I could have moved next to, I get that twit," Christian said.

"Quit complaining. He doesn't like me either," Brad smiled. "Hey, toss me the remote. Let's see what's on right now."

Two football practices a day took a toll on Christian's body. That night's practice signified the end of the twice-a-day hell he had endured for two weeks. When school started on Monday, practices would be at 3:30. Most of the team planned to meet up at a farm house outside of town to celebrate the beginning of the school year, but more importantly, the end of "two-a-days." The upperclassmen discussed it in the locker room as they got ready for practice. Christian stayed in his secluded corner with the other freshmen, trying not to draw any attention to himself. After hastily putting on his gear, he made his way out the back door and up the steps to the parking lot where he sat down to lace up his cleats.

Brad settled down beside him and began to put on his own shoes. They paused there for a while, looking out across the parking lot to the practice field, where some of the players were tossing footballs and cracking jokes.

The high school sat in the middle of an open field, and Christian could see Highway 34 curl out of the hills on the northwest edge of town. The road weaved through farms before disappearing from view at the bridge over the Nishnabotna River. It reappeared from behind some buildings to the north of the Red Oak Community High School, where it met a slow incline before vanishing from view as it passed the high school. Christian wished he was on that road because he had a bad feeling about practice.

Straight west of the high school sat the Montgomery County Fairgrounds. White farm buildings fanned out across the area to the south, while on the north side of the complex stood two stadiums. The compound sat a mile from the high school, and a stand of ten cottonwood trees lined the street between the high school property and the fairgrounds. Above the tree line, huge metal towers rose to the sky, each containing a handful of lights. The closer of the two stadiums was the baseball field, darkening with the setting sun. The other stadium was for football, and the lights glowed more intensely as the sunlight faded. Tonight, the coaches planned to scrimmage in the stadium under the lights. Christian should have been excited about the opportunity to get out of the drudgery of practice and actually get some time playing in a game-like atmosphere, but Calvin Robinson's clenched teeth, and that look from earlier in the afternoon made him nervous.

Of course, the last two-a-day practice began with a one-mile run to the stadium. Upon their arrival, the players spread out in lines and began the pre-game routine. The sun had all but disappeared over the horizon, and only a smattering of orange, red, and purple illuminated the sky. Christian could make out thunderheads in the west, and the tinge of color in the background created a silhouette of ominous clouds. He shuddered, remembering the last time he had been out in the open during a storm.

Most of the players shouted at each other, bashed helmets, and bumped pads, as they pumped each other up in preparation for the game. Christian did not partake in this pre-game football ritual as his preparation turned more inward. In middle school, he usually read a little before a game. While the stereo in the locker room blared some incoherent heavy metal, he sat on the bench and blocked out all the noise. Christian closed his eyes and mentally pictured what he needed to do to be successful. Every once in a while, his teammates in middle school would come over and yell at him to see if he was ready to "GO TO WAR" or some other catchy phrase, and Christian would pound their pads and yell something back over the blast from the speakers and then return to his mental imagery. He picked up mental imagery at a baseball camp a couple of years earlier and used it ever since.

After stretching, the offense ran through a couple of plays, and then the entire team headed to the sideline. The football field in the stadium ran north/south, and the home sideline sat on the east side of the field below the press box. Many fans ventured out to watch the evening scrimmage. Everyone on the sideline looked serious, except Brad Matthews, who picked his way carefully through the belly bumps and chest pounding to stand next to Christian. They both looked out across the field.

"Yeah, they're all pumped up now," Brad whispered, "but look who we're playing."

Brad pointed to the empty sideline on the west side of the field.

"I guess when you're coming off a 2-7 season, you've got to be excited when you know you can win this one," Brad added.

Christian laughed.

Red Oak football had seen some rough times in the last couple of years. Being the new kid, Christian did not know much about the tradition. For years, Red Oak had been a shining program, but in the last decade, the other schools in the conference had grown in size, while Red Oak had fallen off in growth. A turnstile of football coaches had come and gone, totaling eight in the last ten years. Of all the coaches in all the sports Christian played, he liked his new coach the most. A bulky Mississippian by the name of Ted Lilly took the reins of this year's Red Oak team.

Brad told Christian that the hire of Coach Lilly was the first decision his dad had to make as the new athletic director, and Christian thought this young, fiery coach was a good choice.

Coach Lilly called the team over to huddle around him. The red-haired Ted Lilly stood about six feet tall, but he was thick. It was not a body-builder kind of muscular thickness; he was solid mass. In practice, Coach Lilly would cover up his mop-like, fiery locks with a helmet, and without pads, he would line up in a three-point stance to show a lineman the right technique. He would even line up at quarterback or running back, and if a player did not hit him hard enough, Lilly would get in that defensive player's face and chew him out. Christian hit Coach Lilly with everything he had in a goal-line drill earlier in the week, but Christian paid the price. He saw stars for the next two plays, but Coach Lilly bounced right up and slapped him on the helmet, telling him, "Great hit!"

Shawn Cozad, the defensive coordinator, stood next to Coach Lilly. In comparison to Lilly, Coach Cozad ranked second from the top on Christian's list of his coaching favorites.

"Second team offense, yer with me," Lilly shouted over the excitement. "First team defense, go with Coach Cozad."

Coach Lilly constantly grinned from ear to ear, and everyone could tell he loved football. Coach Cozad took a more reserved approach to things, and he chose his words carefully for maximum impact. He actually served as a library media specialist with the school district, so Christian was pretty confident that Coach Cozad had both brawn and brains.

"Biggest, baddest librarian in the country," Coach Lilly had taunted once.

Coach Cozad stood about three inches shorter than Coach Lilly, but Cozad carried a lot more muscle. In the eyes of most of the players, Cozad looked too big to have played defensive back for a college in the South. Christian learned more from him about coverage techniques in the first week of practice at Red Oak than he learned in all the years he played football up to that point. The most important characteristic for both coaches was their ability to relate to the players.

"Okay, men," Coach Cozad stated, growing in intensity as he continued, "No one crosses our goal line. We did not come here for an offensive display! We came here to put up zeroes! EVERY YARD…"

"IS A BATTLE!" the defense answered.

"EVERY PLAY…" Coach Cozad continued.

"IS A BATTLE!" the players responded.

"THIS IS NOT A GAME!" Cozad yelled.

"THIS IS WAR!" the team answered in a frenzy.

The players charged the field like crazed warriors and swarmed in a writhing mass at midfield. Christian's adrenaline caught fire, and the defensive unit held the offense to only two first downs for the entire first half of the scrimmage.

Late in the second quarter, Christian tipped a pass on a crossing route and Calvin Robinson scooped the ball up before it reached the ground. Christian turned and blind-sided a wide receiver planning to tackle Calvin. The block opened up the sideline and Calvin took it back for a touchdown. When the two boys got to the bench, Christian went over to congratulate Calvin on the return.

"Nice pick," he told Calvin.

"After that return, I should have the strong side corner position back where it belongs," Calvin bragged.

"I sprung you with the block, genius," Christian replied, angrily.

"Yeah, but I took it to the house," Calvin sneered.

Coach Cozad grabbed Christian from behind and gave him a huge bear hug. Then, he called the entire first team defense over.

"That is exactly what I am talking about, men!" Coach Cozad smiled. "Pearson stayed in the play. He didn't stop once the ball was deflected, and he found someone to hit. Never stop, men!"

Even behind the facemask, Christian could see Calvin's face turn red. Calvin's clenched his fists at his sides, and Christian savored every second of it. Even if Calvin Robinson failed to see Christian's strong team play, the coaches did.

In the second half, the offense broke through for two touchdowns late in the scrimmage. The first came on a long drive that involved mostly running plays, and the second touchdown came on the following drive.

On second and long during the second drive, Christian deflected a pass near the sideline. As he got up, a streak of lightning caught his attention. He noticed the approaching storm and arrived late to the defensive huddle. Since he did not see the signals for the defensive call come in from the sideline, Christian asked the first player he saw, Calvin Robinson.

"Cal, I didn't get to the huddle or see the signal from the sideline," Christian told Calvin.

Calvin hesitated then said, "It's 44 stack, tackle twist, strong tiger!"

"Strong Tiger?" Christian asked. "Are you sure?"

"Positive, Strong Tiger!" Calvin hollered, as he backed away to take his position on the opposite side of the defense.

Christian sprinted across to the strong side of the field. The base defense, "44 Stack" was four down linemen, four linebackers, two corners, and a safety. "Tackle Twist" meant the interior linemen on the defensive were going to cross, one behind the other, to confuse the offense's blocking and create pressure up the middle. "Tiger" was the blitz call from the cornerback position, and "Strong" meant Christian's cornerback position. For this defensive call, Christian had to disguise the blitz by acting like he was in coverage. Then, he would attack the quarterback from the blind side.

As Christian blitzed from his corner spot, the middle linebackers did the same from behind the tackles, which meant Christian was out of position. He should have covered deep down the strong side of the field, while the safety and weak-side corner had the other two-thirds of the field covered. With Christian blitzing, the receiver on his side of the field slipped off the line uncovered. The quarterback saw the open target immediately, and Christian had no ability to stop it. The ball sailed over Christian's head and into the hands of Jack Jacobson, a second string wide receiver, who raced sixty yards to the end zone. Christian received relentless verbal abuse from his defensive teammates.

"What are you doing?" one voice shouted.

"Stupid freshman!" another scowled.

"Coach is going to kill us for this," another said.

"Then we take it out on Pearson in the locker room," said a familiar voice.

Calvin Robinson grinned at Christian.

Christian did not say a word, even though he knew Calvin had given him the wrong coverage. Christian wanted to crush Calvin right there in front of the entire team, but he held back his emotions.

"Nice going," a voice said from behind him. The shove came from the same direction, and Christian fell forward into Calvin.

"What's the matter, Christina?" Calvin laughed. "Can't you remember the coverages?"

"Christina, I like that," said Jeff Eaton, the player who pushed Christian from behind. "Looks like you got yourself a new name, Christina!"

Jeff Eaton reigned supreme over the junior class. Red Oak's best linebacker was not a guy anyone wanted to tick off. Eaton was dumber than a box of rocks, but on the football field, he was king, and Jeff moved close to Christian's face. Based on the look in Eaton's eyes, Christian could tell Jeff wanted to rip him apart.

"Listen, Christina, if we have to run because of this, I'm going to make it my personal mission to make your life miserable," Eaton said.

He shoved Christian hard and coaches' whistles blared as the players turned to see Coach Cozad's reddened face approaching.

"Lilly decided to end it on that high note for the offense," Coach Cozad started. "Since you boys have enough energy to shove each other around after giving up that bomb, then you have enough energy to hoof it back to the high school."

No one dared to respond.

Cozad continued, "We'll let the offense ride the bus home, and you guys can run behind it. Nobody walks! Now, go get some water."

Christian lagged behind the rest of the team. He had no desire to fight for a drink after being the goat of the scrimmage, so he turned around and watched the approaching storm.

"Christian," Coach Cozad called to him.

"Yes, sir," Christian responded.

"What happened on that coverage?" Coach Cozad asked. "You're smarter than that. What in the world possessed you to blitz?"

Christian wanted to tell his coach that Calvin relayed the wrong call, and he wanted to tell him that Jeff Eaton planned to rip his head off. Above all, he wanted to tell him that he hated this miserable little cow town, but Christian held back.

"I screwed up, coach," Christian answered, dejectedly.

"Well, that just isn't like you," Coach Cozad replied. "I was thinking about sending the signals in to you, making you the quarterback of the defense. You seem to be the only one who knows all the calls and who understands where everyone is supposed to be, but after that play, I am going to have to rethink it."

Christian wanted to say something about what really happened, but all he mustered was a dejected, "Sorry, coach."

He walked to the end of the line, where Brad Matthews waited for him. After a minute, they were the only two getting water.

"Look on the bright side," Brad said.

"What bright side?" Christian replied.

"Not everyone on the defense hates you," Brad pointed out.

"Who doesn't hate me on the defense?" Christian asked.

"Me," Brad said. "Coach just switched me from the offensive line to the defensive line."

Christian smiled and took one last drink. They walked to the back of the bus, and the entire defense stared at their approach. Some mumbling drifted from some of the upperclassmen, but Christian could not understand anything from his position in the back of the group. The bus started up, and the entire defensive unit started running behind it. They jogged the whole mile back to the high school, in the dark, in full pads. By the time they reached the school parking lot, the bus had emptied and left. The sounds of laughter and jokes wafted up the steps from the open doors of the locker room while Christian sat down and took off his cleats.

When he got to his locker, the door sat open and his clothes were gone. His locker had been emptied, and Calvin Robinson strolled around the corner holding a stick in his hand. Christian's wet clothes hung from the stick and Calvin dropped them on the bench beside him.

"I decided to wash your clothes for you," Calvin said. "All the showers were being used, so I had to improvise."

"He used the toilet," shouted Jeff Eaton from the other side of the lockers.

Laughter erupted from the upperclassmen.

Christian shot off the bench and tackled Calvin, who yelped when his back smashed into the padlock of one of the locker door handles. Calvin and Christian rolled onto the concrete, and some of the players gathered around them in a semi circle.

"Get him Robinson," Christian heard Eaton say as he let go of Calvin and got to his feet.

Calvin backed off a couple steps, and more players joined the circle.

"I don't like you, Pearson," Calvin growled.

"I don't care," Christian responded.

"No one here likes you," Calvin said.

"Quit talking and pound him," Jeff snorted with a laugh.

Christian could tell Calvin's tough guy appearance wavered, and he could read the fear in Calvin's face. Calvin tried to show off in front of the rest of the team, to move up in the football pecking order by taking on the kid no one liked, and Christian realized Calvin did not expect him to react the way he did. If they were alone, Christian would have kept hold of Calvin after he tackled him; but in this crowded locker room, he had more enemies to worry about than just Cal Robinson.

Calvin's voice cracked, "Bring it on, Christian."

Calvin hesitantly moved back as he spoke. Christian inched forward, his blue eyes fixed like a leopard measuring its prey, and Calvin backed up a little more.

"Pound him!" Eaton growled in a menacing voice, keeping his volume low to avoid drawing the attention of the coaches who were meeting behind closed doors in the coaches' office. The locker room quieted.

"Knock it off!" a voice shouted from the circle.

Brad stepped in between Calvin and Christian. "No one is going to pound anyone!"

"Move out of the way, froshy," Jeff Eaton ordered, "Let Robinson beat the tar out of him."

"Maybe you should thank Calvin for the extra running," Brad responded.

"What are you talking about?" asked Jeff.

"Cal told Christian the wrong coverage," Brad explained. "I heard it from the sidelines."

"That's crazy," Calvin said.

"Listen froshy," Eaton said as he moved in on Brad. "Why don't you move so these two can duke it out."

Brad hesitated and then straightened, "If Calvin wants to get to him, then he's going to have to go through me."

"You ain't worth it," Calvin muttered backing away.

Calvin found his a way out of the fight.

"What's goin' on?" Coach Lilly shouted, as he came crashing out of the coaches' office.

"Nothin' coach. We're just discussing tackling techniques," Jeff joked, and some older boys laughed.

"Well, you boys best clean up and git," Coach Lilly said, his southern accent twanging the last word.

Coach Lilly turned back to the office.

"Oh, and Pearson, I wanna see you in my office before you leave," he called over his shoulder.

"Yes, sir," Christian replied.

The boys returned to their lockers since the fireworks ended, and Christian sat down in front of his locker and looked down at the pile of wet clothes on the floor. Brad sat down beside him.

"Eaton could've killed you," Christian whispered.

"Nah, he wouldn't touch me," Brad said in a hushed voice, "and besides, I would hate to see you get suspended for fighting Robinson."

"Fight him, I would have destroyed him," Christian smiled.

"Yeah, and you would have destroyed your chances at playing football for a while," Brad added.

Brad was right. It would have killed Christian to miss out on playing football because of some stupid fight.

"What do you mean Eaton wouldn't have touched you?" Christian asked. "That guy has way too much testosterone to back down from a little guy like you."

Brad replied, "Being the son of the athletic director does have a couple of advantages. Eaton is dumb, but he ain't stupid, and Calvin, well, he knows that you could own him. You should have seen the look of surprise on his face when you planted his back into the lockers."

"He did kind of yelp when I lunged into him," Christian grinned, "and did you notice how he was backing away while I was moving toward him?"

"Yeah, but I also saw that look in your eyes," Brad said.

"What look?" Christian questioned.

"Oh, you have a look," Brad answered. "It only comes out in the heat of battle, and I see it occasionally at practice."

"Come on," Christian said, waving his hand to dismiss the notion that he had a "look."

"You get this focus," Brad explained, "like the whole world doesn't exist. You lock in on a target, which in this case happened to be Calvin Robinson, and your face goes to stone. It's expressionless, and those blue eyes of yours burn."

"How do blue eyes burn?" Christian asked, confused by Brad's explanation.

"It's tough to explain," Brad answered. "I once saw a man working on a car with an acetylene torch, welding the frame back together. The torch had this blue flame in the middle, and the sparks shot off white. When you're in the zone like you were with Calvin, your eyes spark blue like one of those torches."

The visual registered with Christian because he saw eyes like that a couple of weeks ago. Grandpa Pearson had eyes like that when Christian showed up on the Lake Albert Dam after spending half the night under water.

"Like Grandpa Pearson," Christian whispered as his thoughts drifted back to that night.

"Like who?" Brad asked, jarring Christian back to the present.

"Nothing. It must be hereditary," he said.

Brad shrugged and stood to close his locker.

"Dad is waiting up in the athletic office. He'll take us home when we're all cleaned up," Brad said.

"I've got to talk to Coach, then I'll come up after that," Christian responded as he closed his locker.

The locker room emptied quickly, since everyone wanted to get out to the farm house party. Christian planned on missing it, and he knew Brad would avoid the party after what just happened.

"Will it end?" Christian asked. "I mean, will we ever be accepted?"

Brad thought for a moment, then responded, "Are you planning on backing down any time soon?"

"No," Christian answered emphatically.

"Me either, so it could be a long year," Brad said, flashing his yellow-toothed grin with a shrug.

Christian washed his clothes in the shower, but he decided to wear his sweaty shorts and undershirt instead. He asked Coach Lilly for a bag when he stopped in the coaches' office.

"I been talkin' to Coach Cozad," Coach Lilly started, "and it seems to us that you're the best at signals. We're gonna start relaying calls to you instead of Eaton. That boy can hit like a truck, but he ain't got the brains to remember all the signs."

"Thanks, Coach," Christian said as he turned to leave.

"One more thing," Coach Lilly added, interrupting Christian's departure.

"Yes, sir," Christian replied as he turned to face his coach.

"What play was called in the huddle?" Lilly asked.

"I didn't get to the huddle in time, coach," Christian answered.

"Then what did you do, guess at the coverage?" Coach Lilly questioned, putting his hand on Christian's shoulder.

The way Coach Lilly squinted when he said "guess at the coverage" gave it away. Coach Lilly must have had an idea about what happened on the field. He may not know the particulars, but Christian could tell Lilly knew someone had given him the wrong call. A no-win dilemma kept Christian from answering his coach right away.

If Christian confessed to Coach Lilly that someone gave him the wrong call, then Christian would have to tell Coach Lilly who the perpetrator was. If he told his coach that he guessed or got greedy, Coach Lilly would know Christian was lying to him, so Coach Lilly had Christian over a barrel.

"Well, Coach, I guess I just lost my wits," Christian said, remembering what Grandpa Pearson told him in the truck. Christian hoped he could knock Coach Lilly off the trail by confusing him a little bit. He wanted to find a way out of this situation without drawing attention to his problems with Calvin and being labeled a snitch by his teammates. Christian was already alienated enough.

"Lost yer wits?" Coach Lilly smiled with a puzzled expression on his face.

"Yes, sir," Christian said. "If you lose your wits, you got nothin' when things go bad. It's an expression my grandfather uses, and I guess I lost my wits when I didn't know the call."

"I see," Coach Lilly said, skeptically.

Christian could tell his coach wasn't buying it, but Lilly stopped pressing the issue and the questions ceased. Lilly just smiled as he let go of Christian's shoulder.

"Can I go now, Coach?" Christian asked, hoping Coach Lilly would not pry any further.

"Yeah, just don't stay out all night lookin' for 'em."

"Lookin' for 'em?" Christian repeated the last part of what Coach Lilly said.

"Yer wits," Coach Lilly replied. "Don't be spendin' all night lookin' for yer wits. Geez, Cozad, how many times have I told you to get one of them English-Hillbilly dictionaries in that library of yours? These Midwest boys can't understand a darn thing I say."

Coach Cozad smiled and responded, "I've tried, but none of those hillbillies can write."

Christian saw this as the perfect moment to make his exit. As he left, he could hear Coach Lilly fire back something about Cozad getting all those muscles from hauling books from the library to read, and Coach Cozad answered with a "you might be a redneck" joke. Christian exited the locker room through the gym and walked over to Mr. Matthews's office, which was located near the main office by the east entrance to the high school. Brad and his dad were waiting on a bench in the hallway.

When he returned home, Christian went straight into the back yard. Behind the east wall of the driveway, a wooden fence extended from the hedge to the trunk of the old oak. A light rain fell, but the threat of thunder and lightning had disappeared. Darkness cloaked the backyard, so it took a minute for Christian's eyes to adjust fully. Inside the wooden fence sat one of the few bright spots of this new house, a four-foot deep, above-ground pool. He unlatched the gate and sat down on a lawn chair to take off his shoes. Christian did not bother with taking his shirt off; he simply slipped into the water, calmly sinking to the bottom.

"I hate this town," he thought as he sat. This town was going to kill him. Then Christian laughed at the thought, because if this town did kill him, it wouldn't be by drowning.

He found the bottom of the pool to be the only quiet spot to sit at night and think. No one bothered him here, and he relaxed in the water.

Christian recalled the first time he intentionally took to the pool for a respite from life. It had been over a week since the accident, and the stitches finally had been removed from his hand. He had made it through his first day of football practice in full pads, but soreness permeated his body. The high school game moved much faster than middle school, and the contact was a lot more violent.

The boredom of no athletic activities and no swimming until the wound had healed made life miserable for too long, but the evening of nonstop pounding on the gridiron took a toll, as well.

The chilly night air made the warm water even more inviting. When Christian eased into the pool, he relaxed, but the tension in his neck wouldn't subside. The first time he willingly took a breath from beneath the water, the chlorine burned a little, but the sensation of sitting beneath the surface was amazing. On the bottom of the pool, the sounds of the world faded away, and Christian could relax completely. Any tension coursing through his body just evaporated.

A light popped on above him, and he could tell the glow came from the back porch. Christian surfaced and heard his mom calling from the house.

"I'm in the pool, Mom," he hollered.

"Are you planning on staying out there all night?" his mom asked.

"No, just trying to relax my sore muscles," he answered.

"Well, I know you must be tired," she said. "Don't fall asleep and drown."

"Oh, I won't, Mom," he responded confidently, laughing at the notion. "Give me a minute, and I will be in. Hey, could you bring me a towel?"

"Sure, I'll grab one from the laundry," she replied.

The back door banged on its hinges as Mrs. Pearson disappeared into the house.

Christian's mother did not know about his unique ability. In fact, no one did, and Christian planned on keeping that secret until the day he died. Mrs. Pearson returned with a towel and an ice-cold Dr. Pepper.

"Christian, you doing okay?" she asked in a concerned voice.

His mother always had a knack for sensing a change in his mood.

"I'm all right," he responded. "Just ready for school to start."

"Well, don't stay out here too long. Your father said there are thunderstorms headed this way, and he's all worked up. He plans to drive to Chautauqua Park to watch the lightning, and I'm sure you could go up there with him. Your father loves having an audience when it comes to talking storms."

"Mom, I have had enough storms for one summer," Christian said, chuckling to himself. "Tell him I'll take a rain check."

He walked with his mother into the house. She kissed him on the forehead and told him goodnight. Christian did not bother cleaning up; he just climbed into bed. He awoke to the grinding of the garage door during the night, but Christian couldn't tell if his father was leaving to watch the storm or returning from chasing it. Time collapsed and exhaustion owned Christian for the rest of the evening.

CHAPTER
4

The rain fell the entire weekend before school started, and Christian's father told him about a weather system stalled out over the Midwest that was pulling the warm, moist air up from the gulf. Christian could have cared less about the storm, because when it rained, the clock always seemed to move at a snail's pace. Brad stopped by the house for a while on Saturday, and they watched the Cubs on the cable station, WGN, out of Chicago. With Christian's father becoming a principal, the boost in pay did reap a reward or two. His family did not have cable in Omaha, just a set of rabbit ears on top of the television. Now, he had cable wired in the basement, so he could watch sports in the comfort of his own bedroom.

The Cubs were playing St. Louis, and the Cubs' pitcher was throwing a gem of a game. Christian did not root for his father's beloved Cubbies, but he enjoyed watching this particular player pitch because he was cerebral on the mound. Early in the summer, Christian read an article about him in *Sports Illustrated*, describing how the pitcher, who was a student of the game of baseball, prepared for every contest. He studied batters' swings and looked for weaknesses and tendencies and he kept his own library of stats on the hitters he faced. Most importantly, he remembered it all in the heat of battle during a game. Christian admired this pitcher's astute attention to detail. That was the kind of athlete Christian aspired to be. Christian's dad always said that brains would beat brawn nine times out of ten.

Christian asked Brad, "What do I need to be ready for when school starts on Monday?"

"Oh, I don't think it will be too bad," Brad said. "You are going to take some ribbing, but no one is going to do anything stupid at school."

"Because my dad will be there," Christian said. "I was thinking the same thing."

"Having your dad in the building will be a blessing and a curse," Brad added.

"I know," Christian agreed.

Christian already thought about the nature of his predicament. His dad was the new principal at Red Oak Junior High. Since Christian entered his freshman year, he assumed he would be at the high school. It turned out that Red Oak Community High School had room for only grades ten, eleven, and twelve, and freshmen attended the junior high, along with seventh and eighth graders.

Brad and Christian would ride a bus to the high school every day for football. The upside was that there were no upperclassmen to deal with in the hallways, but the downside included riding a bus with Calvin Robinson and his little henchmen every day to practice. Even though he did not attend school in Red Oak the previous year, Christian could tell that Cal Robinson ran the ninth grade like the self-appointed king of the freshmen. At practice, Cal's cronies laughed at his jokes, even if they were not funny, and they usually weren't. They all waited like puppies around Calvin, and no decision came to fruition without Cal's consent. If Calvin despised a person, then the group despised that person. Christian bet it would be worse at school than it was at football practice.

"Hey, I bet they keep their distance from you for a while," Brad said.

"Yeah, until we ride that bus to football practice," Christian commented with a sigh. "I don't think that two mile ride will be pleasant."

"At least it will be short," Brad said with a smile.

As the game ended on TV, the rain let up a bit. Brad decided this would be his best chance to make it home without getting soaked. As Brad walked up the stairs to the back door, Christian could hear his father holler from the living room.

"You heading home, Brad?"

"Yeah, the rain is pretty light right now," Brad answered.

"I can drive you home, if you want me to," he offered.

"No thanks, it's only a couple of blocks," Brad said.

The back door creaked open and then slammed on its hinges. Christian lay on his bed, thinking about what he could possibly be facing on Monday. He decided his best option meant going with brains and not brawn when it came to Calvin Robinson. Physically, he could take Calvin, but that would get him into trouble a downside of having his father as his principal. His father would know about it before Christian even thought about doing something wrong.

To survive Red Oak, Christian needed to become a student of the dynamics of Red Oak Junior High's student body. He decided he would pay attention to the social structure and become a student of the game. He knew who controlled it from the top, but ninety-two freshmen filled the rolls of the ninth-grade class. Christian passed judgment on only two of them; Brad and Calvin. Calvin's pack of true followers contained only four or five boys. It appeared that most of the other freshmen football players stuck with Calvin out of fear. Christian guessed no one else had ever stepped up to be followed. At first glance, Calvin and Christian may have appeared to be cut from the same cloth on the outside, but inside, they were as different as could be.

Christian spent Sunday morning at church before he watched a Clint Eastwood marathon with his father. They both liked Clint, because the characters were always no-nonsense guys who would shoot first and ask questions later. Even though Eastwood's characters lived life differently than Christian and his father, they enjoyed watching him, because they loved anything with guns and fights. Christian's mom called it "quality male bonding time between a father and a son." She decided to drive to Omaha after church and she took Christian's sisters with her.

"I don't think your daughters need to be exposed to this much testosterone," his mom said. "We'll be back around eight o'clock, so you two are on your own for lunch and dinner."

"We'll make do," his dad said. "You ladies enjoy the shopping."

"Oh, we will," piped his sister Ann.

Ann stood on the precipice of sixth grade at Washington Elementary. She mourned the disappointment that sixth grade in Red Oak meant another year in elementary school. If the Pearsons still lived in Omaha, she would be entering middle school. She stuck her tongue out at Christian over Mr. Pearson's shoulder, as she gave her dad a hug. Christian's youngest sister, Katherine, mimicked her older sister, but she laughed while she copied Ann. Her tongue curled between the open-space where her front teeth should have been. At seven years old, she had made a mint from the tooth fairy over the last four weeks.

"I see you've been kissin' boys again," Christian joked, seeing Katherine's toothless smile.

She giggled and gave him a hug. Then, she planted a big kiss on his cheek, and they both laughed. Ann no longer looked up to her big brother, but Katherine still adored Christian.

"Kat, Ann, you two get into the van, so we can leave the boys to their movies," their mother said.

"Boys are gross, Kat," Ann said, as she led Katherine out of the living room.

"Yes, boys are gross," Katherine repeated.

The two girls giggled all the way through the kitchen and down into the basement. Katherine received the nickname "Kat" at her birth. Ann struggled to pronounce Katherine, so she just used the first part of her name. The name stuck, and everyone called her "Kat."

His mom said, "Christian, you make sure you and your father eat healthy."

"I will," Christian answered with little enthusiasm.

His mother left the living room and walked through the kitchen. Dad leaned over from his chair.

"I thawed some brats and hid a bag of Doritos in the back of the pantry," he whispered, loudly.

"I heard that, Kenneth Pearson," his mom shouted from the kitchen. Christian and his father laughed.

As the van pulled around the house, his mom tapped the horn to say goodbye, and the girls were off to Omaha.

His father fired up the grill, and by eleven they were knee deep in brats, Doritos, and Eastwood. They caught the last minutes of *Dirty Harry* while they ate. After that, the schedule included *The Enforcer, Kelly's Heroes, and Firefox.* They made a trip to the grocery store during *Firefox,* since they both expressed their dissatisfaction with that particular movie being included in the Eastwood marathon.

At the store, Christian persuaded his dad into going a little healthier with the evening meal. They bought some chicken to go on the grill and grabbed some fresh vegetables for a salad. Mr. Pearson said he would eat it, but he would not like it.

"I'll let you pick out two boxes of ice cream," Christian told his father in his best impersonation of his mother, "but only if you don't complain about the salad."

Christian's father smiled as they strolled to the dairy section. His dad was paying for it, and everyone in the house liked ice cream, so Christian could not lose in this situation.

When they returned at four o'clock, the two decided to eat early before settling in for the last two Eastwood movies of the evening. They sat down to eat just in time to see Clint safely land after stealing a secret military jet from the Russians. The two made quick work of dinner before cleaning the dishes and settled in to catch the majority of *Where Eagles Dare*. They finished off the evening with *High Plains Drifter*.

Mrs. Pearson and the girls arrived home just as the movie ended at around nine. Christian carried Kat up to her room and tucked her in. His mother said Kat had fallen asleep outside of Glenwood, and Ann conked out as they passed the high school on the north side of town. His father carried Ann to her room. Christian told his mom and dad goodnight before heading into the kitchen.

"Dad ate a salad at dinner," Christian hollered to his mom as he reached the stairs to the basement.

"Did you have to hold him down and plug his nose to get it down him?" she asked.

"No, he ate it willingly this time," Christian said. "He was a good boy."

Christian could hear his mother recounting the entire shopping experience for his father as he headed down into the basement.

"Today was a good day," Christian thought as he ducked just before he reached the last two steps. He coped with the problems of living in a new house, and he hoped he would learn to cope with the problems of living in a new town. He thought of the high plains drifter that Clint Eastwood portrayed in the movie.

Eastwood dished out a cold serving of revenge on a lot of people and Christian debated whether or not it was justified.

"Is it okay to even the score with someone who has wronged you?" he thought.

He did not possess the swagger of Clint Eastwood, but sometimes he wished he did.

School on Monday exceeded Christian's expectations. His mom dropped him off at Red Oak Junior High at 7:30, before taking his sisters to their elementary school. School did not start until 8:00, but his mother planned on going inside with the girls for their first day. Christian did not mind missing out on the embarrassment of his mother coming into school with him. Besides, Christian could walk up to the second floor and hang out in the principal's office with his dad until the bell rang. His father left the house at six o'clock in the morning because he wanted to be early for the first day with students, so Christian had not wished him good luck on his opening day of school.

The junior high was a three-story building constructed of red brick. Seventh graders inhabited the first floor, while the ninth graders occupied the top level. The school sat on the south side of Corning Street. North of Corning, a chain link fence protected a large concrete area. When Christian visited the building after his family first moved into town, his father explained that the concrete compound served as the field for P.E. classes when the weather suited outdoor activities. South of the main building, a narrow alley cut through the center of the block. It separated the school from the gymnasium and industrial technology classrooms. The addition was completed ten years before. Parking lots flanked the gymnasium to the east and west. The school's athletic teams operated without a football field, a track, or a baseball diamond on campus. Except for two mammoth oak trees on Corning Street and the patches of grass growing in the small area separating the school from the sidewalks, very little vegetation brought nature to the school grounds. Red Oak Junior High looked like it was hijacked from the downtown area of a major city and relocated to this village of 6,000 people. It rested one block north of the town square with small houses surrounding it on the other three sides. The clock of the Montgomery County Courthouse peered down on the junior high from the west side of the square, and the courthouse was the only building taller than the junior high.

Christian pulled open the glass doors and found himself in a dimly lit pink hallway. The interior walls of the building were allegedly painted an earthy tan on Friday, but it appeared the painters had gone with a different color scheme. The walls definitely looked pink.

The hallway extended the length of the building from east to west before emptying out through an identical set of glass doors on the other end. Orange lockers lined each pink wall with breaks at every classroom doorway. Stairs rose from the north side of each entryway into the building, climbing to the next level like switchbacks (the roads used to travel up steep mountain slopes.) The main office was on the second floor, so Christian turned to his right and began the slow climb up to the next level. He could tell that climbing these stairs every day would get tedious in a hurry.

The second story looked similar to the first, orange lockers and pink walls. The major difference between the second floor and the other two was not noticeable at first glance. Instead of classrooms in the middle section of the second level, the media center sat to the south and the main office to the north. Christian peered around the corner into the main office. The top half of the office door gaped open, but the bottom half was closed and locked, like one of those doors used in Grandpa Pearson's old horse barn. The door kept the horse in the pen, but the top half opened so it could look out. The secretary's desk sat unoccupied, but Christian heard his father talking on the phone. Reaching over the little counter on the bottom half of the door, he turned the knob, let himself in, and peeked in to let his dad know he was waiting outside. Mr. Pearson motioned for Christian to enter.

Christian looked around the office, which looked much different than it did when they first moved to town. Frames filled the walls, and his father's certificate from Concordia College for his Bachelor's Degree in Education hung above his Master's Degree in Educational Administration from the University of Nebraska at Omaha. A shelf of books spanned the rest of the area. To the right of his father's desk, pictures of past fishing trips dotted the beige wall. He examined them as he waited for his dad's call to end. Most of the pictures included his father and Grandpa Pearson, but some included Christian and his sisters as well.

A picture of Christian with his dad and his grandfather caught his eye. They had driven up to Pickstown in South Dakota to fish for walleye. Christian hooked a monster, but they had no idea what pulled on the other end of the line. They first suspected Christian snagged a tree or rock, but the snag started moving. The fish pulled the boat a quarter of a mile and stayed deep in the water, and the rod stayed bent in half for most of the battle.

Grandpa Pearson thought Christian had hooked a big catfish, and his father bet a million dollars on a giant Northern Pike. Whatever pulled on the line, the fish did not plan on coming to the surface quickly. Twice, Christian almost lost the lunker as it changed directions and went under the boat. He had to avoid the prop of the motor on one end and the trolling motor on the other, but after twenty minutes of tugging, the fish finally broke the surface. The monster he hooked turned out to be a carp. Grandpa had the net in hand, and Christian guided the fish to him.

The carp overwhelmed the small net. With only the top half of the fish secured, Grandpa tried to pull the net from the water, but he lost his footing and slipped, and the pole, extending to the net, snapped. His father lunged over the edge of the boat to keep the fish from slipping into the water, and it took both men to lift the net and goliath fish into the boat.

During the battle, a couple of other boats in the area gathered around their Alumacraft to watch. When that fish flopped into the boat, they heard hoots and hollers of congratulations from the gallery of fishermen.

"That was an exciting trip," his dad said, as he hung up the phone and noticed Christian looking at the picture.

"I still don't believe we got that giant into the boat," Christian marveled.

"It is the most exciting fishing story I have ever told," Mr. Pearson added.

"Look how scrawny I am in that picture," Christian said, astonished at the skinny boy in a baseball cap struggling to hold up the thirty-pound behemoth.

"Well, that was three years ago, and you were just going into the sixth grade," his dad reminded him.

In the picture, they were standing next to the boat dock.

His father said, "It was a good boat. I talked to Grandpa last night, and he said that he's already bought another one."

"He did, huh. Well, what did he get?" Christian asked.

"Same thing, only much newer," his dad said. "He told me that he plans to keep it out of the water until next spring, since he has spent enough time fishing this year. Grandpa did tell me that he wants you and me to come up to the place this fall after football season. He wants us to spotlight some coons that are hanging out by the corn crib."

Grandpa Pearson's hearing was not the only thing that he was losing. Grandpa struggled to see clearly at night. People do not usually see raccoons during the daylight, so if a man is going to hunt raccoons, he has to do it after the sun goes down. Christian and his father used spotlights to find them. A raccoon's eyes will shine in the beam of light, so locating a coon at night is fairly simple. The powerful spotlight also stuns them, giving a hunter just enough time to get a shot off. A coon hunt usually does not start until after midnight, and it lasts until the sun begins to rise. Spotlighting for raccoons will get a person a ticket in most states, but no game warden in Nebraska would tell a farmer that he doesn't have the right to shoot a raccoon on his own farm. The corn in Grandpa Pearson's bins is worth money, and those raccoons will find Grandma's chicken coop sooner or later. If they get hungry enough, raccoons will take on a dog to get a chicken dinner. Dogs only keep the raccoons at bay for a short time, but Grandpa Pearson doesn't own any. Christian's grandfather had until the end of the football season, because food gets scarce in the winter, and those coons will look for a way into the chicken coop by the early part of November, especially if an early snow blankets the ground.

Christian grew up in the outdoors, spending many days hunting or fishing with his father and his grandfather, only catching or shooting what they would eat. Some of his friends in Omaha were turned off by Christian's stories of hunting with his grandpa, but Christian had first-hand knowledge of the real cruelty of the natural world.

When he was ten, a little younger than Ann now, Christian and his grandma went to check on some kittens that had been born a day earlier. They found what was left of the kittens and their mother near a brush pile by the garage. Grandma guessed a raccoon was the culprit.

"That's the harshness of nature," Grandma Pearson had said. "Coons gotta eat, too."

"Is that why Grandpa shoots them?" a younger Christian had asked.

"Nah, he tries to keep them away from our food and our property," Grandma explained. "He don't go after 'em until he sees signs that they are eating our crops or our cats. I think he may keep a closer eye out for 'em after I tell him about this."

Grandma did not seem angered by what the raccoon had done to her cat and kittens. She was sad, but she took it in stride. She knew it was the way of nature on the farm. At that early age, Christian came to the realization that Grandpa didn't kill animals for fun or because they were bad. It was simply survival, and that was something his friends in Omaha had never really understood.

"Dad, why are your walls tan in the office and pink in the hallway?" Christian asked.

His father grunted, "Those painters just painted over the old paint without priming it or putting on Kilz. The new paint mixed with the graffiti and the old paint to make that lovely shade of pink you saw on your way in. I have been on the phone with the district for the better part of the morning. The painters say it was beige when they left."

"Can they do anything about it?" Christian asked.

"Nope, we are just going to have to endure pink walls until spring break and maybe until next school year," his father explained.

"The pink Tigers of Red Oak Junior High," Christian snorted.

"Did you get your schedule, yet?" Dad asked, changing the subject.

"Yes, I did," Christian answered. "I think I'll find my locker and unload this backpack."

"All right, we'll see you after football practice," his dad said. "I will try *not* to show up in any of your classes, but you may see me in the hallway, so...."

"I know, I know," Christian interrupted, "call you Mr. Pearson. Have a good first day."

"You, too," his father responded.

Christian strolled out of his father's office in high spirits. The school secretary, Mrs. Johnson, scurried around her desk in the office and two students waited at the window. They needed new copies of their schedules. Christian saw other students milling around in the hallway, chatting with their peers, and he waved a hello to Mrs. Johnson on his way out, since he had already been introduced to the office secretary.

"Good to see you, Christian," she said, while pulling schedules off the printer.

Christian let himself out and walked to the right and up the stairs to the freshmen floor on the third level. Only one other student had made it to the third floor, and Christian smiled when he saw Brad, who was unloading his backpack into his locker.

Christian had not noticed it before, but the lockers did not have locks. At his middle school in Omaha, the lockers had locks built into them, but these lockers did not even have a combination padlock. He gave Brad a friendly jab in the shoulder as he passed.

Opening the door, Christian said, "I can't believe we don't have locks."

"Small school," Brad said. "I guess they think no one will mess with other people's stuff, since everyone knows everyone else."

The two boys compared schedules. Brad and Christian had all but one class together, and that was because Christian had to bus out to the high school for math. Brad asked about Christian's weekend, and he told Brad about the Clint Eastwood marathon. It turned out that Brad and his dad watched *High Plains Drifter* last night, as well.

Other students started to show up and Christian looked at his watch. They still had about fifteen minutes before class, so they decided to get out of the hallway and go to the first room on their schedule, English with Mrs. Droll. The classroom was empty, but Mrs. Droll had written out the directions of what to do upon entering.

"1. Please select your own seat. 2. Grab a reading survey from the front table. 3. Write your name legibly at the top of the paper (first and last). 4. Begin filling out the survey."

"Aw, man, a reading survey," Brad complained. "I can't think of the last book I read."

"You have got to expand your mind a little bit," Christian teased.

"Oh, and when do you have time to read, super genius-athlete?" Brad asked.

"I read all the time, but only at night or on rainy weekends when there isn't a Clint Eastwood marathon on TV," Christian explained.

The first day, the junior high followed an early dismissal schedule, and the classes lasted only twenty-five minutes. The students looked forward to getting out of school at 11:30, while the teachers would be in an in-service with Christian's dad in the afternoon. The high school schedule differed from the junior high. They had in-service meetings in the morning, so the students reported to school at noon, and the high school got out at 3:30. That meant football practice would still be at 3:30 at the high school.

By arriving early, Christian almost completed the survey by the time other students started to arrive. He recognized a few faces from the football team, but not many. He tried to be as observant as possible, watching other students, but Christian soon found out that, along with Brad, he was the focus of everyone's attention. During football, they all looked the same on the field in pads and helmets. Here, Brad and Christian stood out, easily recognized as the outsiders in the building. When Mrs. Droll asked about the last book Christian read, he told her it was *Rumble Fish* by S.E. Hinton. Excitedly, she told the class that they would read a book called *The Outsiders* by the same author.

"Score one for me," Christian thought.

He had read *The Outsiders* in seventh grade. The story revolved around the Greasers and the Socs, two social groups that clashed all the time. The novel opened Christian's eyes to the way students tended to treat each other based on the group they hung out with. In addition, the book taught him that everyone had their own set of problems. Christian leaned over to tell Brad he was going to love *The Outsiders*. Brad rolled his eyes and muttered "Nerd" under his breath.

Christian's second period class took him to the other end of the hallway. The sign over the door said, "Every day will be a battle of the minds; please don't come unarmed." Christian chuckled at the sign as he approached the room. Mr. Button was an imposing figure standing outside his classroom. He towered over everyone as he waited at the doorway to greet each student. Mr. Button knew everyone's name and firmly shook the students' hands as they entered his room. Brad and Christian took turns introducing themselves before entering. Mr. Button's slender frame reached at least 6' 7", and he had glasses with small, circular frames, which looked like the glasses John Lennon of the Beatles used to wear, only Mr. Button's spectacles were not tinted like the rock star's.

The walls of Mr. Button's room were completely blank, except for a sign on his bulletin board that said, "No, I don't play basketball, but I am one heck of a mini-golfer." Christian knew that social studies would be full of surprises, and Mr. Button would keep the students entertained.

The board at the front of the room instructed the students to take a number from the jar and sit at the corresponding seat. Numbers labeled each desk in order up each row, starting with one in the front right desk. The next row to the left started with six and next to that, the number eleven. Christian had drawn number ten. He did not mind the back of a row, and Brad sat next to him in seat number fifteen. As far as sitting next to each other, they were two for two. As Christian watched the students enter the room, most of them talked excitedly with one another; this time they paid no attention to Christian or Brad. Christian prayed the "new kid" shine was losing its luster.

"Most students get excited for the first day of school," Christian thought.

Calvin Robinson appeared in the doorway, his hair matted down on his head. His eyes surveyed the assembled students who had already found their seats, and he fished around in the jar until he found the number he wanted. Calvin settled into seat number thirteen which sat two desks in front of Brad. Christian waited for some kind of remark or at least an evil stare, but nothing of the sort came from Calvin's direction. Christian knew for certain Calvin saw him, but Christian did not interest Calvin at this time. Cal picked a seat in the middle of the room, and pretty soon, a couple of his buddies settled in next to him, one on each side. Christian knew both of them from the football team.

Miles Jones sat in seat eight, and Devin Rammick plopped down in seat eighteen on the other side. Miles and Devin both played offense on the second team and they were decent athletes. Miles's lanky frame matched his blonde hair and pale complexion. He stood a couple inches taller than Christian, but Christian had about twenty pounds on Miles in weight. Even though Miles was a rail, the coaches must have thought he would fill out, because they had him playing tight end, a position usually reserved for bulkier kids. Miles Jones paid attention to detail in practice, which landed him on the second team and the kick off team. He definitely would develop into a pretty good football player once he added a few pounds. For his slender build, he turned out to be more coordinated than Christian originally thought he was.

Devin Rammick sat two seats up in the row next to Brad's. Devin was a couple inches shorter than Christian, and his skin had a dark, copper quality. Christian assumed Devin spent a lot of time in the sun over the summer. The daily dose of sunshine darkened his already tan skin. Devin's face brightened with a contagious smile under dark, almost black, eyes. Rammick played wide receiver, and made the second team because he ran like a deer. He spent most of his time at practice cracking jokes and laughing, since he really had no desire to move up on the depth chart. Christian thought Devin showed up to football because he wanted to be around his friends. In that way, Devin reminded him of Brad.

Not once during social studies did any of them turn around. In fact, Devin spent most of the twenty-five minutes tossing wadded up paper at a couple of girls sitting in seats in front of him and to his right. Miles took notes while Mr. Button spoke about what they would be studying this year in his class. Every once in a while, Cal Robinson tapped Miles on the shoulder to whisper some wisecrack, but Christian never fully heard what Calvin said. Calvin laughed quietly at his own humor and Miles returned to his notes with a fake chuckle. Cal turned to urge Devin to toss another piece of paper. This process repeated itself for the entire period and continued in Mr. Wells's science class during third hour.

Brad and Christian did not end up sitting together in this class; instead, they found their seats on opposite sides of the room. Christian sat in a back corner next to Miles, behind a girl he did not recognize from any classes he'd had yet. Mr. Wells passed out a pretest of thirty questions and instructed them to do their best. He planned to use the test to see how much the students already knew about physical science.

Most of the questions pertained to things Christian studied in middle school, so he breezed through it. Christian finished it with about ten minutes to spare, so he decided to observe the other students for a while. A couple of girls stared at him when he looked up from his finished test. When Christian met their eyes, they giggled and quickly averted their own. Most of the students continued to work on the test. Miles completed question fifteen when Christian glanced over at his paper. Calvin sat on the other side of the room, whispering to another student Christian already knew. Mitch Maxwell, a bottom-of-the-barrel offensive lineman, nodded his head as Calvin spoke. Mitch spent his practices holding blocking dummies for the first and second teams' workouts, and Cal referred to the big ball of goo as "Stay Puffed" after the giant, marshmallow man in the movie *Ghostbusters*. Mitch had a big mouth filled with braces and rubber bands. When he laughed, saliva leapt out of his gaping maw, like one of those sprinklers Christian used to run through as a kid. Mitch snorted at full volume as he smacked a sign that read "DORK" onto another student's back.

Mr. Wells commanded, "What is so funny, Mr. Maxwell?"

Mitch's laugh changed into a spray of words as he said, "Nothing, Mr. Wells," in a sing-song voice.

Maxwell's snickering erupted into a roaring guffaw, when the recipient of the sign failed to reach the sign in the middle of his back. Mr. Wells settled the class just as the bell rang. He instructed the students to place the tests in the tray on his desk and they would find out their scores tomorrow morning.

Christian's math class meant a trip to the high school, but the bus would not be taking him there because of the different first-day schedules with the junior high attending in the morning and the high school in the afternoon. He decided to check out the library before going to gym class. The library had a closed sign on it, so he walked across the second floor hallway to the office.

"Is Mr. Pearson in?" Christian asked as he poked his head through the open half of the door.

"I'm sorry, Christian. He had a meeting at the district office, but he should be back in about half an hour. Do you need something?"

"No," Christian said, "I was looking for a place to hang out until my next class."

"Oh, that's right," she said, realizing that his fourth period class was at the high school. "How's the football team looking this year?"

"We won't know until the first game," Christian said. "Do you mind if I sit in his office until the bell?"

"Sure, go right ahead," she replied.

He plopped down in a chair and leaned his head back. The day progressed much better than he thought it would. Calvin and his little pack seemed to be ignoring the fact that he went to school here, and Christian guessed they had plenty of targets to choose from, anyway. Of the three in Calvin's little posse, Miles Jones showed the most promise of friendship. Miles seemed to be bugged by Calvin during social studies, and he worked his tail off in science on that pretest. Devin Rammick craved socializing too much to leave Calvin, but Devin seemed pretty harmless. Mitch Maxwell proved to be an idiot who acted on Calvin's every whim. Christian knew that Calvin acted like a clean-cut kid around adults, but Cal worked covertly behind the scenes. Calvin was too smart to let anything get pinned on him.

Christian waited for the bell to ring before he headed to the corridor, which passed from the second floor of the middle school to the adjoining gymnasium. A little kid came in crying as Christian left, and he figured the kid was a seventh grader. Christian waited in the hallway for Brad, who hurried over to him when he turned the corner.

"Remind me to tell you about math class when we are on our way home," Brad said excitedly.

"Okay, why not now?" Christian asked.

"Well, I am not sure who's safe to talk around and who isn't," Brad explained. "I know small towns, and I don't want to discuss this out in the open."

They turned to walk to P.E.

"What in the world happened during Brad's math class?" Christian wondered.

Brad had a strange look on his face, an expression which danced between fear and elation. The last three classes of the day passed slowly, as every minute clung to the clock, refusing to let go. Gym class was the same everywhere, so Christian did not pay much attention to Mr. Mauer drone on and on about lockers and appropriate attire for the art of physical education, and Mr. Arnold's safety lecture in industrial technology contained the same monotony.

"Don't stick your hand into the table saw, always wear safety goggles, and always remember that power tools are dangerous."

During study hall in Mr. Button's room, Christian tried to get Brad to tell him what happened, but Brad hushed him, and so did Mr. Button. Brad received an assignment in math, so Christian decided to help Brad with his homework. Mr. Button walked over to check on them. He left the two boys alone when he realized that Christian really was helping Brad with his homework, a review of some pre-algebra, solving for variables. The last time Christian saw algebra was in seventh grade, so it took him a couple minutes to figure out how to solve the problems. Christian never gave the answers to Brad, but he did a lot to steer Brad in the right direction.

Brad finished as the bell rang. They stowed their books in their lockers and headed for the stairwell. Christian stopped by the main office, but his dad had gone upstairs to discuss a discipline issue with a teacher.

"Probably Ms. Mack," Brad whispered, as they left the office.

"So spill it," Christian demanded in a whisper.

"Not until we are out of here," Brad insisted in a hushed tone.

They hurried down to the main floor and headed out the glass doors on the east side of the school. Students filed into cars, and a large group waited by the parking lot next to the gymnasium. Red Oak had quite a few students who lived in the country on farms. Christian's dad said three buses picked up students outside the gym every day. A fourth bus would pull up on the east side of the school to take freshmen to athletic practices at the high school, but not today. The first country bus pulled into the fire lane as Brad and Christian cut across the grass to the street corner.

The two boys crossed and began the journey up Corning Street to Brad's house. The strong wind bent branches in the trees above. The hot, August air roared out of the south, so they only felt it until they traveled far enough for a house to shield them. The two boys lagged behind a group of chatty seventh-grade girls, because Brad wanted to have a buffer of privacy before he told Christian what happened.

"Man, this is a steep hill," Brad complained.

"At least we don't have any books to carry," Christian reminded him.

"Yeah, but when football is over, I think I'll wait for my mom to pick me up after the elementary kids get out," Brad said.

"We're clear of anyone else, so spill it," Christian ordered.

"Okay, I was sitting in the front row in Ms. Mack's math class. She was going on about how this was geometry, but we would be doing some review over simple algebra before getting into that."

"Wow, that's exciting," Christian joked, pretending to yawn. "It's good you didn't share that where people could hear you."

"Do you want to hear the story, or not?" Brad snapped.

"Sorry," Christian said, and he motioned for Brad to proceed.

Brad continued, "Well, Ms. Mack looks like she is about eighty-years-old and built like a bell. Her hips are huge! I mean, she almost had to turn sideways to fit her can through the door to her classroom. Anyway, she has stacks of papers sitting on a table at the back of the room. She just finished explaining that we were going to staple together the papers on the back table into a review packet like an assembly line, and she was sort of modeling how to do it. She put together a stack and tried to staple it, but the stapler was empty. She grabbed another one on her desk, but that stapler was also out. She rifled through her desk and couldn't find any staples in there, either."

Brad paused a little, and excitement flashed in his eyes. Then a car pulled up beside the two boys and honked. It was Christian's mom.

"You boys want a ride?" she asked.

"Thanks, Mom, but I think we'll walk," Christian answered.

A car roared past her on the left and honked.

"Christian, don't stay at Brad's house," she said.

Christian was hoping she would leave, so he could hear the rest of the story.

"Why not?" he asked, as another car blew past.

"I have to run you out to the high school at 1:25 for your math class," she said.

Christian had completely forgotten about the math class. His mom had received a letter from the high school, stating that he would need to come over in the afternoon for his math class on the first day of school.

"I forgot," Christian said. "I'll come straight home."

"See you in a bit," she said as she pulled away from the curb.

Christian's sisters were in the back seat and they both waved as the car drove away.

"Sorry about that," Christian said to Brad.

"Where was I?" Brad thought aloud. "Oh, yeah, so Ms. Mack squeezes her big butt out the door to go get some staples. As soon as she leaves, Devin Rammick walks over to get a drink from the water fountain right outside the room. He comes back in and says that Ms. Mack is down the hall in Mr. Button's room, so Mitch Maxwell pushes his lard butt out of his desk and lumbers back to the table with all the papers. The whole time, he is laughing so hard that saliva is spraying everywhere. You know when that kid laughs, he looks Chinese."

"So, what did he do?" Christian asked with anticipation.

"He opens a window, and starts grabbing stacks of papers and throwing them out," Brad said almost in disbelief.

"Out the window? No way!" Christian shouted.

"Yep, he was chucking those papers out that open, third-floor window as fast as his chubby hands would let him. Then he sits down in his seat."

"What did Ms. Mack do?" Christian asked.

"Well, Mitch turned to this little kid sitting in front of him and told the kid he would kill him if he tells Ms. Mack who did it. Then he punches the kid hard in the shoulder. Calvin starts laughing, and Rammick says, 'Here she comes.' I couldn't believe what was happening."

"What happened next?" Christian said, hanging on every word.

"Ms. Mack grabs the stapler off her desk to refill it with staples, and she doesn't even notice that all the papers are gone. That little kid that Mitch punched, well he's the first one in the row. I think his name is Tom." Brad paused a moment.

"No, it's Tim… Tim Kirth. Anyway, Tim doesn't know what to do when she tells him to start the line to make the packets. Ms. Mack says, 'What's the matter boy; didn't you hear me?' Tim stands up and she hands him the stapler. He starts walking to the back of the room. Mack explains that the other students need to follow Tim. She was kind of getting irritated at the class, because no one moved, when all of a sudden she sees those papers are gone. She asks Tim where the papers are, and he looks at Mitch. I could see Mitch from my seat, and he can look mean when he wants to because he's so big. Think about it. If you were a little guy, wouldn't you be scared to death?"

Christian shrugged his shoulders. He didn't think Mitch looked tough at all.

"So, Tim looks at Ms. Mack and says, 'They aren't on the table.' Ms. Mack is fuming, and she tells Tim that she can see that the papers aren't on the table. By this time, snickers are gurgling up from a couple of students around the room, but no one is saying a word. Ms. Mack pushes her way to the table and looks underneath it. She turns around and faces the class from the back of the room. Tim is still standing there with that stapler in his hands."

Brad paused as the two boys crested the top of the hill. They had gone about four blocks from the school, and Brad turned around to make sure no one followed them. The girls in front of them turned off a block earlier, and the only people they could see on the sidewalk were back near the school. This must be big, because Brad looked a little nervous.

Brad began again in a whisper, "Tim is still standing there with the stapler in his hand. He doesn't know what to do, so he hands it to Ms. Mack. She was real angry, and she kind of slapped at his hand. Well, he was so jumpy standing there; his natural reflexes kicked in and that stapler went flying."

"Did it hit someone?" Christian asked.

"Nope, it flew up into the window and shattered the top pane. A couple inches lower and it might have broken the bottom window. Instead, the stapler struck the bottom of the pane of the top window and CRASH! Glass went everywhere."

Christian looked back at the school. Brad was not checking to see if people followed them; he looked back at the third-floor window. Christian spied the third floor from where they stood atop the hill, and someone leaned out of the window on the far right. From his location, Christian could not tell if the window was broken, but he guessed the man leaning out the window was his father.

"So, what did she do?" Christian asked.

"Well," Brad continued, "Ms. Mack got real still and said, 'Now look what you've done,' to Tim. She tells him to go see your dad, but Tim just stands there. 'Get moving, Tim,' she says, but he doesn't move. Tim said something about the fact that he didn't do anything, and Ms. Mack says, 'Well, then who broke the window?' Tim stands there for what seemed like forever before telling Ms. Mack that she broke the window. Just then, those papers that Mitch chucked out the window started swirling outside the third floor."

"No way!" Christian exclaimed in disbelief.

"Yep, that wind must have kept a couple of those papers swirling around outside, and some of them floated around the windows right when Ms. Mack had her back turned to the outside. Calvin Robinson started to cackle, and Ms. Mack..."

"Cal was in there, too?" Christian interrupted.

"Uh, huh, and Calvin was behind the whole thing," Brad said.

"So, what did Ms. Mack do then?" Christian asked.

"Cal starts laughing like a hyena, and Mitch loses it when those papers float up. Ms. Mack asks what happened to the papers, and Devin starts looking in trash cans."

"Devin says, 'Did you check the trash cans? Maybe they got thrown away.' Ms. Mack walks over to her desk and looks in the trash. When she turns around the floating papers are gone from view. She turns on Tim again and says, 'Why are you still standing here? Now get down to the principal's office!' Tim starts bawling and leaves the room. Ms. Mack grabs the only remaining stack of papers on the back table and tells us that we need to take one for homework. The bell rang shortly after that, and we all scrambled for a paper and then the door. Nobody wanted to wait around, and as far as I know, nobody else was called down to the office for it."

"So how was Calvin behind it?" Christian asked, remembering what Brad said earlier.

"Students were talking about this big math assignment, and when I got into class, Calvin was just coming out from behind Ms. Mack's desk. He didn't see me, as he walked back to the table and emptied the stapler into the garbage can. I also saw him throw a box of staples into the trash. When Mitch and Devin came into the room, it looked like we had all walked in together, even though I had been standing at the door watching. Calvin motioned for them to come over by him, and I walked to a desk as far away as possible. I had no idea what they were doing, and I didn't want any part of it."

"So Calvin put Mitch and Devin up to it?"

Brad nodded.

"Calvin did the same thing in science," Christian said, remembering the sign Mitch put on another student's back.

"That was the same kid," Brad said.

Christian felt sorry for Tim Kirth, but he felt relief at the same time. With Tim as the target, Calvin left him alone, and Brad must have been thinking the same thing.

"I guess that's why Calvin isn't getting even for Friday," Brad said.

"I guess so," Christian answered.

They stood in front of Brad's house.

"See you at practice," Brad said as he crossed the street to his driveway.

"Hey," Christian called to him, "Tim Kirth won't be out on that field during football practice."

Brad replied, "I know, and I won't be on that field, either, so you'll be dealing with those things on your own."

Brad smiled and walked up the driveway, and Christian turned and jogged the rest of the way home. He wondered if his father would bring up the events of school at dinner tonight. Christian entered uncharted waters with his father, since he had never been in the same building as his dad. As much as he wanted to talk to his father about what happened, he was not in Ms. Mack's classroom, and he did not plan to "rat" on Calvin Robinson or Mitch Maxwell. Christian did not like keeping secrets from his parents or lying to them, but sometimes staying quiet led to the only way out. The line between right and wrong got fuzzy in a situation like this one. In the last few weeks, the black and white answers to questions turned a muddied gray, and Christian had a feeling that trend would continue.

His trip to the high school was pretty uneventful. The math class was a yearlong class of Algebra 3 and 4. Christian took Algebra 1 and 2 in seventh grade, and geometry comprised his eighth grade math class. In Red Oak, Algebra 3 and 4 was usually for juniors, but the class Christian had been placed in was an accelerated math class for sophomores. The small class contained only twelve students. Again, Christian played the role of outcast, because he was the only freshman in the group, but Christian had grown accustomed to being an outsider.

Mr. Penton, the high school principal, eagerly walked Christian down to Mrs. Dvorak's room for math class. The petite fifty-year-old teacher had wiry, gray hair with streaks of black running through it to a ponytail. Rectangular bifocals with slightly rounded edges on the rims perched atop her forehead. Her pointed nose and wide, dark eyes reminded him of an owl.

Mr. Penton made the introductions, and Christian awkwardly offered his hand to her when she moved hers forward toward a handshake.

"Don't worry," Mr. Penton said. "Mrs. Dvorak always looks that serious, but I think you will enjoy having her as a teacher."

Mrs. Dvorak smiled genuinely. When Mr. Penton left, she showed Christian to his seat.

"I've never had a freshman before," Mrs. Dvorak commented.

"Oh, good," Christian said, only half-joking. "That means I'll be an outcast in two buildings at the same time."

"Outcast?" she said with a puzzled furrow of her brow. "There are no outcasts in my room. We only have twelve students, including you, so everyone will have to be a participating member of society."

"Yes, ma'am," Christian uttered with a little nervousness seeping out on the latter part of the phrase. "I didn't mean to offend you."

"No offense taken, Christian. There is no need to be nervous. I think you will do just fine," she said, trying to put him at ease.

The bell rang, and students began to slowly file into the room. Christian failed to recognize any of the first nine students, but the last two to enter were people he knew. Omar Raja, the football team's kicker, and Jesse Thompson, a second-string offensive lineman, seemed interested in the fact that Christian joined them for class. Their conversation stopped the moment they spotted him.

Neither of them said a word to Christian, while Mrs. Dvorak ran through the course syllabus. The bell rang for the next class, and Christian gathered his things. When he looked up, Omar and Jesse stood over his desk, and they both had grins on their faces.

"We didn't know you were in this class," Omar started.

"You're a freshman, right?" added Jesse.

"Yes, I'm a freshman, but I took Algebra and Geometry in seventh and eighth grade in Omaha. I was in an accelerated math program there," Christian stated.

"Well, if you can do school like you do football, you're going to be fine up here," Omar said.

Things were looking up for Christian, as he walked out of the classroom with Omar and Jesse. A couple looks of bewilderment arose from other sophomore football players in the hallway. In addition, a few of the girls sent appraising looks to the new kid with Omar and Jesse. Christian strolled the short distance from the main office to the front door, noticing he would not have to be spending a lot of time in the high school hallways. He decided his daily field trip to Red Oak Community High School would not be that bad after all.

Football practice was exhausting. Cal spent most of his time bragging about the incident in Ms. Mack's class, gaining some stature with the upperclassmen. They were impressed with Calvin's gutsy prank. Christian became accepted as one of their own, but for different reasons. His visit to the high school had spread through the team.

Mid-way through practice, Jeff Eaton started in on Christian, "Hey genius, quit leaving that brain of yours at school. I ain't running for another one of your stupid mistakes." Eaton slammed his facemask into Christian's helmet.

"Back off, Eaton," a familiar voice called. Jack Sampson, an imposing defensive lineman, stepped in front of Christian. Even though they were not in the same class, Christian helped Jack on a math problem before practice. Unfortunately, Sampson's brains failed to mirror his massive biceps in ability. By himself, Jack could not dissuade Eaton physically, but Sampson held his ground, silently.

Another teammate's deep voice added, "It was a rookie mistake. Let it go, Jeff."

Jeff Eaton still did not like Christian much, but he backed down and took it easy on him the rest of practice. Christian chalked up the change in his teammates to his ability to excel in school for their benefit.

At home, his father did not mention one word about the broken window on the third floor, and Christian avoided bringing it up. However, his dad did throw a curve ball at him after dinner.

"Mr. Wells stopped by to see me this afternoon," his father said.

"What about?" Christian asked, thinking it involved Tim Kirth and the sign on his back or the flying stapler.

"It turns out that you aced his pretest," his father said.

"Well, that was easy," Christian responded. "Most of it covered what I studied last year."

"He's worried about you getting bored with the same material," his dad said.

"I guess I'll have to plow through it with everyone else," Christian responded.

"I don't think so," his father replied. "I called the district and the high school. You are going to be placed in a third period biology class. I believe the teacher is Mrs. Bloom."

Christian puzzled about how to approach this new development, but with the events of the day shedding a more positive light on life in Red Oak, Christian agreed to the schedule change. He had nothing to lose with the switch. In fact, he wanted the opportunity to be challenged a little more at the high school, and he liked the high school, but Christian did not want to tell his father that. He didn't want his father to have any inkling that things were not as rosy as they should be at the junior high.

The remainder of the week was tame compared to Monday's thrills. Christian adjusted to the junior high/high school dynamics and observed more of the same behavior from Cal, Devin, and Mitch during the school day. Christian found more football teammates in biology, and since he had brains, other players called on him to help with assignments. He even became a hot commodity when they chose lab partners for an experiment on Thursday.

Calvin and his henchmen continued to bully various kids during the week. They harassed an anti-social girl about her bad teeth during English class on Wednesday. They called her "Snaggletooth," and Mitch handed her a gnarled toothbrush that appeared to have spent its days scrubbing a bathroom floor.

Thursday, Tim became the target again.

Friday, Christian witnessed a "sprinkler" for the first time during P.E. While showering after gym, a couple of Calvin's cronies peed on the unsuspecting victim who had closed his eyes to wash the shampoo out of his hair. Christian did not know the name of the student who received the sprinkler, and honestly, he was just glad he had not received it.

The week ended with a shortened practice on Friday. Calvin and Christian got into a little scuffle during a tackling drill, but a couple of upperclassmen split them up before it got out of control.

As the weekend descended upon Red Oak, Christian felt pretty good about his improving situation. Brad seemed to be fitting in with some of the students on the periphery of Robinson's group, and Christian met more people at the high school. The two boys were still pretty tight, but Christian could see that their circle of friends grew larger each day.

A sophomore cheerleader gave Christian her phone number after practice on Friday, and she told him to give her a call over the weekend. Christian made up a lame excuse about homework and family obligations, because she did not seem to be his type. It made Christian feel good that a cheerleader noticed him; however, he did not want to be rude, so he lied. Sometimes, a lie ended up being the only way out. He saw no point in hurting her feelings.

Christian looked forward to next week. The change in his school schedule turned out as a plus, and a girl in his first two classes of the day at the junior high started to notice him. This time, the girl was more his type. She enjoyed learning, and she was cute, as well. In addition, the team had its first football game of the season and it was a home game.

"Monday is going to be a good day," Christian said to himself as he lay down to read before going to bed on Friday evening.

Little did he know another storm brewed on the horizon, and Monday was not going to be what he anticipated it to be.

CHAPTER
5

By Monday morning of the second week of school, Christian had an established routine set in place. The alarm went off at 6:45 a.m., and he grabbed some clothes and hustled up to the shower. Christian's attire always consisted of a pair of shorts and a t-shirt, nothing too fancy. His dad was always finished in the shower, so the two never played tug-o-war with the hot water. Christian showered quickly before he headed to the kitchen for two bowls of cereal. A quick brushing of the teeth and hair, and he completed the routine of getting ready for school. By the time he finished, Mrs. Pearson had both of his sisters roused from bed, and Christian fixed each sister a bowl of cereal before heading out the door to Brad's house. The entire process from start to finish took less than 30 minutes.

The weather had been excellent the first week of school, so the walk to Brad's house was no big deal. Today, however, it rained, so instead of making the short trip to the Matthews's house, Christian waited for Mrs. Matthews to swing by and pick him up. With no paper to read, since the Red Oak Express circulated only on Tuesdays and Fridays, Christian decided to flip on the television and check out the news. An Omaha station had a morning news program, and the weatherman entered the screen, forecasting rain for most of the week, including thunderstorms on Friday night. Of course, the chance for rain today was only thirty percent. Christian looked toward the window and thought the weatherman should have changed that to 100 percent. For Tuesday and Thursday, the chance of rain increased to forty percent, but Wednesday looked to be clear and sunny. Friday contained another chance of rain at fifty percent.

Christian's father sat down in the recliner next to the couch.

"Looks like a wet week ahead," his father said.

"Yeah, but those guys never get it right," Christian commented. "I'll bet you a million dollars that it rains on Wednesday."

"I'm just glad the rain held off until today. We had a broken window on the third floor that needed to be replaced," his dad said.

Mr. Pearson paused.

"We had it boarded up," he continued, "but they put in a new pane on Saturday. I am sure you heard about it at school last week."

Christian heard all about it from Brad, but it surprised him that his father waited until now to bring it up.

"Yeah, I heard about it," Christian said, leaving it at that.

"You know, Ms. Mack thinks it was a couple of football boys who were behind it, but she doesn't have any proof," his father said.

"Oh!" Christian faked surprise in response to his father's comment.

"I don't expect you to be an informant," his dad said. "I know that would put you in an awful position. It's bad enough your dad is the principal, but I do expect you to stay out of trouble. If I catch word that you are causing any trouble for other students or teachers, it will not be pleasant living in this house."

"I know, Dad," Christian said, understanding the point his father tried to make.

"I know you understand," Mr. Pearson continued, "but I wanted to remind you. See you at school."

Christian's father got up from the recliner and walked into the kitchen. He heard his dad tell his sisters to have a great day at school, and they gave him loud kisses that were easily audible from the living room. Christian's mother told her husband to have a good day before Mr. Pearson headed down the stairs to the basement. A moment later, the garage door whined its discontent. The garage door grumbled again as Mr. Pearson left.

Brad's mom dropped them off at school, and before long, Christian found his seat in Mrs. Droll's English class. They finished up a review last week, so she handed back the quiz from Friday. Brad glowed when he got his back with a large 95 written in red and circled. Christian did not bother to show Brad the 110 percent on his paper.

"Why ruin his shining moment by making unfair comparisons?" he thought.

While Mrs. Droll discussed the components of writing a friendly letter compared to a business letter, he caught a glimpse of his father walking down the hallway. Next to Mr. Pearson, a tall, slender man glided effortlessly. Christian did not get a very good look at the man, but Christian saw that he wore black slacks, a white button-down shirt, and a tie. Three teenagers followed behind Mr. Pearson and the sharply dressed man. The overhead fan, along with Mrs. Droll's words, kept him from hearing the discussion in the hallway. Christian's father never mentioned anything about visitors to Christian this weekend or this morning before school.

They stopped in front of Mrs. Droll's door, and Christian heard his dad explain insignificant details about the school, but that was it. Before they ventured out of view, he got one last glimpse of the teenagers. One boy and two girls stepped out from behind the man in the tie to look through the doorway, then they disappeared.

Brad leaned over to ask Christian, "Who was that?"

He shrugged, noticing Mrs. Droll giving him the teacher-look. Christian guessed the three teens were new students, but he wondered if all three of them were in the ninth grade. He would have to sneak into his father's office before catching the bus to the high school for biology and math. Hopefully, he could get some information from his dad.

The hallway buzzed with discussions about the visitors during first period. Christian pieced together that his dad gave a tour to three new students who had the same father. No one knew which one would be joining the freshman class. His father's office stood empty after the second period bell, but Christian did not have enough time to wait for him.

By the time he returned to the middle school for fifth period lunch, the guessing game ended. One of the teachers told a class that three new students toured the school this morning. A boy and two girls were joining Red Oak Junior High as freshmen.

Christian heard Cal Robinson announce from his lunch table, "Well, I hope he doesn't plan on going out for football; we don't need another new kid screwing things up around here."

Christian did not bother turning around to look at Calvin because he knew who Calvin referred to. Everyone did.

"Moron," Brad muttered under his breath.

As Brad uttered the words, a marinara meatball landed hard on Christian's tray and spaghetti sauce exploded everywhere. The meat projectile had passed within inches of Christian's ear. When he looked down, Christian saw his t-shirt had little streaks of red on it. Brad took a little shrapnel on his own sleeve, but it blended in with Brad's black t-shirt. Fortunately, no one sat across from Brad and Christian, so they ended up as the only victims of the meatball assault.

Christian slowly turned around and saw Maxwell laughing and spitting all over his own lunch. Devin pointed at Maxwell calling him "China man," and Cal tried to contain his own joy. A couple of the other idiots laughed, too. The only one at Calvin's table who failed to even crack a smile was Miles Jones.

"Do you need a napkin?" Cal sneered at Christian from his table.

Christian stood up but opted not to say a single word. Watching Calvin and his buddies the previous week, he realized that reacting incited more Calvin wannabees to join in the fray. Christian just stared at Calvin as he calmly walked over to his table and reached for a napkin next to Mitch Maxwell's tray. In doing so, Christian intentionally knocked over Mitch's milk, which poured onto Cal's lunch tray.

"I'm sooo sorry, Calvin," Christian said in a steady voice. "Here, use this napkin."

Christian wiped some sauce off his own shirt and then tossed the napkin into Calvin's lap. Then, Chistian turned around and strolled back to his seat to finish his meal. Brad looked at Calvin's table as Christian sat down with his back to them and proceeded to finish his lunch.

The laughing at the table stopped the moment Christian knocked the milk carton over. In fact, the entire lunchroom quieted, but Christian didn't care. He endured it on the football field in practice, and over the last week, he witnessed what Calvin and his friends did to other students. Cal's group strode around like they were entitled to do whatever they pleased, like everyone had to bow to the thugs. One good week of school made Christian realize that he refused to allow them to take any joy away from him. On his own, Christian could take any one of Calvin's entourage, including Mitch Maxwell. Christian was not concerned about his safety. He did not plan to make a stand. When that meatball landed on his tray, he intended to walk over to Calvin Robinson and punch him in the face. Fortunately, the words of his father cracked through the thick thinking of his angry mind as he stood up.

"If I catch word that you are causing any trouble for other students or teachers, it will not be pleasant living in this house," his father had said.

Christian planned to grab a napkin and return to his seat at his table, but when he saw Mitch's milk carton, he nudged it just right to make a mess but not to draw attention from the lunchroom supervisors.

"Are they still looking over here?" Christian asked Brad.

"Uh-huh," Brad said dumbfounded.

Christian grabbed his milk and turned toward the group of boys. He raised the milk carton as if to toast Calvin's shocked table. Cal's muscles tensed and he stared at Christian, who turned back around appearing disinterested, and Brad did the same. The cafeteria returned to normal, and soon Christian heard Devin telling a joke. Christian sensed Calvin was not laughing this time.

Christian and Brad emptied their trays and returned to their seats. As they walked back, Cal's entire table decided to dump their trays, as well. Calvin Robinson glared at Christian, as he and Brad approached Calvin's pack. Calvin mumbled something about Christian's sexual orientation, and the Calvin cronies laughed. Christian gave no response; he just smiled and took his seat.

The students were dismissed from lunch before heading to the gym. Students at Red Oak had P.E. every day, which Christian did not mind at all. He was sitting in front of his locker and changing his clothes when Miles Jones entered the locker room and selected the seat next to Christian. On occasion, when Calvin's pack wasn't around, Christian found Miles to be unlike the rest of his group. The two weren't friends, but Christian liked him.

"Robinson is really pissed at you," Miles said.

There was genuine concern in his voice, like he almost cared about Christian becoming a target. When Miles found out Christian switched to a different science class at the high school, Miles had approached him after a football practice. Miles told Christian that science was tough for him and he asked if Christian would be willing to help him with his homework. Of all of Cal's friends, Christian appreciated Miles. Christian was beginning to appreciate him and he told Miles he would get a copy of the ninth grade science book from his father.

"Call me at home any night. Nobody has to know," Christian told him.

Miles called him on Thursday and once over the weekend. The two boys did not talk about anything that friends talked about. Miles just asked Christian about the questions he failed to figure out or the things he did not understand, and Christian tried his best to help him. The tutoring was almost businesslike.

Now, they sat together in the locker room, changing for gym class as Miles warned Christian about Cal's anger.

Like I couldn't figure that one out on my own, Christian thought.

"You know what, Miles? I really could care less if Cal's mad at me," Christian said. "Why do you hang out with him? That guy's a jerk!"

Christian did not pull any punches this time as he said it loud enough for anyone in the locker room to hear it. Christian pulled on his P.E. shirt and stood up. Brad closed in behind Christian as they rounded the corner to go into the gym. Calvin pushed his way through the door with his head turned, looking back at Devin and laughing. Christian emphasized his distaste for Calvin by leaning his shoulder into him, catching him off guard. Calvin's head swiveled back around as Christian lowered his shoulder, and Calvin Robinson's body jolted the locker room door.

"I'm sorry, Calvin," Christian said apologetically. "I didn't see you."

Calvin responded with a weak shove as Christian cut through the rest of Calvin's friends and settled down on the first row of the bleachers, waiting for class to start.

"Do you have a death wish or something?" Brad asked.

"Look, why should he be able to make my life miserable, or anyone else's for that matter?" Christian answered.

Brad shrugged and changed the subject, "Hey, do you know who the three new students are?"

"Nope," he replied, "but I plan to ask Dad about it tonight; sooner if I can get to the office while he's in there."

"There is a rumor that they're triplets," Brad said.

"Well, I didn't get a good look at any of them except for my dad and that tall, slender guy in the tie," Christian said.

"I wonder how they'll fit in?" Brad asked.

Christian had not thought about that. Three new students were going to be entering the building tomorrow. Christian felt even better about what he had just done to Calvin. No one should be subjected to Calvin Robinson.

"At least Cal will leave them alone," Christian said.

"Why is that?" Brad asked with an expression of puzzlement.

"Well, after what I did to Calvin, he'll be focused on me for awhile," Christian explained.

"And that's good?" Brad asked incredulously.

"Yep," Christian replied.

"Sometimes I don't understand you," Brad said, as he stood up to walk to the water fountain.

Calvin came out of the locker room and stood directly in front of Christian. Devin and Mitch stood, flanking Calvin, one on each side, while Mr. Mauer, the gym teacher, lingered in the locker room. Christian leaned back on the bleacher row behind where he sat and faked a yawn.

"What's up Cal?" Christian said.

"You're lucky I don't…" Calvin started and then paused.

"Lucky you don't what, Cal?" Christian responded.

Mr. Mauer entered the gym from the door to the locker room. Other boys filed out, and Mr. Mauer barked orders about getting into stretching lines. Christian jumped up from the bleachers and walked right through the three boys standing in front of him. They parted as Christian passed by, nudging Cal with his shoulder.

"You're a punk," Christian whispered toward Calvin, so only he heard it.

The class played wall ball for the entire period. The game mimicked kick ball, but players had to run around the bases twice to score a run. More than one person occupied the same base at a time, and Christian enjoyed playing it, especially since Cal ended up on the other team. On two separate occasions, Calvin tried to drill him with the ball and missed. After gym class, Cal made a couple more comments to him in the locker room, but Christian just ignored him. In addition, Cal tried to drop a shoulder into Christian in the hallway, but Christian saw it coming and moved.

Christian started paying more attention to the other students in his remaining classes. In industrial arts, Brad and Christian paired up with two "Square Rats." Square rats, or skate boarders, tended to hang out near the town square. Brad and Christian built a birdhouse with the two of them.

In study hall, Christian got a note from the cute girl in his English class, Ruby James. A friend of Ruby's dropped it on Christian's desk while he concentrated on his math homework. The note explained her level of boredom in art and how she thought Christian was cute. She asked Christian if he had a girlfriend, and then told him to write back.

He jotted down that he had no girlfriend and left it at that. He gave his response to her friend, Molly, and told her to deliver it for him. Molly giggled and nodded.

After dinner that night, Christian asked his dad about the three new students he saw during first period. They finished clearing the dishes from the table, but more work had to be done. Even though their family owned a dishwasher, they needed to scrub the remnants of the meal off their plates. The dishwasher needed to be upgraded, but that particular item sat a long way down the list of to-dos.

"Oh, yes, I was wondering if you saw them," his father said. "They moved into town over the weekend. They're renting a farmhouse a couple miles out of town to the south. I think it is somewhere on 'J' Avenue."

"I have no idea where 'J' Avenue is," Christian said. "Are all three of them in ninth grade?"

"Yep," his dad responded.

"The rumor mill is on full speed," Christian said. "Some of the students are saying they're triplets."

"They're not triplets," his father answered, grunting, "Rumors," in disgust. "Mr. Banner does survey work for construction companies. The county is planning to do some roadwork this fall, and Mr. Banner has been brought in to work on the upcoming road project."

"I didn't see his wife," Christian thought aloud.

"His wife passed away years ago," his father explained. "Mr. Banner is raising those three on his own."

"If they aren't triplets, how does he have three kids the same age?" Christian asked.

His father paused, and Christian guessed he contemplated just how much information to release to his son.

Mr. Pearson answered, "They all have the same last name."

He gave Christian only a little information to work with.

"So… they are all his kids then," Christian said.

"I guess so," his dad shrugged. "They were all very polite and well-mannered. Mr. Banner was also polite. He appears to be a well-educated man."

"Do you remember their names?" Christian asked.

"Well, why are you so interested?" his father quizzed. "Did you think one of the girls was pretty?"

Mr. Pearson jabbed his son in the stomach playfully.

"Nah," Christian answered, "I was just curious. Most of the school is curious."

"The boy's name is Raymond," his father started to give more details, "but he goes by Ray. He's a good lookin' kid. He looked athletic, but when I asked him about sports he said that he wasn't big on sports. The taller of the two girls is Alexis. She had the dark black hair. The other one is Samantha. They are both cuties, don't you think?"

"I didn't get a good look at them, remember?"

Christian handed scrubbed plates to his father who loaded them into the dishwasher. As they cleared the glasses from the table, Christian could hear Kat whining from the bathroom as her mother tried to get her into the tub. Ann finished her evening shower ritual and sang along to some teenybopper song playing in her bedroom.

"But, Mom," Kat pleaded, "I took a shower yesterday!"

"Yes, but you spent the day working hard at school," her mother contested. "Besides, you played in the backyard when you got home and made those mud pies with your friend."

"But I'm clean," Kat continued to argue.

"I can smell you from the kitchen!" Mr. Pearson hollered.

"See," Mrs. Pearson pleaded, "even your daddy thinks you need a shower."

"Why doesn't Christian take a shower?" Kat whined, but she already knew the answer.

"Honey, Christian will take a shower in the morning, like he always does," Mrs. Pearson said as she started the water running.

Katherine gave in, and once she got in the shower, she refused to get out. The irony of the entire episode repeated almost every night. After his mom spent all that energy getting Kat into the tub, Kat did not want to get out, so Mrs. Pearson stormed out of the bathroom and plopped onto the couch in disgust next to her husband.

"I got her in there," Mrs. Pearson announced, "so you can get her out."

Christian's father gruffly rose from the sofa and made his way up a couple of steps to the bathroom. In a minute, the water quit and Kat and her father laughed. Christian's mother brushed Kat's hair in the living room before she ushered both of the girls to bed.

The phone rang, and Mr. Pearson answered it.

"Yes, he's here," he said. "It's for you, Christian."

"I'll grab it downstairs," Christian said. "It's probably Miles with a question on his science."

Christian's father covered the phone.

"It's a girl," he said with a huge grin on his face.

"Then I'll definitely take it in the basement," Christian replied.

He flew through the kitchen and down the stairs.

Christian grabbed the phone on his nightstand and yelled, "I got it!"

He waited for the click from upstairs before he spoke into the phone. Christian's parents still had not bought a new cell phone for him, even though his phone lay on the bottom of Lake Albert. A new cell phone ranked below a new dishwasher on the infamous family to-buy list.

"Hello, this is Christian," he said.

Giggling filled the phone line, and it sounded like more than one girl.

"Hey, Christian," the voice answered. "This is Molly Weston. I gave you the note in study hall today."

"Yeah," he responded, nonchalantly.

Christian did not know what to say, since his experience with girls was limited. He dated a couple of different girls last year, but nothing got real serious.

"Well, there is someone here who wants to talk to you," Molly said, giggling again.

"Okay," Christian said, nervously.

Another voice came on the line, "Hi, Christian, do you know who this is?"

Christian recognized the sweet voice of Ruby James in an instant. She was the cute girl in his English class, and her voice matched her petite frame, soft and hesitant.

"Hello, Ruby," Christian managed to utter.

He felt himself blush even though he had no mirror to check for sure.

"Is it okay that we're calling you after eight o'clock?" she asked with genuine concern. "I don't want to get you in trouble with your dad."

"I probably shouldn't talk for long," Christian said, "but you can call anytime before nine. My folks don't think it's polite to make calls after nine o'clock."

"Oh, that's good to know," Ruby said.

Even Ruby's voice had a cute tone to it.

"Anyway, what can I do for you?" Christian asked.

"Well, I was wondering if you wanted to go see a movie with Molly and me tomorrow," Ruby said.

Her words sent his heart into palpitations.

"I'll have to ask my folks," he responded. "With it being a school night, I'm not sure what they'll say. How about if I let you know tomorrow in English?"

"Sure," Ruby replied.

Christian heard a voice in the background, "Come on! Ask him!"

The prodding voice belonged to Molly.

Ruby said, "Okay, okay, geez!"

"What does Molly want you to ask me?" Christian said.

"Do you think Brad would come with you?" she asked. "Molly thinks he's cute."

The phone banged around on the other end of the line, and Christian could hear Ruby laughing.

Ruby picked up the phone and said, "Sorry about that. I guess I wasn't supposed to tell you that part."

"I can ask Brad if he wants to go," Christian said. "What time is the movie?"

"Seven o'clock," Ruby replied.

"I'll call Brad and let you know at school," he said.

"See you tomorrow," she cooed.

"Yeah, see ya tomorrow," he repeated.

Ruby hung up and Christian quickly walked upstairs. His mother lay on the couch and his father leaned back in the recliner with his feet up. His mom read a book, while his father watched T.V.

"I know tomorrow is a school night, but can Brad and I go to the movies with a couple girls?" Christian said, waiting for the argument bound to come from his question.

"What time is the movie?" Mr. Pearson said before Christian's mother had a chance to squelch any hope.

"Seven o'clock. We would meet them down there and then have someone pick us up as soon as it was done," Christian answered quickly.

"What movie?" Dad asked.

Christian did not even know what movie they planned to see.

"I don't know, I guess whatever movie is showing," Christian said with a shrug.

"Football goes until six o'clock, so you won't have much time to eat and shower before the show," his mom chimed in. "If you have homework, you'll have to do it after the movie. I don't know about this, Ken."

His father said, "I don't like you doing homework that late, and we always eat as a family."

"Come on, Dad!" Christian pleaded, fighting a losing battle. "I always get good grades, and I am usually up until eleven or so anyway. You know I'll get my homework done, if I have any."

"Boy, she must be cute!" Christian's dad flashed a smile at him. "Who is it?"

Christian knew his parents would not let him go if he did not reveal to them who the mystery date was. He also knew his father would harass him about her for the rest of the week.

"Ruby James," he said after a long pause punctuated with a sigh.

"She hasn't caused any trouble at school, yet," his father said, turning to his wife.

Christian's father may be the junior high principal and the breadwinner of the family, but his mom made the big decisions. Christian saw her going through the what-if scenarios in her mind.

"We're just going to the movies," Christian begged.

"All right," she said, "but you better have your work done for school the next day."

"I will!" Christian shouted as he hustled down the stairs to call Brad.

Brad told Christian he would talk to his parents, but Brad thought it would not be a problem. Mr. and Mrs. Matthews were a little more lax with the rules than Christian's parents. Brad called back a couple of minutes later to let Christian know he could go. They talked a little bit about Molly, and Brad refused to call it a date because he thought Molly lacked in the looks department.

"You owe me for this one," Brad complained.

"I'll buy your ticket," Christian said.

"And a Pepsi," Brad added.

Christian worked on biology in the dining room. The phone rang again, but this time it was Miles Jones on the other end of the line.

"Can you help me with my homework?" Miles asked.

"It's Miles," Christian told his parents. "Sure, I could use a break from biology."

Christian grabbed his copy of the ninth grade science book, and he helped Miles with two problems that seemed pretty easy, even for Miles. When Christian made a comment about it, Miles got serious.

"Christian, Cal is really ticked about what happened today in the cafeteria and gym," Miles stammered. Miles talked in a hushed voice, like he worried about someone trying to listen in on their conversation.

"Give me a second," Christian told him before running downstairs and lifting up the receiver in his room. After hurrying back upstairs to hang up the phone in the kitchen, he rushed back down to his room.

"I need to get cordless phones for Mom and Dad this Christmas," Christian thought, tired from the trips up and down the stairs for phone calls.

"Okay, Miles. I'm in my room, now," Christian said.

"Cal was talking after practice about getting even with you," Miles said. "Now, you have been really nice to me, even though I hang out with him. I mean, you've been helping with my science, so I sort of feel like I owe you."

"Don't worry, Miles," Christian said, "I won't tell anyone that you talked to me."

That seemed to relax Miles a little bit. Christian could read his discomfort around Calvin and Mitch when they bullied other kids, but Christian also knew Miles was in that group. If someone found out that Miles was calling Christian, Miles would end up in a dangerous predicament.

"I just wanted to make sure you wouldn't tell anyone," Miles said, nervously.

"Did he say how he was going to get even?" Christian asked.

"Nah, he's just really ticked about how you stood up to him, I guess," Miles said. "Cal isn't used to someone doing that. He pretty much gets his way, but you should know that he used to date Ruby."

"Aw, crap," Christian said.

That made the situation more complicated for Christian.

"Yeah, and I know she likes you because Molly can't keep her mouth shut about anything," Miles continued. "Molly said something to me while Devin and I were waiting for the bus to football after school. I just wanted to let you know."

"Thanks, Miles," Christian said.

"Just know that if Molly knows something," Miles chuckled, "the whole town is going to know it."

"See you at school tomorrow," Christian said.

He hung up the phone.

Christian finished his biology and put his backpack by the front door. The excitement about the movies waned due to the phone call from Miles. Christian almost hoped his parents would change their mind.

The next morning, Christian walked up to Brad's house. The rain in the forecast ended and clear skies and sunshine appeared. The muggy air slowed Christian's steps as he trudged up the driveway to the Matthews's front door.

Brad greeted him on the front steps and said, "Let's walk."

They had plenty of time, and Christian guessed Brad wanted to discuss Molly and the movies without his mother eavesdropping. Christian did not mention a word about the discussion he had with Miles, but he did take time to tell Brad that he thought Molly had a big mouth.

"No kidding," Brad laughed. "I think she is the queen of gossip in our class."

"Good," thought Christian. *"Brad will be careful about what he says about Calvin and the other boys."*

Christian filled Brad in on what he learned from his father about the three new kids. He told Brad their names and that their father worked on road construction.

Brad asked, "Are they triplets?"

"I don't think so," Christian said, "but they do all have the same last name. It's Banner. Dad didn't give me much more to go on."

"That Ruby James is cute," Brad said, changing the subject.

"Yeah, but she used to date Cal," Christian said.

"What!" Brad exclaimed. "Who told you that?"

"My dad said he heard that when I told him who asked us to the movies," Christian lied.

"And the plot thickens," Brad commented.

"Hopefully it's no big deal," Christian added.

"Knowing Calvin Robinson," Brad smiled, "it will bug the crap out of him."

Yesterday, Christian traveled past the point of no return with Cal. He ended any hope of making a go at friendship when he dumped the milk on Calvin's tray. Christian rethought the stand he decided to take, as he and Brad crossed Fourth Street and stepped onto school grounds.

He decided to skip the office and headed to the third floor. Mr. Button stood outside of his room talking to the three new students. Christian needed to go the opposite direction to get to English, but Mr. Button called him over when he saw Christian at his locker.

"Christian, come here," Mr. Button said. "I want to introduce you to our new students."

"Hello," Christian said.

Mr. Button began the introductions, "This is Ray, Alexis, and Samantha."

He pointed to the boy and then each girl as he said their names.

Ray matched Christian in height, but Ray appeared more muscular. He had blonde hair that looked almost white and buzzed sides with a flat top. His skin was pale as well, and a few tan freckles mingled with red pock marks. Christian assumed they were the remnants of zits. Puberty attacked some kids more violently than others, and puberty appeared to be Ray's number one enemy. Ray's eyes were a mix of green and hazel, and he wore blue jeans and a long-sleeved shirt.

"Aren't you hot?" Christian asked, remarking on Ray's attire. "It's going to be at least 90 today with humidity close to 80 percent."

"I haven't unpacked my shorts yet," he said in an unexpectedly deep voice.

"He has a skin condition," said Alexis. "The sun is tough on his skin, so he likes to wear long sleeves and jeans when it isn't too hot."

Ray rolled his eyes and looked away, seeming a little bothered with his sister's volunteering of information.

Alexis had a warm smile. Her jet black hair matched her olive skin, which stood out because she wore a bright orange tank top and khaki skirt. She was tall and lean and her arms and legs were muscular and taut. As she reached out to shake Christian's hand, her cat-like movements reminded him of a panther moving in to pounce. She shook his hand firmly but with a feminine touch.

"Pleased to meet you both," Christian said as he released his hand from hers and turned to greet the third member of the Banner family.

Samantha stood barely over five feet tall and a good six inches shorter than Alexis. When Christian turned to greet her, he stopped cold. Her deep blue eyes fixed on him suspiciously. They dazzled below locks of curly brown hair with streaks of sandy blonde mixed in. Her furrowed brow puzzled Christian for a second. She blinked, and the hardened features of her face melted into a genuine smile. He noticed a blush in her cheeks, like Christian caught her sneaking a peek at Christmas presents. Samantha wore khaki capri pants and a blue blouse. Her skin had an almond quality to it. Both girls were quite attractive, but in different ways.

Samantha reached out her hand and said, "Call me Sam."

Christian shook her soft, delicate hand, which felt very different from Alexis' grip. For three kids with the same father, they sure did not look alike in any way. Christian did not get a good look at the man in the hallway the day before, but he could not see any family resemblance in any of the siblings.

"So, are you all related?" Christian asked.

"Sort of," said Ray.

"We're all adopted," explained Alexis.

Mr. Button interrupted, "If the three of you have any questions, this guy is probably the best student to ask. He's pretty reliable."

"That's good to know," Sam said. "Christian, I'll be sure to find you before this day is over."

The three teens walked past Christian and found their lockers.

Mr. Button leaned close to Christian and said, "I think she was flirting with you."

"Come on," Christian said, embarrassed.

He turned around to head to English class, and Mr. Button chuckled as he watched him leave.

Sam turned to watch Christian pass by.

"Maybe she was flirting," he thought.

Brad caught Christian before he entered English and started quizzing him about the three new students.

"So, I heard you talked to the three new students," Brad commented raising his eyebrows.

"Yeah," Christian answered, "they seem pretty normal to me."

"So, are they all from the same family?" Brad asked.

"Yes," Christian stated without giving Brad any more information.

Christian knew it would bug Brad.

"Yes... and...?" Brad quizzed, waiting for Christian to give more details.

"And what?" Christian asked.

He enjoyed making Brad squirm a little bit.

"So, how are they from the same family?" Brad asked, his impatience growing.

"Oh," Christian paused, acting like he just realized what Brad wanted to know. "They are all adopted by the same man. They're not triplets, they're not related by blood, and they all seemed pretty nice to me."

"Names? Do they have names?" Brad questioned.

"Yes, they do," Christian responded.

He turned to point out who was who of the three new students.

Christian continued, "The boy's name is Raymond, but he goes by Ray. The shorter girl standing next to him is Sam, short for Samantha. The other girl has black hair, but I don't see her. Her name is Alexis."

In the distant end of the hallway, he found Alexis; her eyes set squarely on him. Her skin seemed darker under the blazing orange top in the poor lighting of the hallway. She glided effortlessly down the hall, avoiding students, but keeping her eyes fixed on his conversation with Brad. As she approached Ray and Sam, an uncomfortable feeling crept into the pit of Christian's stomach. Alexis leaned in close to Sam's ear and whispered. Samantha Banner immediately looked in Christian's direction.

He did not know what to do, so like any freshman boy caught looking at a girl, Christian turned away from Sam quickly.

That pit in his stomach grew larger and heavier. Christian could still feel the weight of Alexis's eyes, even though he looked the other way. When Christian turned back toward the girls, Sam and Alexis continued to stare in his direction.

Samantha smiled and waved at Christian.

He waved back, relieved that the look from Sam was friendly. Alexis did not wave as she continued to eye him with a sinister glare. At that moment, he realized what prey must feel like when it locks eyes with a predator. Alexis did not appear to be angry, but her hard black eyes cut through him. No matter how much Christian wanted to look away, his eyes disobeyed. He feared taking his eyes off Alexis, terrified that the minute he looked away, she would race after him like a cheetah giving chase to an antelope on the African savannah.

"Dude, what has gotten into you?" Brad asked, snapping Christian back to reality.

"What do you mean?" Christian asked, turning his head away from Alexis, reluctantly.

"Well, for starters, I have been talking to you for the last minute, and you haven't answered a single question," Brad said in irritation. "You keep staring at those three new students."

"I was?" Christian said in confusion.

Brad seemed a little baffled. "Yeah, I told you that the two new girls were hot. Then I asked about the movie with Molly and Ruby. After that I told you that my mom would drop us off, if your mom would pick us up. Then I asked if you had seen the alien spaceship land in front of the school."

"I'm sorry," Christian responded, "I was zoning out."

"Well, Sam's wave seemed friendly, but what is with the tall girl?" Brad asked.

"So, you saw it, too?" Christian said, excitedly. "How she was staring at me?"

"Yeah, what was that about?" Brad said. "She just stared at you the whole time."

"I don't know," Christian replied, "but it kind of creeped me out."

"If I had two good-looking girls looking at me," Brad said, "I don't know if it would creep me out." He laughed and punched Christian in the shoulder. "We better get to English."

As the students filed into the various classes, Brad and Christian fell in line behind a couple of students entering Mrs. Droll's classroom. They still had a few minutes before the bell, so Christian stopped by Ruby James's desk to give her the good news about the movies.

"We will have to meet you guys at the theater because of football practice, but Brad and I both got the okay from our parents," Christian informed Ruby.

She blushed a bit and smiled.

"Great!" she said. "I can't wait until tonight."

Christian started to walk to his desk, but Ruby's hand reached up and lightly touched his arm, beckoning him to wait a moment longer. She gently pulled on Christian to get him to kneel down beside her desk. Ruby touched him softly as he knelt closer. Christian could smell the fragrance of her perfume as she leaned close to his ear.

Ruby whispered, "We may not watch much of the movie."

Then, she let go of his arm.

As Christian staggered back to his desk, the aroma of her perfume lingered with him for a few moments. Normally, a boy sent that kind of message from a cute girl spent the day in a foggy haze. Christian headed down that path until he sat down at his desk. The fog lasted all of ten seconds.

From the other side of the room, Christian felt the gaze of a panther on him. Alexis took up residence in the second seat on the far end of the classroom. Her deep, black eyes cut into him once more.

Brad leaned over. "What did Ruby say?"

"I'll tell you later," Christian whispered.

Alexis turned her eyes to the front of the room as Mrs. Droll started class.

CHAPTER
6

Christian wanted to be on cloud nine because he had a date with Ruby James. By the sound of it, Ruby planned on doing more than just watching the movie, but the uncomfortable interference of Alexis Banner interrupted Christian's euphoria. However, by the end of second period, he no longer feared Alexis. Actually, Christian became intrigued by her. She possessed this uncanny ability to look in Christian's direction any time he had a serious conversation with Brad. It happened twice in English. After first period, Brad stopped by Christian's locker. Brad babbled on about how cute Alexis was and asked Christian for his opinion of her. When Christian looked up to answer, Alexis stared at them from her locker, which was at least sixty feet away.

"She is kind of mysterious," Christian whispered.

"Mysterious," Brad laughed. "She's hot!"

In social studies, all three of the new students joined the class. They filled in the last three seats in the row closest to the door. Alexis sat in the third seat with Samantha behind her and Ray behind Sam. During class, Brad leaned over to tell Christian that he planned on asking Alexis out. As soon as Brad uttered those words, Christian noticed Alexis stiffen a bit before she continued to write down the notes from the board.

Brad Matthews took notice of Alexis like a number of other boys in the ninth grade, and Christian overheard Calvin Robinson make a comment to his cronies about Alexis' level of appeal. Calvin motioned for Devin Rammick to throw a piece of paper at her, and of course, Devin did just what Cal asked.

Alexis whirled around in her seat to face the offender, but the look she gave to Devin differed from the look Christian observed in the hallway and in Mrs. Droll's classroom. Alexis glared at Devin in utter disdain, and Christian sighed in relief upon seeing the difference.

"Please refrain from making childish gestures of flirtation towards me while I am trying to do my work," Alexis snarled in a low voice.

"Devin!" Mr. Button said as he turned from the board, "Would you please meet me outside the classroom for a moment?"

Mr. Button did not ask. He demanded.

Calvin contained his laugh as Devin rose from his desk and walked to the door. Mr. Button followed behind Devin, and the door closed. The entire class listened intently as Mr. Button chewed Devin out. Then, Alexis turned on Calvin.

"You know it takes a weak boy to make another student do his dirty work," she stated. "If you wanted to ask me out, you should have done it in a more mature manner. I hate to tell you, but my answer will always be a resounding NO!"

Alexis emphasized the last word.

"I don't want to go out with you!" Cal protested, emphatically, but Christian sensed disappointment in Calvin's voice.

"Whatever," Alexis responded, holding up her left hand and looking away to her right. "Our conversation is done."

"I wouldn't be caught dead with you," Calvin replied to her snub. "You freak! You're all freaks!"

"You better watch your mouth, punk," a deep voice from the back of Alexis' row growled.

Ray's pale face changed over to a light shade of red.

"It's okay, Ray," Alexis said in a soothing tone. "Don't even waste your breath. He isn't worth the trouble."

Ray's face cooled as the redness faded, but he still eyed Calvin with distaste. Alexis went back to finishing her notes as Devin returned to the classroom.

"Sorry for the interruption," Mr. Button stated calmly. "I think the disruption has been dealt with."

Christian enjoyed the poetic irony of it. Yes, the disruption had been dealt with, but not in the way Mr. Button thought it was handled. Alexis did an admirable job of handling Calvin Robinson all by herself.

By the time Christian returned from his trip to the high school, the new students acquired a nickname, and all of the ninth grade referred to Alexis, Sam, and Ray as "The Three." Brad filled Christian in on what he missed while he was away.

Mitch Maxwell received his introduction to Alexis during science. After hearing Devin tell an off-color joke, Mitch started spitting like he always does when he laughs. After collecting some of the spray on her arm, Alexis told Mitch he should "wear a bib to school to keep the slobber off his shirt." Alexis walked away, and when Mitch tried to follow her, Ray stepped into his path. Mitch pushed into Ray, and Ray pushed back firmly.

"It was just some shoving, nobody threw a punch," Brad said, as the two boys sat down to eat lunch. "So no one got into any trouble from Mr. Wells."

"I wouldn't want to tangle with Ray," Christian said. "He looks pretty tough."

"Speaking of The Three," Brad commented, "I wonder where they're going to sit for lunch?"

The Three grabbed their lunches and surveyed the cafeteria.

"With us, of course," Christian said, as he waved for The Three to sit at their table.

"What are you doing?" Brad whispered with concern.

"They're in the same boat we are," Christian replied, "new students."

Brad did not return Christian's charitable smile.

The Three joined Brad and Christian at the table.

"Thanks for inviting us to sit with you," Samantha bubbled.

Samantha's brown hair bobbed with enthusiasm, as she sat across from Christian. Alexis and Ray took the two remaining seats. Ray sat quietly next to Brad, and Alexis chose the seat next to Christian. Christian debated if Alexis wanted to sit by him or if she chose that seat to avoid sitting next to Brad.

"It's nice to eat with someone besides him for a change," Christian commented, as he motioned to his only friend in Red Oak. "Have you all met Brad?"

"We have not been introduced," Samantha said with a smile. "I am Samantha Banner, but you can call me Sam."

Had Sam been closer to Brad, Christian thought she would have put out her hand to shake his. Now that Sam sat close to Christian, he seized the opportunity to view her up close. Besides their meeting in front of Mr. Button's room, Christian had not had any real conversation with Sam. In fact, he failed to converse with any of them.

"Brad, this is Alexis and Ray," Christian said as he pointed to each of them. "Guys, this is Brad Matthews."

Ray stuck out his hand to shake.

"Pleased to meet you," Ray said, before releasing his grip to take a bite of his sandwich.

Christian noticed Brad's discomfort ease after shaking Ray's hand.

"Don't let Ray scare you," Sam said. "He really isn't as gruff as he looks."

"What is there to do in this town?" Alexis asked. "Is there a movie theater?"

Brad pounced on her question.

"Yes, there is a theater. We're going to go to the seven o'clock showing of Epicenter," Brad said, as he transformed from meek to enthusiastic.

"I hear that is supposed to be good," Ray said.

"You guys could join us," Brad responded.

Christian's anxiety level grew.

"Is it just the two of you going?" Alexis asked.

Christian knew what Alexis hinted at behind that smile, as she emphasized the word "two."

"No," Christian said, "a couple of girls were going to meet us there."

"And it would be great if you three joined us!" Brad added, enthusiastically.

Christian kicked Brad under the table.

"We would love to join you," Sam said. "It's a date!"

"So, you don't mind if The Three join you out in public?" Alexis said, looking at Christian for his response.

"That would be great!" Brad answered, almost shouting.

Alexis' gaze continued to pry at Christian, as he accepted the fact that he would be seeing the entire movie after all.

"Fine by me," Christian said, wondering how Ruby would react when he told her The Three planned to join them on their first date. At least he didn't have to pay Brad's way into the movie anymore, but he would wait to inform Brad of that detail in study hall.

"Do you like movie theater popcorn?" Sam asked Christian from across the table.

Her deep blue eyes sparkled as she spoke. Alexis had drawn all of his attention up to this point, but now Christian saw Samantha's beauty at least equaled her sister's looks.

"Yes, I do enjoy good movie popcorn," Christian responded.

"Great!" Sam exclaimed. "I can't eat a jumbo tub by myself, so we can share one. I'll buy."

Christian noticed Sam's flirtations.

"Great," he thought to himself, *"Ruby doesn't want to watch the movie because she has other ideas, and Sam wants to share a tub of popcorn with me, and Brad has the hots for Alexis, not to mention that Molly is going to blab the events of the evening to the entire school tomorrow. This trip to the movies is going to be an absolute fiasco."*

Christian dreaded study hall for good reason. Molly started in on Christian as soon as he arrived, because Brad already broke the news that The Three would be joining them for the evening. What did Brad care? He didn't like Molly, and Alexis planned on going, anyway.

Christian ended up apologizing to Molly for the mix-up, even though it was not his fault. He met up with Ruby after school and explained how Brad invited The Three to the movies. Ruby appeared a little bummed by the news, but she seemed okay with it.

"I guess we'll have to watch the movie, then," she said with a flirtatious smile, before Christian left for football practice.

The Red Oak Tigers would open the season on Friday against Rock Port, Missouri, so the freshmen offensive unit ran some of Rock Port's offensive sets to help the team prepare for the different looks they would see on game day. Coach Cozad referred to them as the "scout team" during practice. Rock Port's offense traditionally ran out of the I-formation. Christian understood this offense. Not only did his beloved Nebraska Cornhuskers run a similar offense in the past, but his team in Omaha ran the same one, too.

Rock Port ran the option. Basically, two backs lined up behind the quarterback in the shape of an "I." The fullback lined up behind the quarterback, while the second back, the I-back, stood three yards behind the fullback. This gave the quarterback three options. He could hand off to the fullback on a dive play up the middle. The second option meant the quarterback kept the ball himself. For a third option, he could pitch the ball to the I-back on a sweep to the outside.

To stop this offense, the defense had to remain disciplined. As the cornerback, Christian had to support the run, and if the quarterback turned in his direction, Christian had to take the I-back on the pitch play, while the defensive end had responsibility for the quarterback. Rock Port threw the ball very little, so most of Christian's practice consisted of getting around the block of a lineman.

Mitch Maxwell eagerly took on the task of blocking Christian for the scout team on the option plays. Christian spent all afternoon locking horns with Mitch on the option. Christian had athleticism on his side, but Mitch proved to be a big obstacle to get around. For the first five plays, the scout team offense ran directly at Christian, and Mitch overpowered Christian every time. Mitch rubbed it in by calling him "Christina" or lying on top of Christian well after the play had ended.

Coach Cozad sensed Christian's frustration.

"Get off your heels," Coach Cozad said, pulling Christian aside after Mitch bowled him over for the fifth time in a row. "Sure, he's bigger, but he's much slower. Don't back up! Attack him and push him back into the I-back."

"But how do I get away from him to make the tackle?" Christian asked.

"That's why you have teammates," Coach Cozad responded. "If you can shed his block, then make the tackle. Otherwise, string the play out and give your teammates time to help you out. You can't beat the option alone, and this isn't one-on-one coverage against a pass. You have to keep the ball from getting past you. If you slow it down by staying in the way, then your teammates can pursue the ball carrier and finish the play. Now, attack that pulling guard and use Mitch to your advantage."

Christian felt stupid. For five plays, he tried to do it all by himself. Christian prided himself on being a team player, but he forgot to use teamwork, and he wanted to show Mitch up on the field. Christian was trying to beat Mitch single-handed, so Coach Cozad simply stated the obvious.

"Do you really want to spend all day letting that marshmallow push you down the field?" Coach Cozad hollered as the defense huddled up.

Jeff Eaton smacked Christian on the helmet, "Come on Christina, you gonna take your skirt off and hit someone or what?"

Calvin Robinson laughed when Eaton referred to Christian as Christina. As the defense broke the huddle, Mitch Maxwell glanced over at Christian. Mitch had an immense grin on his face, and spittle hung from his facemask. Mitch was enjoying pushing Christian around.

The quarterback took the snap and faked to the fullback, and Mitch Maxwell pulled from his lineman position. Christian shed the block of the wide receiver, but instead of waiting for Mitch to pound him, Christian exploded forward into Mitch. Catching Maxwell off guard, Christian created enough leverage to push Mitch backwards. The defensive end closed in on the quarterback, so the quarterback pitched the ball to the I-back. The pitch arrived at the I-back the same time Mitch and Christian arrived. Mitch Maxwell and the ball carrier ended up on their backs, while Christian stood over them howling in victory.

Coach Cozad smacked Christian on the back of the helmet. "That's how you do it, Pearson!"

More teammates congratulated Christian, as they huddled up for the next play.

"You finally got lucky," Eaton said.

"Nope, I finally figured it out," Christian replied. "Luck had nothing to do with it."

Eaton smiled and thumped Christian's helmet with one of his huge hands.

"Good," Jeff said.

The small compliment from Jeff Eaton encouraged Christian.

The defense progressed enough for the day, so Coach Cozad decided to go light on the conditioning. Practice ended early for the defense. Brad and Christian left the locker room at 5:42, and they made it home in record time, 5:50. After a quick shower, Christian ran to Brad's house, scarfing down a sandwich on the way. Since the two boys were ready to go, Brad's mom drove them to the theater early. The courthouse clock read 6:25 when she dropped them off in front of the Twin Cinema. Brad told his mother to call Mrs. Pearson and tell her they were going to walk home, so she didn't need to pick them up.

The theater occupied part of a row of buildings between Third and Fourth Street on Coolbaugh, about half a block east of the town square. Coolbaugh Street ran only one direction, so cars on both sides of Coolbaugh pointed to the east. Only a few cars were parked on the street. Three doors up from the square, the movie posters of coming attractions lined the windows. A triangular awning pointed out from the second story of the building, and a white light illuminated the black letters on the billboard.

"Now Showing: Epicenter"

The Twin Cinema did not have two theaters, but sometimes it would show two different movies on the same night. On Fridays and Saturdays, two movie times were available. Epicenter was a late arriving summer blockbuster, so it was the only movie showing this week.

Since the two boys had time to kill, Brad and Christian decided to walk around the square before going into the theater. A green park filled the middle of the town square, which was surrounded on all four sides by businesses. The traffic on the square ran one way in a counterclockwise direction. Coolbaugh Street ran along the south side of the park and Reed Street on the north side. Second Street formed the boundary line to the west with Third Street along the east side. Brad and Christian stood on the corner of Coolbaugh and Third. Cars parked in spaces next to the park in the middle of the square or in front of the buildings. Marquees for a hardware store, a bank, Brown's Shoe Company, and some clothing stores dotted the brick structures. Most of the square appeared vacant because the businesses closed at six o'clock. The only cars parked on the square probably belonged to business owners or patrons of the two bars. A pizza place remained open, and a couple of cars sat in diagonal stalls in front of it.

The door to the pizza place reflected the setting sun as it opened, and Alexis, Sam, and Ray were stepping out. Brad had glanced back up Coolbaugh Street toward the movie theater, so he failed to see The Three at first. As Ray and Alexis came through the door behind Samantha, Christian swore that Alexis and Ray were holding hands. The Three turned in Christian's direction. He pretended not to see them at first, as he turned to look down Third Street. From where Brad and Christian stood, the top of the junior high peeked over the second story of the Red Oak Savings and Loan. Christian heard Sam yell his name, so he turned back toward The Three.

"Hey Christian!" Sam waved as she hurried her steps toward them. "We decided to get some pizza before the movie."

"I hope you still have room for popcorn," Christian said, looking past Sam to Ray and Alexis, who no longer held hands.

Maybe I was just seeing things, Christian thought.

"Of course," Sam replied, "I didn't eat the last piece of pizza because I knew I would be sharing a tub of that buttery goodness with you."

Sam's smile melted Christian. As she looped her arm in his arm and squeezed, his heart fluttered a little at Sam's embrace, but he pulled away in surprise. Samantha let go, sensing she caught Christian off guard by her touch.

"Sorry," Samantha said, "I've always been a hugger."

Even though Alexis towered over Sam, Christian had at least five inches on Alexis. Sam looked at Christian, scrutinizing him as he stood over her. A brown thread of Sam's curly hair dropped in front of one of her dazzling blue eyes. Sam's brow furrowed a bit, as she pushed out her bottom lip and blew air out of her mouth at the dangling curl. Christian laughed when the curl lazily dropped back down over the same eye. Sam pouted a bit and then brushed the hair back in place alongside the other brown and blonde curls.

"Darn humidity," Sam said, as she shot him another smile.

"I have the same problem," Christian said, as he smoothed his hand across his short hair.

Christian and Sam laughed as Alexis and Ray strolled up to them.

"Shall we?" Sam cooed as she looped her arms in Christian's arm again and then Brad's. They strolled toward the Twin Cinema, and Brad glanced back at Alexis and Ray trailing behind them.

Sam gave Brad and Christian details about the pizza place when the boys explained that neither of them had eaten there.

"It's called Bread Dough," she said, "but it is spelled B-R-E-A-D-E-A-U-X."

"Wouldn't that be pronounced Braid-e-ox?" Christian said.

"Call it what you want," Sam said, "but the taco pizza is fantastic."

The five teens bought their tickets. Brad paid his own way, and Ray bought a ticket for Alexis. Sam stayed true to her word and purchased a jumbo popcorn with extra butter, and Christian decided to buy Sam a soda, since she bought the popcorn.

No one had ventured into the theater yet, so the group had their pick of the seats. Sam chose a row about half-way down. Christian forgot about Ruby and Molly joining up with them for the movie, but they walked in before the group figured out who would sit where. Since Sam and Christian shared a tub of popcorn, Sam sat to Christian's left near the wall. Ruby sat on his right, and Molly picked the seat next to Ruby. Ray and Alexis sat on the end of the row near the isle. Brad worked it so he sat next to Alexis, which also put Brad next to Molly, so Christian decided no one would have hurt feelings.

Christian was disappointed in himself for thinking it, but he wished Ruby had not come. In a very short time, Christian was starting to like Sam, and that seemed unfair to Ruby, who had invited him to the movie in the first place.

Of course, Ruby was cute, but Sam had a special quality. Sam's personality sparkled, which Christian first noticed during lunch earlier in the day. He talked easily to Samantha Banner, and he didn't have to explain things to Sam, like he had to do with the girls he dated before. Sam seemed to see the world through intelligent, observant eyes. Christian was facing the reality that he might be falling for Sam, and Ruby never stood a chance.

The movie was a solid action flick. Jack Benson served as a government agent in an anti-terrorism unit, and he tried to stop a terrorist who wreaked havoc on the east coast of the United

States. The movie contained plenty of gunfire, explosions, car chases, and hand-to-hand combat, so Christian enjoyed it. Sam enjoyed it, as well, which came as a pleasant surprise to Christian.

On a couple of occasions, Sam leaned near to whisper, "That was cool," when the special effects went above and beyond her expectations.

Ruby tried to hold his hand a couple times during the movie, but Christian let go each time to reach over and get a handful of popcorn from the tub on Samantha's lap. During a couple of intense scenes, Ruby grabbed Christian's right arm and hugged it while turning her face into his shoulder. During those same scenes, Sam squeaked a little and then laughed at the fact that she had been startled by the dramatic action.

On a few occasions, Christian leaned forward to look down at Brad. Brad watched the movie intently, and the third time he peeked in Brad's direction, Brad held Molly's hand in his.

The movie ended when the hero thwarted the final plan of destruction by the mastermind terrorist. Jack Benson killed the terrorist, saved the city from disaster, and rescued a woman from certain death. It was predictable but good. The credits rolled, and Christian stayed seated. If Christian enjoyed a movie, he always waited in his seat while the credits played at the end. If his father accompanied him, they always discussed the quality of the show while everyone else exited the theater.

Sam leaned over and whispered, "That was a good one."

Christian nodded in agreement.

"They left it open for a sequel at the end," Christian said, "because the terrorist's brother survived."

"I was thinking the same thing," Sam responded.

The others got up and headed for the exit, but Sam and Christian stayed seated until the credits finished. They rehashed their favorite scenes and finished the last few handfuls of popcorn before finding the exit.

"Sorry about pushing my way into your date," Sam said, as they stood up to leave. "I hope she isn't jealous."

"Yeah, well, I'm sure Ruby was a little disappointed about you guys coming," he said.

"She seems nice," Sam added.

"I really don't know her that well," he explained. "This was the first time I was going to go out with her."

"Oh, then I am really sorry," Sam frowned. "I put you in a tough spot. I figured you guys had been dating awhile."

"No, she isn't my girlfriend," Christian quickly clarified. "Molly likes Brad, so we decided to double."

That last statement contained truth, but it lacked the total truth, and it just sounded better the way Christian decided to word it.

As they left the darkness of the theater, Christian saw Alexis hovering at the door.

"It's about time!" she chided, looking at her watch.

Sam replied, "Sorry Lex, but you know how I like to replay the highlights after a movie, and Christian gave me an audience."

"Great," Alexis said with an overemphasized roll of her eyes, "We have two movie connoisseurs to deal with."

Alexis added a warming smile, and Christian realized Alexis was taking pride in giving him a hard time.

Brad and Molly stood by the concession area.

"That was a pretty good movie," Christian commented to Brad.

"It sure was," Molly said, grabbing Brad's hand.

"Where is Ruby?" Christian asked, looking toward the entrance.

"She left," Brad answered.

Molly added with a hint of disgust in her voice, "She only lives a couple blocks up from the school. She decided to wait for us on the square."

Molly leaned close to Christian and whispered, "I don't think Ruby cares for *her*." Molly pointed to Samantha.

"Brad, you ready?" Christian said, ignoring Molly.

Brad answered, "I was going to walk them home. It turns out that Molly lives a couple blocks from my house, and Ruby's house is on the way. I thought maybe you would join us, since it's only 8:35. We were going to walk home anyway."

"Wow, the movie was only ninety minutes," Christian said, as he turned to The Three. "When is your ride coming?"

"We're walking," Ray answered.

"Do you want to join us?" Alexis asked.

"Which way are you going?" Christian questioned.

"We live just outside of town," Ray said, "so we will be walking this way."

Ray pointed in the direction of Christian's house, up Coolbaugh Street.

Christian looked pleadingly at Brad.

"Do you mind if I walk with them?" Christian asked.

"Nah, I'm a big boy," Brad said. "I can find my way home all by myself."

Molly pleaded, "Come with us, Christian. Ruby will be disappointed if you don't."

"How far up Coolbaugh are you going?" Christian asked Ray.

"Well, our father was going to be watching a ball game with someone he works with. They live on Kelly Circle," Ray explained, "but I'm not sure how far we have to go to get to Highland Street. That's where we turn."

"That is just up the street from my house. I know exactly where Kelly Circle is," Christian responded, excitedly.

Molly interrupted in indignation, "I think you should really come with us, Christian. Ruby is waiting for you."

"It would be great to have someone who knows where we're going," Alexis tugged back, flashing a glare at Molly.

Molly backed down instantly. Alexis made anyone feel uncomfortable with that look of hers and her physical stature.

"I'll see you in the morning," Brad said.

Brad grabbed Molly's hand and headed out the glass doors. The new couple turned toward the square and disappeared.

"I don't care for that girl," Alexis grumbled.

"At least she occupied Brad and kept him from flirting with you," Ray joked, as he squeezed her shoulders.

Alexis gave Ray a playful elbow in the stomach and smiled. Christian swore they acted like boyfriend and girlfriend, even though they were siblings. He realized Alexis was probably out of Brad's league. She seemed a lot more mature than a freshman, and Brad must have figured that out, too. Maybe Brad decided to cut off the chase with Alexis and give Molly a chance.

"So, I guess that settles it," Sam cheered, as she bounced to open the front door for Christian. "After you, young man," Sam said, as she stood at the open door with her hand held out to point him in the right direction.

Alexis sighed, "You are so weird."

They stepped out of the controlled comfort of the air-conditioned movie house and walked into the muggy night air. The air clung to Christian's skin.

Most of the cars had deserted the street outside the theater. Christian looked for Brad and Molly, but they already made their way out of sight, so he turned to follow Ray and Alexis. Samantha walked beside him, and no one said a word as they approached Fourth Street. The night quickly turned darker as the last rays of sunlight disappeared behind them, and the lights of various shops popped on, making it easier to see. They passed the last window before crossing into the residential part of town.

Here, the trees canopied the street in a more sinister darkness. Locusts buzzed from the trees above. If Christian walked alone, it would have been a little creepy, but with four of them together, the eerie sounds became white noise. The four teens walked uphill, so they trudged rather slowly. Alexis started laughing at something Ray said, but those two traveled too far ahead for Christian and Sam to hear what was so funny.

"I'm glad you decided to walk with us," Samantha said, as an air conditioner hummed to life next to the house on the right.

"Me too," Christian replied.

They strolled past a couple more houses. Sam slowed her pace, so Christian slowed to match it. She grabbed his hand, and this time he did not pull away.

"I have a secret," Sam said, as she stopped and turned toward Christian.

"What is it?" he asked.

"I like you," Sam said, as she turned to walk again. "And I am positive you like me, too."

"I see," Christian said, his heart fluttering. "I guess *my* secret is out, then, too."

Sam let go with her hand and looped her arm in his arm, as they walked.

"Do you have any other deep, dark secrets?" Sam asked playfully.

Christian sensed Sam dug for a bigger secret. He quietly thought about how hard it was to go through life with the secret ability he possessed. Christian had only known Sam for about twelve hours, but he already felt in tune with her. He talked easily to her, but he had concerns. Sam would see him as a nut if he told her about his ability to breathe under water. Boys do stupid things when they're around girls, but Christian did not want to jeopardize what seemed like a pretty good thing with Sam.

"I would tell you," Christian joked, "but then I would have to kill you."

"Ooooo, it must be a really big secret," Sam mocked.

"It is," he said seriously. "It could affect national security."

Christian quoted Jack Benson from the movie.

"Well, then you better keep it to yourself *for now*," she responded.

"*For now*," Christian thought.

Sam placed a lot of emphasis on those two words. Was there some hidden meaning to it? Did Samantha Banner know his secret? How could she know? Christian mentally slapped himself back to reality and changed the subject.

"What's with Alexis?" he asked.

"What do you mean?" Sam said, quizzically.

Alexis and Ray increased their distance to about half a block ahead of them.

Alexis turned around and hollered, "Hey slow pokes! Do we need to come back and carry you two?"

"That," Christian said. "She turned around just as I asked you about her."

Sam stopped and looked at Christian, and he could tell she searched for something in his expression. Her brilliant blue eyes darkened in the faint glow of the street light hidden behind the branches of an oak. Sam studied Christian intently, and she seemed to be confused by something.

"What emotion are you feeling right now?" Sam asked, seriously.

Christian laughed, "What do you mean?"

"Just what I said," she responded in a matter of fact tone. "Are you nervous? Elated? Excited?"

"Huh," he stammered, "Uh, I don't know. I guess I'm happy."

"I can't tell," Sam said, and then she turned to continue on the walk, but Christian held her there.

Samantha did not resist.

"What do you mean by you can't tell?" Christian asked. "I'm smiling and holding your hand. Samantha Banner, I have enjoyed your company this entire evening. In fact, I don't want to keep walking because I don't want the night to end, but I know that eventually it will. Can you tell how I am feeling now?"

"I'm sorry," she said. "I didn't mean it that way."

Sam reached up and put her arms around Christian and hugged him, and the embrace felt like more than two friends hugging. Passion radiated from Sam's body. Christian lifted her light frame off the ground and spun her around a half turn before putting her down.

"Can you tell now?" Christian whispered, as he placed her gently on the ground.

"Yes," she said.

Sam planted a light kiss on his lips.

Christian hoped for that kiss, but it still caught him off guard.

"I guess you are going to have to hang out with The Three more often," Alexis shouted from a block away.

"How does she do that?" Christian whispered into Sam's ear.

"It's a secret," Sam whispered, as she let go of Christian and loped off toward her siblings.

CHAPTER 7

Wednesday started with a boom as lightning from a thunderstorm shook the house just as Christian's alarm buzzed. He walked upstairs to take a shower, while his father sat in the living room and watched the news.

"Severe thunderstorm warning," his father said.

"Any tornadoes mentioned?" Christian asked.

"Nope, just a lot of rain," his dad answered.

The thunder boomed outside again.

"And lightning," his father added.

"I guess you owe me a million dollars," Christian said as he walked toward the bathroom for a shower.

"That's right," Mr. Pearson replied. "You did bet me that it would rain today. Double or nothing that it rains again tomorrow."

"What does the forecast say?" Christian asked.

His dad responded, "Sixty percent chance of thunderstorms."

"They'll be wrong," Christian said, "and I'm up at least $10 million, so it's a bet. No way it rains tomorrow."

As Christian showered, the lights flickered. While putting on his clothes, the power went out completely. Enough light came in through the small window to the bathroom, so it was no big deal. The rain poured outside, and something tapped on the roof. Christian recognized the familiar sound of hail.

Christian's sisters woke up and bounced with excitement that the power was out. After settling them down, his mother readied bowls of cereal for the girls. She asked if Christian had eaten, and he told her no, so she got a bowl out for him, too.

"Good thing it wasn't storming like this when you walked home last night," his mother commented.

Mrs. Pearson was still bugged a little that Christian walked home instead of calling for a ride.

"Yep," Christian answered.

Rehashing last night's events served no purpose. His father saw no harm in Christian walking after dark, but Mom constantly worried about him. Even though he returned home by nine o'clock, her mind played out a number of what-if scenarios. Most of them involved Christian getting kidnapped or hit by a car. His father calmed his mother's anxiety last night, but Dad left the house already, so Christian's father could not defend him.

"Well, I'm glad you made it home okay," his mother said, reiterating the fact that she worried about him.

"Mom, we just walked home from the theater. I told you last night; there were three other people with me. Now, who would want to kidnap four high school freshmen?" Christian said, a bit irritated.

His sister, Ann, smiled at Christian's last statement.

"One is bad enough," Ann said.

"Yeah, one is bad enough," echoed Kat.

Christian reached over and rubbed Kat's head, messing up her bed head even more.

"One is bad enough," he copied Kat in a girly voice.

Kat giggled.

"And two sisters means double trouble," Christian continued, as he reached over Kat and playfully pushed Ann's bowl of cereal away from her.

"Hey," Ann complained, "brothers are a pain!"

A roll of thunder shook the house again, and hail hammered the pavement on the driveway outside the back door. Christian hurried to the door and moved the curtain to peer outside the window.

"Wow, that is some big hail," he said.

Small pieces of ice littered the yard from the hail that had fallen earlier, which looked like little golf balls. The bigger crystal chunks fell sporadically, bouncing a foot or two off the grass here and there or smacking the concrete. Christian heard a thud on the roof, and he decided to run down and open the garage to get a better look.

Christian hit the button for the garage door before remembering the power outage. He pulled the emergency release cord and lifted the door manually. The hail was huge!

Sometimes hail fell like rain, covering the ground with a layer of little white pellets of ice. If enough fell, it looked like snow covered the ground. As the hail got bigger, fewer pieces pounded the earth. Hail caused some serious damage when it got bigger than golf-ball size.

"Your father said this was a slow-moving storm, but no tornado warning had been issued," Christian's mother said from behind him.

His sisters followed their mom down to the garage.

"He left right after you jumped in the shower and said he would keep an eye on the weather from school," she said.

"You know why he went to the school," Christian replied.

"Yes, I know," his mother answered in disgust.

"Why?" Ann asked.

"He's probably up on the third floor watching the storm," Christian said.

"Why would he do that?" Kat questioned.

"Because he is loony like you two," Mrs. Pearson said, as she grabbed Kat and tickled her.

"He can see over all these trees from up there," Christian explained.

"Why does he like storms so much?" Ann asked.

"It's his hobby," her mother said.

"What's a hobby?" Kat asked.

"I'll tell you upstairs while you finish your breakfast," her mom said as she corralled the two girls and led them through the basement.

Christian stayed in the garage and watched the hail slam into the pavement. A chunk of ice landed in the grass on the retaining wall to the south. Christian walked over to the edge of the garage and reached out to pick up the cold, slippery object. Hail melted pretty fast after falling to the ground. The size surpassed a golf ball, so he decided to throw it in the freezer, since his dad might get a kick out of it later. Hopefully, the power would return soon, so the prize would stay frozen.

After putting the hailstone in the deep freeze in the basement, Christian went back upstairs and finished his breakfast. He did not plan to walk to Brad's house this morning, so he killed time before Mrs. Matthews picked him up for school. With the electricity out, the television and radio served little use. Christian's dad kept a radio with batteries in the basement, but he decided against the hassle of finding it.

The hail stopped briefly as rain poured, and Christian ran to close the garage door. He did not want to leave it open and let the water flow in, so he pulled the door shut and hurried back upstairs.

"What time is it?" he asked his mother.

"By my watch, it's almost eight," she answered.

The hail resumed.

"I guess they don't want to come out while that hail is coming down," Christian's mother said from the kitchen. "I don't think we'll venture out until it stops either."

Christian heard a cheer from Kat, "No school today!"

"Oh, you will be going to school," Mrs. Pearson called to Kat. "You'll just be late."

Kat moaned her discontent before going up to her bedroom. Thunder boomed outside, and a loud thud struck the the roof, then another. Christian looked out the front window and saw a white baseball crash into the pavement.

"Mom, come here!" he hollered. "Hurry!"

The Pearson family stood at the front window, as white chunks of ice the size of baseballs rained down outside, and a few approached softball size. As the hailstones fell, small branches fluttered from the trees. The barrage lasted for two minutes before another deluge of rain arrived and the hail stopped. A large piece of hail rested outside the front door, so Christian ran outside to grab it before his mom could stop him.

Kat and Ann marveled at the giant hailstone when Christian brought it back in.

"You are soaked," his mom commented.

"I'll change my shirt before we go," he said.

The hail looked like a bumpy softball, as if a bunch of small pieces of hail had been glued together.

"I wanna hold it," Ann said.

After each of his sisters took a turn holding the monstrous ice ball, Christian ran downstairs and put it in the freezer next to the smaller piece of hail. He changed his shirt in the faint light of the basement and headed back upstairs. The electricity returned at about 8:15, and Christian turned on the television to check the weather. The station out of Omaha reported that the storms were pushing off to the east. Reports came in of possible tornadoes outside Council Bluffs. This portion of Iowa and Nebraska could expect rain off and on the rest of the day, but the severe weather was moving out of the area.

The phone rang, and Christian's mother answered it.

"No school today!" she exclaimed from the kitchen.

Kat and Ann cheered.

"What?" Christian said in surprise. "Why is school called off?"

"That was your father," she explained. "He said that they had so much rain, it flooded part of the high school, and half of Red Oak is without power. They decided to call off school in order to clean up. Your father said the hail added to the problem."

"Really?" Christian stammered in disbelief.

"Yes," she said, "and to make matters worse, some of the county roads are flooded. The buses can't get to everyone, and a couple lost windshields because of the hail. Your father said he heard someone say we got almost seven inches of rain in the last four hours."

"Can you take me to school?" Christian asked.

"But you don't have school today," she responded.

"I know that, but maybe Dad could use some help. I don't really want to be hanging out here all day," he explained, motioning toward his two younger sisters.

"Call your father," his mom said.

Christian called his dad, and after fighting through busy signals, he finally got hold of him. His father said Christian could come hang out at school. Christian hoped The Three would be there, and if they weren't, he hoped he could at least get a phone number. He wanted to see Samantha again.

"You will probably still have football practice," his mother reminded him, as she dropped him off at the junior high.

"I'll call you if I need a ride," Christian said as he closed the door and sprinted to the school.

Branches and leaves littered the grounds. As he neared the front door, someone inside pushed it open. Some seventh graders milled around waiting for rides home. Some students were dropped off early because their parents worked, and Christian hoped Sam was one of them.

Christian quickly scrambled up the stairs and checked the second floor. A couple of students stood outside the front office with his father while he directed traffic at the office phone. Christian waved to his father and hollered that he would be back down in a second.

No students occupied the third floor, but Christian heard a couple of teachers talking at the other end of the hallway, discussing whether this day would be made up at the end of the year or if it would count as a snow day.

Christian walked downstairs to the office in hopes of retrieving Sam's phone number, but at that moment, Mr. Pearson was still dealing with kids calling for rides. Christian decided to get a drink of water from the fountain before going into the library. Maybe he could get on the Internet and check last night's baseball scores.

His father hollered, "No one is in there. Mrs. Smith couldn't get off the farm this morning due to the flooding."

"I'm going to read a little," Christian explained. "Come find me when you have some time."

"It may be a while," his father said.

"Not a problem," Christian answered.

Christian selected one of the computers off to the side, where he could see the door to the library. He walked to the window to look outside while the computer slowly ran through the start-up sequence. The window overlooked the alley between the main building and the gym, so the view was limited, but Christian noticed the rain picked up again.

After logging in under his username, Christian clicked on the Internet and checked the weather radar. The severe storms moved east, but it looked like the rain planned on sticking around for a while. Christian's dad popped his head in the library door.

"Give me about thirty minutes, and then we will survey the flooding," his father said with a smile.

The main reason Christian came to school revolved around the hope of seeing Sam, but he also came to school to hang out with his dad. Christian knew his dad would find time to drive around and check the storm damage. His father loved that stuff, and Christian wanted to do that rather than fight with his sisters for the TV remote or computer at home. He also figured his dad would take him out for lunch. Christian checked his e-mail and played some Internet games for a while before logging off.

The hallway was quiet, so he could hear his dad on the phone. Christian waited in a chair in the office. Mrs. Johnson, Dad's secretary, was unable to come into school as well, so her desk sat empty.

Christian heard his father hang up the phone then appear in the doorway with his keys in his hand. Mr. Pearson closed the door to his office and locked it. Then he closed the main door to the office.

"I better not lock it," his father said. "Someone may have to use the phone or run some copies. The doors to the school are locked now, and I think all of the students are out of the building."

"You know," Christian said, "I think the pink is starting to grow on me."

"I plan on painting your bedroom the same color," his dad jabbed.

The two of them walked past the gymnasium and out the south doors. The rain fell, but not nearly as hard as before. They crossed the street to the staff parking lot and his father's pockmarked Mercury, and soon the car pulled out onto Corning Street. They headed north to the high school. Most of the cars that sat parked on the street had hail damage similar to his father's car. Many had cracked windshields, and Christian knew the cracks were due to hail, as well. They drove by a house on Eighth Street that had some of the siding stripped off by the storm. As the car pulled into view of the high school, both of them saw why school had been called off. The circular drive in front of the building had been converted into a small lake.

"The hail must have frozen in the storm drains," Christian's father said. "The water backed up because there was nowhere for it to go. It's draining slowly, if at all."

They turned into the student parking lot that marked the south side of the high school and followed that road to the west. Pools of water dotted the practice fields in all the lower areas. Christian wondered what practice would be like on the muddy plain.

"I am guessing you guys will be inside today," his father said, reading Christian's thoughts. "I don't think they want to tear up the practice fields any more than they have to."

"It's like a swamp out there," Christian said.

"They ended up calling school off because the power is out in a number of areas," his father said. "Power is out in at least two of the four elementary schools, and the main kitchen at the district office had some flooding. They weren't going to be able to serve lunch to all of the elementary school kids. The river is out of its banks west of Broadway, and they aren't letting anybody cross the bridge at Coolbaugh."

"Unbelievable," Christian commented.

"To make things worse, a couple of the windows at the high school were knocked out by the hail, and who knows how many leaks were found during the rain this morning," his dad continued. "We had minor roof leaks at the middle school, but I think the high school had some water gushing into a number of rooms."

"Will we have school tomorrow?" Christian asked.

"I am pretty sure we will, as long as we don't get a repeat of this morning," he said.

"Since we're out, can you show me where J Avenue is?" Christian asked, remembering that the Banners had moved into a house on J Avenue. "That's where Ray's family lives."

Christian hoped his father would not start asking him a bunch of questions about what he thought of Alexis or Samantha.

"Sure," his father replied with a grin.

They took a right on Fourth Street and headed for Highway 34. The fairgrounds sat on their left, and Christian saw that the water covered most of the baseball field, while a moat of water surrounded the football field. Hopefully the field had not been saturated because he had a home football game in two days.

They drove up Highway 34 until the car reached Eastern Avenue. Eastern Avenue ran a block east of Highland Street, so

Christian found his bearings as they approached Summit Street. Summit turned into old Highway 34 and meandered out the east side of town. The new highway was built long before his family arrived in Red Oak, but people still called Summit Street "Old 34." Old 34 met up with the new Highway 34 a couple miles outside of town to the east.

The turn onto J Avenue was a mile and a half further. His father turned right onto gravel. Water filled the ditches, and Christian saw water standing in the rows of corn and soybeans. The car crossed over a set of railroad tracks before coming to a stop at Bluegrass Road. Up ahead on the right, an old two-story farmhouse sat nestled in a horseshoe of evergreens.

"I think that is the Banner place," his dad said, reverting back to the farm lingo he used while growing up in the country.

Mr. Pearson grew up outside a little town in northeast Nebraska called Beemer, so he occasionally used words like "place" instead of house or farm.

His father asked, "Do you want to stop by?"

"No," Christian responded quickly, "I was just curious where Ray lived, in case we end up hanging out some time."

"I would have no problem with that," his father said. "Mr. Banner appears to be a good man, and I have heard nothing but good things about those three kids of his."

They turned right onto Bluegrass Road and took it all the way back into town. Before getting to the railroad tracks, the road turned sharply to the north to avoid a large pond before passing through a one-lane tunnel. In this location, the elevated ground of the railroad tracks divided the country from the city. Rows of houses lined the streets on the other side of the tracks, but they were not visible from the farmland on this side of the hill. The railroad built a wall of earth on this side of town to allow cars to cross through without waiting for the trains that rolled by every half hour. Christian's father said at least two other tunnels, like this one, appeared along the wall of the rail line on this side of town. This tunnel differed from the others because of the one-lane access.

Even though the clock pushed eleven, Mr. Pearson decided they should pick up an early lunch and eat it at the school.

They passed through the square when Christian saw a girl with curly light-colored hair walking into a clothing store. The girl resembled Samantha Banner.

"Hey, do you mind dropping me off here?" Christian asked.

"Aren't you hungry?" asked his father, as he pulled the car into an open stall.

"It's kind of early for lunch, now that I think about it," Christian said. "I'm going to check out some of the stores down here. I'll come by the school, and you can take me out for lunch then."

"How long will you be?" his father asked.

"Give me half an hour," Christian said.

"I can't guarantee I'll be there," said his father. "Here."

Mr. Pearson handed his son a ten-dollar bill.

"You find something to eat on the square, and then you can come to the school and see if I'm around. If the car is gone, call your mother to come pick you up," his father said.

"Thanks Dad," Christian answered.

"Boy, she must be cute," his father said with a grin.

Christian hesitated before he responded, "You have no idea."

The rain drizzled slightly as Christian got out of the car. He cut across the intersection diagonally and ran to the door of a clothing store, and the bell rang to announce Christian's entrance. He visited this place once before when his mom wanted to get him sized for a letterman's jacket. Since Christian planned to play all kinds of sports, his mother decided to order one right away. She ordered it a couple of sizes larger than his measurements because she knew Christian would grow some more.

At first glance, the store appeared to be unoccupied by any patrons. Christian knew Sam could be standing behind any one of the racks of clothes and he would not see her. He made his way past a display of jeans before spotting Samantha, who held up a blouse and pouted as she looked in the mirror. Sam had not noticed Christian stalking her, so he walked around the other way and crept up behind her as she selected another blouse to hold up.

"I like that one better," Christian said, startling Sam with his reflection in the mirror.

Samantha squealed with delight. "Christian! I was hoping that in a town of this size I would run into you, but I didn't expect it to be in the girl's section of a clothing store."

"What are you doing in town?" Christian asked. "I hope you didn't walk all the way in."

"Ray has a school permit, since we live so far out of town," Sam explained.

"Ray can drive?" Christian said in surprise.

"Sure, so can Alexis," she replied. "They both have school permits."

"But we didn't have school today," he said.

"Yes, but we had already driven to town when we found out school was called off," Sam said, "and my father is working all day, so we decided to stay a while."

"So once you drive back home…" Christian started.

"We can't legally drive back into Red Oak, if we go home, unless it's for a school activity," Sam finished Christian's thought. "That would be tough for my father to deal with, since he is working for the department of roads right now."

"So how long are you planning to be in town?" Christian asked.

"I was planning to look for you around school and the square until the rain stopped," she said. "Then, I was going to walk to your house."

Christian sensed her giddiness as Samantha briskly walked the ten feet to him and locked her fingers in his hand.

"Mission accomplished, now let's go eat," Sam said as she led Christian out of the store.

They strolled under the awnings of the stores to avoid the raindrops. Since Sam had been shopping all morning, she told him various details about each store as they passed by the windows along the way. When they crossed Coolbaugh Street, she explained to Christian that she didn't go into the bar. They both laughed. The couple reached the pizza place, and Christian opened the door for her. Sam pecked him on the cheek to thank him for holding the door open like a true gentleman.

Sam had on tight-fitting blue jeans and a green blouse, and Christian stole a glimpse of her from behind. She had a cute butt, too, but Christian chastised himself for sneaking that peek. They ordered a medium pizza and took a booth along the far wall. Christian decided to sit across from her.

"Ray and Alexis were going to meet me here for lunch," she said. "They decided to hit the grocery store when I started on a second block of stores on the square."

"I don't want to impose," Christian said.

"Don't be ridiculous," Sam laughed. "It was their idea to come looking for you."

"Really?" he said in surprise, "Why would they want you to find me?"

She motioned for him to come over to her side of the booth. Christian moved around next to Sam, and she leaned close to his ear.

"They think we make a cute couple," Sam whispered.

The pizza arrived at the same time that Alexis and Ray strolled in. They sat across from Christian and Sam. Neither Alexis nor Ray craved pizza, so they had picked up sub sandwiches from a sub shop on the main drag before arriving. The four ate and laughed. Christian finished off the last piece, and they headed for the door.

"You want to see our house?" Alexis asked, as they walked out into the sunshine. The rain had stopped, and the sun pierced a few remaining clouds.

"I would have to check in at home," Christian replied.

"No problem," Ray said. "We can stop by there on the way out of town."

"I'm not sure if my mom will be cool with it," Christian said, "and I have football practice at 3:30."

"I'll give you a ride when I come in for volleyball practice, so it will be legal," Alexis announced. Christian witnessed Alexis roll her eyes even though her face looked away from him.

Ray drove them to Christian's house with Christian up front and the girls in the back.

Christian told his mom that he wanted to go to Ray's house.

"He can drive?" his mother said in surprise.

"Yes, he has a school permit, and he was in town waiting for the storm to quit. I bumped into him at the square," Christian explained.

"Call your father to see if it's okay with him. He probably knows the driving rules better than I do," Mrs. Pearson said. "How will you get back for football?"

"He has to bring his sister into town for volleyball practice," Christian replied as he dialed the school.

His father had no problem with it, when Christian explained that he could get his own ride back into town. Christian guessed his mother was willing to get one kid out of the house on an unexpected day of no school, as he kissed his mother goodbye and headed for the door. Soon, the car passed Kelly Circle and turned left to go through the tunnel to Bluegrass Road.

"Isn't it amazing how it's all houses on this side of the tunnel," Christian said, "and then it's nothing but farmland when you come out the other side?"

Alexis and Ray roared in laughter.

Alexis chuckled, "You two were made for each other."

Ray added, "Sam said the same thing when we drove into town this morning."

After driving a mile, the car turned right onto J Avenue, and Sam pointed to the same two-story house Christian's dad pointed out earlier in the day.

"That's it," Sam said.

The car pulled into the gravel drive between rows of soybeans. As they neared the house, Christian realized he underestimated the size of the home. The white, two-story farm house had received a new paint job, and it looked sharp with the contrasting black shutters. Two windows on the second floor gave the appearance of eyes, and a porch extended the length of the front of the house. A white railing ran the length of the porch, opening up in the middle for the three steps leading up to the door. The railing matched the picket fence that ran from the right side of the building to the line of trees that formed a windbreak on the north side of the property. The pines circled the house in a horseshoe around the back and up the south side, where the driveway ran between the trees and a small barn, which matched the house's color scheme. When they pulled around the back side, Christian realized the barn was a large, detached garage. The double door rolled open, and Ray pulled the car into the middle of three parking spaces. To the right, a tarp covered another vehicle.

"This reminds me of my house," Christian commented. "We have to drive around the back of the house to get to the garage."

The back of the house had a second veranda-styled porch. A couple other outbuildings hid in the trees, but most of them needed paint and repairs.

"This is home," Sam said, as she grabbed Christian's hand and led him around to the front porch.

Alexis and Ray entered the house through the back door.

"It looks a lot nicer from up close," Christian said.

"Have you been by here?" Sam asked.

"Dad and I drove by here once," Christian explained. "The trees really hide the place from view."

"That's why Dad picked it," Sam said.

Christian wondered why her father wanted a house with an obstructed view. He guessed Mr. Banner wanted his privacy.

"So, he isn't your real father," Christian said, wincing as he said it.

He did not want to say the wrong thing; it just sort of slipped out.

"Sorry if I shouldn't ask something like that," Christian said sheepishly.

"Well, my boyfriend should know all about me, shouldn't he?" Sam said with a flirtatious smile.

"Oh, is he here?" Christian said, while acting like he looked around for someone to appear.

"You are so strange," Sam cooed, as she put her arms around Christian's neck and pulled him close.

Instead of a kiss, she looked into his eyes.

"But everyone has some strangeness to them, an odd quirk, or a hidden talent," she whispered.

Sam studied his face for a reaction, but he had already become accustomed to left-field questions from her. Christian remained stoic.

"You are a tough one to read," she smiled and let go of his neck, slowly backing to the swing hanging on the far end of the porch.

Sam sat down and patted the seat next to her. A light breeze bounced a few brown curls into her face, and she smoothed them back with her hand. He sat down, and they rocked on the swing. Samantha's blue eyes penetrated Christian. Again, she seemed to search him for some clue to a riddle she struggled to figure out.

"What is the deal with the eyes in your family?" Christian asked.

Sam looked puzzled, "What do you mean?"

"Well," he started, "first, I spend the whole day yesterday trying to avoid the stare from your sister."

"Alexis!" Sam laughed aloud, "She can make the toughest high school boy cower with some of her looks!"

"Exactly," Christian said. "Every time I saw her, it was like I was being interrogated without her saying a word. It was creepy at first, until I saw the way she glared at Calvin Robinson. Then I realized it wasn't an angry look from her that I was getting. There was more to it."

Christian's last statement seemed to make Sam a little uncomfortable. He noticed her shift her weight as she stared out across the bean field, avoiding eye contact with him. Part of his statement must have struck a chord with Sam, but he didn't press the issue.

Christian continued talking, "And then I meet you."

Sam looked back into his face with the same searching eyes he experienced moments before.

"You look at me differently," Christian explained. "It isn't a suspicious interrogation. In fact, it's a warm and friendly scrutiny, like you're looking for clues in the evidence presented before you, and you want to make sure you have all the facts straight."

"Is that bad?" Sam asked, sincerely.

"No," Christian said. "Well, with Alexis, it's a little unnerving, I must admit, but with you, it's totally different. It's relaxing to look into your eyes, and I get lost in the sparkling blue."

"For a freshman, you sure do know how to talk to a girl," Sam said.

"What are you searching for?" Christian asked.

"Someone odd to be my soul mate," she replied.

Christian laughed, but Sam didn't join his laughter. She searched Christian for clues again.

"How odd do I need to be?" he asked.

"Are you applying for the job?" she fired back, eagerly.

This time, Sam laughed at Christian's seriousness.

"What makes you look at me the way you do?" he asked, keeping the serious façade.

"I just want to know everything about you," she said. "From the moment we met in front of Mr. Button's room, I knew there was something special about you."

"What do you want to know?" Christian asked.

"Your favorite color?" Sam said.

"Forest green," he answered.

"Favorite food?" she asked.

"Seafood," he responded.

She studied him intently, as if seafood held the key to unlock a mystery.

"Favorite music group?" she asked.

"Steven Curtis Chapman," he said.

"That is one singer, not a group," she claimed.

"Okay, then I would have to say... Genesis," he said.

"Genesis?" Sam looked puzzled.

"Come on," Christian chided, playfully. "Don't tell me you've never heard of Phil Collins, perhaps the most versatile musician on the planet."

"Yes, I know who Phil Collins is," she said, irritated that he gave her a hard time. "I just didn't know his band was called Genesis."

"My turn," Christian said.

"No, no, no," she exclaimed, "this is me learning about you."

Christian tried his best to pout, but pouting did not match his grinning face. Sam laughed and motioned for him to bring it on.

"I'll give you one, so make it good," she said, " and then I get to scrutinize you some more."

When Sam smiled, Christian noticed a little dimple on the right side of her mouth.

"Let me think about this one," he stalled. "Let me see... let me see... Okay, I got it."

"You only get one," she reminded him.

"What is your hidden talent?" Christian asked.

Sam turned to him and searched his eyes with a different look than before. He could tell she mulled over the possible answers in her mind. The dazzling blue in her eyes appeared to brighten, as she paused before answering.

"I can see how people feel," Sam said.

"Like they have the word sad painted on their forehead?" Christian responded.

"Nope, and that is two questions," she stated. "You were only allowed one. Now you owe me a deep question."

"Go ahead and ask," Christian said.

"Not now," Sam responded. "Some day. Let's go inside, so I can show you around the house."

Sam opened the screen door and a heavy oak door, and they stepped into the foyer. The wood floors shone like they had just been refinished. The stairs to the second floor climbed up to the right, and the living room sat to the left. Christian saw the kitchen down the hall in front of him.

"My dad had the floors refinished before we moved in. He also had the house painted," Sam explained. "That is the dining room, and down this hallway is the kitchen."

She led him into the kitchen.

Sam continued to talk as they toured the house, explaining little intricacies about each room. She explained what had been fixed and what needed to be fixed. Christian's brain sensed something odd about each room, but he failed to put his finger on the exact reason for the strange feeling.

As they headed upstairs, Sam shouted, "Everybody decent up there?"

"Yes!" chorused Alexis and Ray.

They looked into Alexis' room first, which overlooked the front porch. Not a single item looked out of place in the neat and tidy room. No clothes littered the floor, and Christian guessed he could not have found a speck of dust anywhere, not even the ceiling fan, even if he looked all day.

"Wow, this is the cleanest room I have ever seen," Christian commented.

Alexis lay on her bed, reading. She had already changed for volleyball, and her olive skin was still dark, even when compared to the black athletic shorts she wore. She had an orange t-shirt with "Red Oak Tiger Volleyball" printed across the front. Even though she rested on the bed reading a book, Christian thought he would not want to tangle with her in an argument. She looked tough, even while she read.

"Have you read this, yet?" Alexis asked.

"*The Outsiders*? A couple times. It's one of my favorite books," Christian said. "I read it in seventh grade English."

"Awesome," Alexis said, "I may have you help me with it. I have never been good with fiction."

"What page are you on?" Christian asked.

"Eleven," Alexis responded.

"It's an easy read," Christian said. "Once you get a couple chapters in, you won't want to put it down."

"I hate to break up the nerd party," Sam interrupted, "but I need to continue the tour."

"Bus leaves in a couple hours," Alexis hollered, as Sam and Christian crossed the hallway to another bedroom.

"This is Ray's room," Sam announced.

Ray did not keep his room as clean as Alexis' bedroom, but it still appeared tidy. Again, something odd gnawed at Christian, but he could not decide what it was. Ray listened to some music through his headphones and read a sports magazine. Ray did not appear to be in the mood for conversation.

Sam and Christian left Ray to his tunes and walked down the hallway. First, she opened the door to the right.

"This is Dad's room," she said. Christian took a quick peek before Sam closed the door.

"Ta Da," Sam said with a little flair. "This is my humble abode."

"Very nice," Christian said as he looked around the room. Of the three siblings, Sam's room proved to be the messiest, but by no means a pit. Some clothes hung over the chair at her desk, and the trash can needed to be emptied.

"I would hate for you to see my room," Christian said. "It isn't a mess, but I don't know if it would be up to Banner standards."

Since Mr. Banner was not home, Sam and Christian talked in the bedroom for a while before Sam led him back downstairs to the living room. Sam offered him something to drink and walked to the kitchen. As he surveyed the living room, Christian realized what was missing... pictures. No pictures of any of the Banner family adorned any of the rooms. Not a single family portrait hung from a wall. No vacation photos or school pictures perched on any shelf. The entire house stood void of photos. Now, why would a family fail to have pictures as part of the décor of their house?

Christian quietly walked to the hallway to see if he missed something, but no pictures occupied the walls there either. He moved to the stairs and peeked over the rail. Nothing ornamented the walls next to the steps leading upstairs. Maybe they did not have time to empty the box of picture frames after moving in, but the house had no basement. Sam pointed out that no lower level sat below the main level when they first toured the house. Christian thought about the storage capabilities of this house, and unless it had a hidden attic, the Banners had no ability to store any unpacked boxes, and he had not noticed any boxes in any of the bedrooms.

Christian heard a giggle upstairs, so he leaned stealthily toward the railing. Ray and Alexis whispered in the hallway, and Christian could tell they stood outside Alexis' room. Then, Christian heard the distinctive sound of what sounded like a kiss.

Christian quickly moved into the hall, and Sam asked if he wanted lemonade or sun tea.

"Lemonade," Christian said, distractedly, thinking he heard another kiss. Christian quickly moved to the kitchen. Sam finished the pouring of his lemonade when he rounded the corner.

She turned to Christian, and he leaned over and planted a kiss square on Sam's lips, which caught her totally off guard, and she almost spilled the glass of lemonade. When Christian pulled away, he heard the same soft sucking sound he heard moments before in the upstairs hallway, and his head spun out of control. He *had* heard Ray and Alexis kiss!

Before Christian wrapped his mind around the notion, Sam swung her arms around Christian's neck and returned the favor.

She pushed her lips tightly against his. Now, he was the one caught off guard, as she pressed against him. The counter kept Christian from tumbling backwards. His emotions fogged, and he was lost in a passionate haze. Their lips parted for a second time, and the sound took Christian back to the reason he kissed Sam in the first place. Fortunately, Sam did not search his face for clues this time. Instead, Samantha Banner turned her head sideways and melted into Christian's chest. They slow danced without music, and Christian prayed that she would not look into his eyes.

He needed time to calm his emotions.

"S… sorry about almost knocking the glass over," Christian stuttered.

"You are strange," Sam cooed.

After a while, she let him go and handed him the glass.

Sam and Christian watched part of a movie for the remainder of the time, and Christian did not say much. Alexis bounded down the steps, her ponytail swinging from side to side.

"Train's leaving," Alexis said.

Christian gave Sam a peck on the cheek and told her that he would see her tomorrow. Christian followed Alexis out the back door to her car. During the quiet ride, neither Christian nor Alexis said much. Alexis remembered the exact location of his house, so Christian did not even have to discuss that. He just wanted out of that car.

"Thanks for the ride," he said as he opened the door.

"You all right?" Alexis asked.

"Yeah, just a little tired," Christian said, nervously.

"Sam can wear you out," Alexis responded. "Hey, do you need a ride home from football practice tonight? It's on the way."

Alexis was being unusually nice.

"Nah, I'll catch a ride with Brad," Christian said. "Thanks for the offer."

"Hey," Alexis stopped Christian from closing the door, "I am sorry if I made you feel uncomfortable yesterday. I'm cautious about who my sister likes, and I don't want to see her get burned."

"That's all right," Christian said, wondering if Sam mentioned something to Alexis about how uncomfortable Alexis usually made him feel.

Christian recollected that Sam spent the entire time with him and did not have any opportunity to say anything to Alexis with him around. Alexis must have truly felt bad about the uncomfortable stares.

"I suppose I'll be protective of my sisters as they get older," Christian said, hoping that Alexis would let the conversation end there.

"Well, anytime you need a ride, just holler," she said.

"I'll hear you," Alexis added, as Christian closed the door.

Christian turned to the house thinking about the added "I'll hear you" at the end of Alexis' statement.

"What if she is in the girls' locker room, and I am in the boys' locker room?" Christian muttered, sarcastically to himself.

Christian knew two things for sure. After two days, he had fallen head over heels for Samantha, and he also knew something strange surrounded the Banner family.

CHAPTER

8

Thursday brought sunshine and heat as the temperature climbed into the nineties. At least the weatherman got the temperature right. As Christian rode the bus back to the junior high for lunch, he laughed to himself about the rain he saw in the forecast. Did weathermen just flip a coin to decide what to report each day? For the third day in a row, the prediction missed its mark, badly. Christian decided he would have to remind his father sometime this afternoon that he owed Christian another million dollars on the double or nothing bet.

Christian spent the morning avoiding The Three, after the apparent kiss between brother and sister from yesterday. He lounged around in the principal's office until the last second before rushing to English. Christian washed his hands three times before exiting the bathroom before Mr. Button's class, and he avoided Alexis like the plague, averting his eyes from hers by any means necessary. His trip to the high school for algebra and biology refreshed him like an oasis before he returned to the junior high.

He knew lunch was going to be tough, and that concern slowed his steps from the bus to the front doors of the school. Christian trudged up to the third floor and opened his locker. A note had been wedged into the door, and it fell to the floor. He looked to see if anyone else watched in the hallway as he stooped to pick it up.

Above his name on the front, a heart dotted the i's, and little curls swooshed off each letter. A girl definitely had written the note. The bell rang, so Christian put the note in his pocket. Sam stopped by his locker.

"Everything okay?" Sam asked.

"Yeah, I guess I'm just not feeling well. Science and algebra kicked my butt at the high school today." Christian lied.

"Alexis is a whiz in math," Sam said, "and Ray and I could help you with science."

Christian looked quizzically at Sam as she leaned in close to him.

"School comes pretty easy for us," Sam whispered. "Except for Alexis and her fiction issues."

"But I'm not taking the same classes you are for math and science," Christian explained.

The ninth grade floor cleared out, because no one wanted to be late for lunch, and Sam waited for a few stragglers to hit the stairwell.

"We've all taken algebra. In fact, Alexis has taken trigonometry. Biology was a breeze for all three of us," Sam said, flashing her cute smile.

"Wait a second," Christian said, "then why aren't you guys taking those classes at the high school?"

"Well," she paused to choose her words carefully, "we don't want to draw unneeded attention to ourselves."

"Unneeded attention," Christian repeated in a whisper, thinking about how strange that statement was.

Actually, his anger percolated.

"Unneeded attention about what?" he hissed.

Sam stared at Christian hard for what felt like an eternity. She looked concerned, and he relaxed as he peered into her face. Christian had no reason to be angry with Sam.

"For our safety," a hard tone came from behind him.

Christian whirled around to see Alexis standing halfway down the hallway. Ray stood at the far end of the hall behind her, and Ray appeared to be checking the stairwell for anyone who might come up to the third floor.

Sam whispered, "Follow me," as she led Christian past Alexis to the other end of the third floor.

"No one is coming up this side," Ray said in a low voice.

Sam shot a look back to Alexis.

"I'm positive the floor is empty," Alexis said. "The teachers are in the lounge for their own lunch."

Alexis sprinted toward Christian and Sam as Ray met them at the door to the auditorium. Christian had forgotten about the little theater that served as the junior high auditorium. The speech teacher, Mr. Neil, used it as his classroom, but he only taught seventh and eighth period at the junior high. The auditorium drapes cast long shadows, and only threads of light filtered through the tattered coverings of the three large windows at the back of the spacious room.

The Three had pulled Christian into a dark room, and he had no idea why. He hoped someone planned on giving him an explanation.

"What the hell is going on?" Christian demanded.

"Lower your voice, please," Sam pleaded in a tone just above a whisper.

"Then tell me what is going on," Christian said more quietly.

Alexis, Sam, and Ray looked at each other in silence. Their hesitation allowed Christian to settle his emotions.

"What did you mean when you said 'For our safety' in the hallway?" Christian asked in a calmer tone.

"Are we sure we can we trust him?" Ray asked.

Alexis shrugged, and Sam did not make any indication one way or the other. Sam walked slowly toward Christian. Her face hid in the darkness with the only light coming from the windows behind her. She reached her hands delicately up to the sides of his face, and Christian smelled the sweet aroma of her skin. Sam smiled. Christian could not see the smile, but he could see the light glint off the changing musculature of her smooth cheeks, which rounded up, and he caught a glimpse of her teeth under her button nose. Christian wanted to push Sam away and kiss her at the same time.

"Yes," Sam whispered in a low hush that Christian barely heard.

Alexis answered her, "Are you sure?"

"I can't see it," Sam said, "so I'm sure."

Ray moved in close to Christian, as Sam let her hands drop. Sam backed away but only a step.

"Christian," Ray said with a serious tone in his voice, "we know."

"Know what?" Christian asked, curious and confused about what Ray meant.

Sam whispered, "We know you have a secret."

Christian thought, *"This is crazy. Three people who I have never met before show up to tell me that they know my secret."*

Christian's mind raced, and he felt his heart rate jump to a new level as Ray's words registered in his brain. The water... Were they talking about his ability to breathe under water? But how could they possibly know? No! There was no possible way that this was about his special ability! Christian had not told a soul. Christian reeled inside, and he felt the air leave his lungs like he had been kicked in the chest. Panic attacked Christian in waves as he tried to gain his mental balance.

Alexis moved to his side. "We know that the secret you carry is an extraordinary ability."

Christian felt sick to his stomach. Fortunately, he had not eaten lunch yet, or it would have ended up on the auditorium floor. Sam tried to hold his hand, but Christian pulled away from her. He brushed past Ray, who tried to grab his arm, but Christian's strength and adrenaline allowed him to pull his wrist from Ray's strong grasp. Christian marched toward the door, and Sam alone followed him.

"Christian, wait," Sam stammered, as Christian put his hand on the door. He stopped with his forehead pressed to the cool metal. He should have pushed through that door and left them behind him. Christian wanted to leave, but he waited.

"I still have my deep question to ask," Sam stated in a soothing voice.

Christian could feel Sam's smile in those words.

"Then ask it," Christian responded flatly.

"What is your deepest secret?" Sam asked.

"How do you know I have one, if you don't know what it is?" Christian asked, but deep down in his core, he believed that they knew somehow.

"Because of my own secret," Sam said.

Christian pushed the door open and stormed away from The Three. He had no desire to eat, but he walked to the cafeteria anyway. Brad's seat at their usual table sat unoccupied. Instead, Brad decided to sit a couple tables over with Molly and Ruby. Christian had not spoken a word to Ruby since ditching her at the movie, but he did not have many seating options, so he took the seat next to Brad.

"I was wondering where you were," Brad said with surprise at Christian's arrival. "You don't look so good."

"Rough day," Christian said.

"Where are The Three?" Molly asked.

"Who cares?" Christian said, angrily.

"Really!" Molly exclaimed intensely, surprised by the tone in Christian's voice.

"I don't want to talk about it!" Christian fired across the table at Molly.

Christian felt like a wounded animal being circled by a hungry jungle cat.

Ruby asked, "Did you get my note?"

Christian had forgotten about the note in his locker. He assumed Sam wrote it, and after what had happened, the note had escaped Christian's mind completely.

"Yes, but I haven't had a chance to read it," he said.

"Well, my brother is throwing a party at the pond tomorrow night after the football game. It's sort of a tradition in this town," Ruby explained. "After the first game of the year, the junior football players host a party at a farm outside of town. Win or lose, the football players and a bunch of high school girls get together. I'm a freshman this year, so I can go."

"Who's your brother?" Christian asked.

"Jeff Eaton," Ruby said.

"I'm going," Brad told him, "so you can tell your parents you're going to stay the night at my house. My parents will be cool with it, as long as I find my own ride, and I don't come home drunk."

Christian's bewilderment about his run-in with Sam, Alexis, and Ray in the auditorium turned to confused anger as he stewed. He was really hitting it off with Sam and although skeptical, he started to see Alexis and Ray as possible friends, when they turned on him. Suddenly, Christian was mad at his father for moving him away from life in Omaha to this little Iowa village. He was mad at The Three for ambushing him, and he was tired of not fitting in to his new surroundings. Maybe a party with his teammates would fix his problems and allow Christian the opportunity to be accepted.

"Then I'm going to go, too," Christian stated.

After lunch, Christian watched for Sam, Alexis, and Ray. He prepared himself for a repeat of the earlier performance, but he didn't see them the rest of the day. During study hall, Molly said The Three went home from school. She babbled about Mr. Banner coming to pick them up after lunch, and Molly started a rumor that The Three had been caught smoking in the bathroom, while the ninth graders were all eating lunch. But Christian knew better. His father verified the untruth when Christian asked for a pass to go to the office. Mr. Pearson also gave Christian the okay to spend the night with Brad after the football game.

Practice breezed by easily. The Red Oak football team did what is called a "walk through." They wore just their helmets and ran through pre-game warm-ups. They fine-tuned their coverages for their opponent's offensive alignments, and the offense ran through a series of plays. Practice ended in a little over an hour.

Miles called Christian for science help after supper, and Brad called to make sure Christian's mother gave Christian the okay to spend the night with him after the football game. After Christian explained that everything was cleared with his mom, Brad told Christian about making out with Molly. When Brad realized Christian was losing interest in his tales of conquest, Brad starting asking him about what he thought about Ruby.

"Are you and Sam an item or what?" Brad asked him.

"I don't know," Christian said. "We were, but I don't know what we are now."

"Have you called her?" Brad asked.

"No," Christian said.

"Why not?" Brad asked.

"I don't know," Christian responded. He could not explain to Brad what happened in the auditorium at school.

"Well, I hope Ruby is still interested," Brad said, "or you may be all alone at the party."

"That's fine with me," Christian stated.

Brad finally gave up on him, and Christian went to bed. At 8:30, he turned out the lights in his bedroom. Christian needed to get some rest. He pitied anyone who lined up against him tomorrow as he thought about taking out some aggression on Rock Port's football team. Then, the phone rang.

"Yes, he's home," Christian heard his dad say.

His father's steps creaked across the kitchen floor.

"Christian, the phone's for you," his father said.

Christian didn't answer his dad, and his father said Christian's name a second time.

"Samantha, his lights are off. I guess he decided to go to bed early because of the big game tomorrow. Yes, I think he's excited about it. I'm sorry to hear that about your aunt. Yes, I'll wish him good luck for you. I'm sorry you missed him. I'll tell him that you won't be around until Saturday. I'll leave the note where he'll see it. We'll see you on Monday then. 'Bye, Samantha."

Christian tossed in bed for hours, but the images of the day continued to flash through his thoughts. He replayed the events in the auditorium and the discussion with Brad, Molly, and Ruby in the cafeteria. Christian felt as if he had been in bed for half an hour, so he peeked at the clock again. Only a few minutes had passed since the last time he had looked at the clock. Christian's brain wrestled persistently with whether The Three knew his secret or not.

"So much for a good night's rest," he thought.

Maybe he had overreacted to them in the auditorium. How in the world could they know about his ability? He had not leaked a single word about it to anyone. In fact, he didn't really have anyone to share his secret with. Anger is an easy first emotion, but Christian's initial reaction had ebbed and curiosity took control. He tried to recall the exchange with The Three.

Did Sam say, "Because of my own secret," or "Because I know your secret?"

Christian couldn't remember her exact words, and he wrestled with the possibilities. Why would Samantha ask if she knew? If she doesn't know, why would she think Christian has a secret? If Sam has her own secret, what is it? Are the two related somehow?

"Can she read my mind?" Christian whispered.

He laughed uncomfortably at the thought and then dismissed it. Christian decided Sam had said, "Because of my secret," but he had no idea what that meant.

After tossing and turning for an hour, Christian finally drifted off to sleep.

CHAPTER 9

On Friday, school became an afterthought for most of the students. The home opener against the Rock Port Blue Jays kicked off at seven o'clock, and the cheerleaders covered the pink halls of Red Oak Junior High with spirit signs made of white rolled paper. Each football player's locker had a black tiger paw taped to it. In large, white, block-style numerals, the cheerleaders wrote each player's number. Some paws had "Go Tigers" scrawled above the number, while others contained little notes from the girls. Brad's paw read, "Hit 'em hard!" Molly scribbled a heart with her name below the words.

The high school took the school spirit to a higher level, and the building contained double the signage of the junior high. One sign showed a muscular tiger with a blue jay hanging limp from its mouth. Another sign had large cartoon football players drawn on it with printed pictures of the faces of the starting offense. In biology, Omar told Christian about a huge starting defense sign hanging in the opposite hallway. The players found it difficult to concentrate on their studies with the big football game broadcast on every wall, and everyone eagerly wished for the school day to end. Mrs. Dvorak glared over her bifocal glasses to remind Christian's class twice during algebra that she had no problem giving them extra homework for the weekend if they failed to get through the day's lesson. Christian enjoyed her as a teacher, but Mrs. Dvorak took a page out of Alexis' book when it came to staring people down.

With the lesson completed, Mrs. Dvorak loosened the reigns and let her students collaborate on the problems she gave to them, so Jesse and Omar moved closer to Christian. With an easy homework assignment in front of them, they chatted about the upcoming party at Eaton's place.

Christian's thoughts drifted toward The Three. He disliked them for the way they had cornered him, yesterday. They crossed a line, and he could feel the turmoil welling up inside of his body again, but he calmed as he remembered the soft voice of Samantha.

"Because of my secret," Sam's curious words echoed through his thoughts.

What secret could she have? What secret ability could she possess that would possibly allow her to know about Christian's own secret?

"This is crazy," Christian thought to himself, but he actually said it aloud.

Omar and Jesse turned from their conversation.

"How in the world can you disagree with me, Christian?" Jesse chastised.

"Huh?" Christian said, not sure what Jesse was talking about.

Omar responded to his look of cluelessness, "Well, Captain Obvious here," Omar pointed to Jesse, "was stating that Emily Thompson was the hottest of the cheerleaders even though she is only a sophomore, and you then told him that he was crazy. Defend your statement."

The two boys stared at Christian, waiting for a witty response or a reasonable explanation.

"Who is Emily Thompson?" Christian asked.

Jesse and Omar contorted their faces in response, as if Christian had grown horns from his head and his skin turned green.

"Who is Emily Thompson?" Jesse mimicked in disbelief.

"You haven't seen her?" Omar said in the same voice inflection. "Well, we need to remedy this immediately. We will try to find her for you when we leave class. I think her locker is in this hallway."

"She does," Jesse said. "I try to keep up on important matters like this."

The three boys finished up the final problem of their assignment as the bell rang. They wound through the other students in the hallway, and Christian spotted the football players more easily since they all wore their jerseys for school. On any other day, Christian would not have recognized the student in front of him as a football player, because on the field, he only saw helmets and numbered jerseys. If Christian attended school at the high school all day, he would probably recognize all of his teammates.

"I don't see her," Jesse said with disappointment. "I guess you'll have to wait until after the game. I overheard her say to some friends that she would be attending tonight's festivities, even though she broke up with Eaton last night."

"Seriously, what does she see in that guy?" Omar commented.

"If she was dating Jeff," Christian whispered, "she must not be that bright."

"You don't have to be smart when you are *that* hot!" Jesse said, giving Omar a high-five.

"Looks aren't everything," Christian said.

"Nope, looks are the *only* thing," Jesse replied, his tongue hanging out of his mouth as he high-fived Omar a second time.

"Then I guess you're screwed," Christian said to Jesse with a smile.

Omar let out a laugh, and Jesse tried to punch Christian's arm, but Christian quickly jumped away from Jesse, who whiffed on the swing. While dodging Jesse, Christian inadvertently bumped into another football player.

"Watch it, froshy," a deep voice bellowed.

Christian looked up at the number 69 on Johnny Stratton's chest.

"Sorry, Strat," Christian said apologetically.

The senior offensive lineman towered over him, and Strat pushed Christian up against the lockers.

"Watch where you're goin' little boy," Strat snarled.

Little pieces of chewing tobacco littered his clenched teeth.

"I don't like freshmen, especially a freshman who comes to the high school during the school day. Go back to the junior high where you belong."

Strat pushed Christian to the ground and lumbered down the hall. Other senior boys laughed as they followed in Strat's wake, and a couple of them turned around to get another glimpse at Christian lying on the ground.

"Are you all right?" a soft voice asked from beside Christian. Christian turned in the direction of the voice, where a cheerleader knelt next to the lockers. She collected Christian's books that spilled when he bumped into Strat. Her blonde hair seductively covered her face.

"Yeah, I guess I picked the wrong time to not look where I was going," Christian muttered.

"Strat does that to everybody," she said. "He acts like he rules the place."

Christian grabbed his books and got to his feet. He expected the girl to move on down the hall, but she continued to stand in front of him. Her well-tanned legs caught his eye, and she pushed her hair from her face revealing beautiful green eyes.

"I'm Christian," he said.

"I know," she responded with a roll of her eyes, pushing her hair behind her right ear. "It's my job to know who the football players are; I'm a cheerleader."

"Right," Christian said. "Are you going to the party tonight?"

"Yes," she answered, as her right hand dropped to her hip with a sigh of impatience.

"Maybe, I'll see you there," Christian said, not sensing that he was in her way.

"Could you moooooove?" she announced in irritation. "You're standing in front of my locker."

"Oh, I'm sorry," he said, as he stepped to the side. "Thanks for helping me with my books."

"Just be more careful when you walk down the hallway," she said as she opened the door to her locker, relieved to finally have access to it.

"Oh, I don't know, I may let Strat throw me into your locker again on Monday," Christian replied with a grin.

Her irritation slipped away and she tried not to laugh, but a smile slipped onto her lips.

"See you later," Christian said as he turned to leave.

Jesse and Omar stood a few feet away.

"You all right?" Omar asked.

"Yeah, who was that?" Christian questioned, referring to the blonde bombshell he had just been thrown into.

Jesse put his arm around Christian and explained, "That, my friend, was Emily Thompson."

"I apologize, Jesse. You're not crazy," Christian said, as he left them to catch his bus.

During study hall back at the junior high, Christian asked Mr. Button for a pass to the library to do some research for biology. He lied, but Christian felt like avoiding Molly's inquisition about Ruby and The Three being absent from school. The Three angered him, but he still felt the paradox of needing to defend them. In addition, he really liked Sam.

As he waited for the log-in screen to appear on the computer, Mrs. Smith asked if he planned to be in the library for a while.

"Yes," Christian answered, "I have some research to do for one of my classes at the high school."

"I was going to leave early to catch my son's football game in Menlo, near Des Moines," Mrs. Smith said. "I have a two hour trip, so I was hoping to head home before school ended."

"No problem, just let my dad know I'm in here. He is my ride home today," Christian said. "I will stay in here the whole time."

"I trust you," she said. "I'll tell your father he can find you here."

Mrs. Smith left, closing the door behind her, and Christian's dad walked in a couple of minutes later.

"Biology," Christian explained.

"I may have to stay a while after school to finish some stuff," his father said. "Do you want to call your mother?"

"Nah, I'll hang here until you're done."

Mr. Pearson closed the door.

Christian decided to check his school e-mail account. All Red Oak students had an account through the school district. They could send e-mails, but only to other accounts on the district network, not to outside e-mail accounts like hotmail or yahoo. And the school limited students to a certain number of e-mails a day. Teachers sent reminders about assignments and upcoming tests, and students could check their e-mail accounts from home. Principals sent reminders about parent-teacher conferences and other school news.

Christian had one new message.

Christian,

Good luck during the game tonight. Go Tigers!

The Cheerleaders

He was about to log out, when a number one appeared in his inbox telling him that he had another message. Christian clicked on the link and saw a message from "sbanner." The subject was blank. Sam sent the message to him within the last couple of minutes. Christian thought about deleting the e-mail without reading it but changed his mind.

I am so sorry about yesterday. We didn't mean to make you angry with us. Please don't hate me. You are still my boyfriend, whether you like it or not. :) We kind of ganged up on you, but it's important for you to know that I am on your side. We all are. I hope you win your game. I wish I could be there, but I think it's better if I stay home. Please do one thing for me before I see you on Monday. Look up the definition of "phenomenon" for me.

Phenomenon? He knew what phenomenon meant, something that is out of the blue, something that doesn't fit the pattern. Christian decided to double-check his definition with dictionary.com, so he typed in the word and waited for the definition to pop onto the screen.

Phenomenon – 1) a fact, occurrence, or circumstance observed or observable. 2) something that impresses the observer as extraordinary. 3) a person having some exceptional ability or talent.

Christian closed the e-mail and opened up the internet. He typed "phenomenon" and clicked search. The list of websites on the first page of about 24 million links included mainly TV shows, a John Travolta movie, and future music superstars. Christian narrowed the search by typing in "phenomenon + human ability," which allowed him to search only those links that included human traits. He scrolled through the links. Sites for human enigmas and paranormal abilities flashed on the screen. One mentioned the occult in the summary, and another claimed to be a UFO website, which was getting Christian nowhere.

He scrolled through page after page of websites. After about twenty pages, Christian rubbed his eyes and leaned back in his chair. He clicked on the next button every couple of seconds, and a new list appeared. A link at the bottom of page 43 caught his eye. "**Phenomenal child can withstand extreme temperatures** – *boy is a phenomenon… the human ability to maintain body temperature in those extreme temperatures is virtually impossible…*"

Christian clicked on the link and found an article dated three years earlier from a newspaper in Montana. He skimmed the article. *"An unnamed teen had survived a car accident during a blizzard… Both his parents were killed in the accident… The car had slid off the road… Authorities said the boy had been in the car for twenty-four hours in below freezing conditions wearing only jeans and a long-sleeved shirt… Doctors were amazed that he suffered no ill effects from his time in the harsh cold."*

The boy's name never appeared in the article, but Christian thought about Ray. The only reason his mind jumped to Ray was due to Ray's typical attire. Ray always wore jeans and long sleeves, and then it hit Christian. Could Ray have been adopted because his parents were killed in a car accident in Montana?

Christian searched the article for the names of the boy's parents. He found the names and wrote them down. Then, he clicked on the newspaper's home page and typed in "Obituary Doug Tines" in the search box.

Christian found an archived obituary for Doug and Stacy Tines, and he scanned the article until he found the surviving family members. Doug and Stacy were survived by one son, Raymond Tines.

Christian searched the site for any other reference to Raymond Tines or Ray Tines, but he had no luck.

Christian's father popped his head into the library.

"You all done?" Mr. Pearson asked, startling Christian.

"Yeah, just let me shut down," Christian said, a bit shaken.

"I'll be in my office," his father replied.

Christian had not heard the bell or the students in the hallway. His search for answers had engrossed him.

He shut down the computer and grabbed his books off the table. Christian had a feeling that Ray Banner was Raymond Tines of Montana, and he planned to ask Ray on Monday, if he got a chance. He looked at his watch. It was four, and he had to get home to eat because the players needed to be in the locker room by 5:30.

The Rock Port Blue Jays took the opening kickoff back for a touchdown, but a solid kick return by the Tigers gave the Red Oak offense good field position. Seven plays later, the Red Oak quarterback, Ricky Downs, hit Chris Johnston for a twenty-two yard touchdown pass to knot the score at seven apiece. From that point on, the defenses took over, and the stalemate continued through the second quarter. Red Oak stymied the Blue Jay rushing game, holding them to only three first downs in the first half, but Rock Port's defense tightened up, as well. They held the home team's offense in check until late in the second quarter. With less than two minutes on the clock, Ricky hit Johnston for another long pass to put Red Oak's offense inside the twenty yard line. But two plays later, Ricky fumbled the snap, and Rock Port recovered the ball at its own fifteen.

With the clock winding down, Rock Port abandoned their ground game and tried to throw the ball. After a twenty yard gain to Rock Port's own thirty-five yard line, Jeff Eaton deflected a pass. By chance, the ball ended up in Christian's hands, and he broke a tackle along the sideline before getting shoved out of bounds at the Rock Port thirty yard line. Coach Lilly played in close to the vest by running the ball in the middle of the field. On fourth and two from the Rock Port twenty-two, Omar kicked a thirty-nine yard field goal. Red Oak went into the locker room with a 10-7 lead.

Johnny Stratton stood at the door to the locker room as the players entered, and he screamed at his teammates.

"Come on!" Strat yelled at the offensive players. "We are getting our butts handed to us out there. We need to get some intensity!"

Eaton fired, "Yeah, the defense is getting tired of doing all the work around here!"

Strat shoved Jeff, "Up yours, Eaton!"

Eaton held his ground and glared at Stratton.

"Is that all you got?" Eaton growled.

Stratton moved toward him and shouts arose from the other players standing around the two behemoths.

"Break it up!" Coach Cozad shouted as he stepped between each player. "Break it up!"

Cozad's muscles throbbed as he grabbed hold of the front of Strat's shoulder pads with his right hand and Eaton's facemask with his left. Then Coach Cozad shook them like rag dolls.

"You two are on the same team!" Cozad exclaimed as the rest of the players quieted to a whisper. "Instead of running your mouth, Strat, maybe you should thank the defense for covering for your lack of effort out there."

Coach Cozad turned to Eaton and said, "We have two more quarters of war with Rock Port, and you want to pick a fight with your teammate. What the hell is wrong with you?"

Cozad pushed Johnny and Jeff to opposite sides, as Coach Lilly entered the room.

"Listen up!" Lilly stated. "For two quarters, they've manhandled y'all on the offensive line. We need to maintain our blocks. We can't just hit 'em and let go. We've got to hit 'em and hit 'em and hit 'em. Sustain those blocks so Ricky can find his receivers. The poor kid is running for his life back there. Now, they been stunting with their tackles and freeing up a linebacker to blitz. Damn it, running backs, you need to see that blitz and pick it up. You wanna add anything, Coach Cozad?"

Coach Cozad walked to the front. "Defense, excellent job in the first half, but we still have two more quarters to play. Stay with your assignments and keep stringing out their option. Look for them to run play-action in the second half. Our linebackers have been doing a good job stuffing that fullback dive, so safeties, be ready for them to dump a pass off play-action in that middle zone behind our linebackers. Defensive ends, if that tight end lines up on your side, you need to lock him down and keep him from slipping behind our linebackers. With our success in stopping the run, they are going to take some shots through the air. Be ready."

Coach Lilly moved back to the front. "We have twenty-four minutes of football left, and I know you're tired, but we need to leave it all on the field, boys." Coach Lilly's voice rose to a yell, "Defense, we came here to put up zeroes! EVERY YARD..."

"IS A BATTLE!" the team answered in unison.

Lilly continued, "Offense, we came here to move the ball! EVERY YARD..."

"IS A BATTLE!" the team answered again.

"EVERY PLAY..." Coach Cozad hollered, as the players rose to their feet.

"IS A BATTLE!" they responded.

"EVERY PLAY..." he repeated.

"IS A BATTLE!" they shouted again in a frenzy of testosterone.

"THIS IS NOT A GAME!" Cozad yelled.

"THIS IS WAR!" the players shouted.

"THIS IS NOT A GAME!"

"THIS IS WAR!" they screamed.

"Now, I know you're tired," Cozad said in a low tone, "and I know you are battered and bruised, but I also know you are winners."

Christian felt the hair on his neck rise as the energy passed through him.

Coach Cozad continued, "When your backs are against the wall, and you feel like you have given everything you have, you need to look across the huddle at your teammates and read the letters printed across your teammates chests. Read that word, TIGERS! A TIGER does not quit!" His voice began to grow. "A TIGER does not give in! A TIGER FIGHTS, TO THE END! THIS IS NOT A GAME!"

"THIS IS WAR!" the team screamed, and Coach Cozad raced through the throng and out the doors of the locker room.

The team followed him, howling like wild animals on the hunt for blood. The spectacle continued on the sidelines as the coaches screamed "THIS IS NOT A GAME" in each player's face. The call to war reverberated up and down the sideline. Christian's adrenaline reached a crescendo in the furious mob.

On the opening kickoff of the second half, Chris Johnston broke free down the Red Oak sideline, as Miles Jones, who earned a spot on the kick return team, sprung him free with a massive block. Miles screamed like a warrior as his shoulder pads rocked the unsuspecting Rock Port defender under the jaw line. The offensive line sustained their blocks, and soon Red Oak struck pay dirt in the end zone.

The defense continued to stop the Blue Jay attack, forcing punts on the first three Rock Port possessions of the second half. After showing promise during the opening scoring drive, the Tiger offense sputtered on the next two drives, failing to convert a first down. At the end of three quarters, Red Oak led 17-7.

Early in the fourth quarter, Red Oak punted from deep inside its own territory. The Rock Port return man broke free for fifty-five yards before getting pushed out of bounds at the nine yard line. On the next play, Calvin Robinson bit on the play-action, and the wide receiver on Cal's side of the field caught a fade route in the corner of the end zone for a touchdown. The Blue Jays missed the extra point. A bad snap caused the kicker to pull it to the left, and the home crowd roared as the ball caromed off the upright, no good. Red Oak clung to a 17-13 lead.

Rock Port attempted an on-side kick, but Red Oak covered the ball at the forty-five yard line. The offense chewed up some clock while grinding out two first downs on the ground. Unfortunately, two holding penalties pushed them back near midfield. Rock Port started burning time outs, and Red Oak punted.

With just under two minutes left in regulation, Rock Port blocked the punt. The ball ricocheted back into the punter before fluttering into the hands of a Blue Jay lineman, who made it to the fifteen yard line before Strat tackled him from behind. Christian had never seen Strat run that fast. With 1:42 left in regulation, the Red Oak defense took the field. Down four points, Rock Port needed a touchdown. With no timeouts, Coach Cozad told his defense to be ready for Rock Port to throw the ball.

After an incomplete pass, Rock Port's quarterback scrambled for eleven yards, making it first and goal from the four yard line. Christian lined up to the strong side of the field in press coverage on the wide receiver. On the snap, the wide receiver clamped down on Christian. The quarterback faked to the fullback in the backfield, and Christian recognized Rock Port's option headed to his side of the field. Christian shed the receiver and closed in on the I-back. The pulling guard tripped, and the Tiger defensive end slipped past the blocking tight end. Christian leapt over the stumbling guard as the quarterback came face to face with the defensive end. The quarterback pitched the ball just before getting leveled, and Christian converged on the I-back as the football arrived. With the running back's head turned toward the ball, he did not stand a chance. Christian lowered his pads while keeping his head up and planted the running back into the turf. The football wobbled from the I-back's grasp. With his legs still pumping, Christian sprung to his feet and scooped up the ball. He could hear the crowd roar, as he raced down the field and crossed the goal line exhausted. Christian's touchdown essentially put the game out of reach, and Calvin Robinson intercepted a pass with a minute left in the game to seal the victory.

In the post-game speech, Coach Lilly praised his team for the determination and resolve to finish the game, and he presented Calvin and Christian with the game ball.

"You'll have to share it," Coach Lilly joked before pulling out a second ball and throwing it to Christian. "Imagine that… two freshmen get the first game balls of the season."

Coach Lilly let out a shout that sounded something like "sue we," and the entire team laughed.

The euphoria of the locker room reverberated off the walls. Players smiled and relived individual moments of the game while taking off sweat-drenched pads. Christian sat in silence in front of his locker. He was beat. He waited for the upper classmen to finish showering before taking his turn. Christian may have gotten a game ball for his play, but freshmen still showered last, so he had to wait his turn.

Brad and Christian threw their bags in Mr. Matthews's car and walked to the student parking lot. Molly waited for them near a blue minivan.

"Nice game, Christian!" Molly said in a loud voice.

Something strange lisped from Molly's speech, and she giggled, as Brad put his arms around her and gave her a kiss.

"Let's go," a female voice called from the van.

They piled into the sliding door, and Molly introduced Christian to her older sister before snuggling with Brad in the back seat. Another girl sat in the passenger seat, but Christian could not see well in the darkness of the vehicle.

"There's a cooler in the back if you wanna beer," Molly's sister explained from the driver's seat.

"I'll take one," Brad said.

Christian heard the ice rattle as Brad fished out a can. Brad motioned to Christian with the beer in his hand.

"No, I'm okay for now," Christian said. "I'll wait until the party."

Christian lied, because he had no plans to get in trouble by drinking at a party or in a car for that matter. Christian knew he wouldn't make friends by staying home on the weekends, but he wasn't naïve to think there wouldn't be alcohol at the party. In Christian's mind, if he wasn't drinking, he wasn't going to be in trouble.

"Suit yourself," Brad said coolly, as he took a swig of his beer. "Nothin' like a cold brew on a steamy night like tonight."

Christian wasn't surprised that Brad drank, since he smoked. Molly giggled again, and Christian rolled his eyes as the van pulled out onto the highway. The radio blared a country tune as they turned onto gravel. Christian had not been paying attention to where they were going, but he recognized the road. Christian saw the sign for Bluegrass Road, and he spotted the lights of the Banner house. As they drove past the farm, he saw the lights on in the living room as well as what he thought was Sam's room. He figured the only darkened window belonged to Alexis.

Shortly after the lights of the house faded behind them, the van turned right onto another gravel road. Christian caught only a glimpse of the street sign, which he thought said 215 Street. About a quarter mile down, they turned into the drive of another farm. The road curled around behind a house. The dim light of a TV shone in one of the front rooms.

The van wound through a stand of trees before coming to an open field. They drove through the field and into another denser grove of trees. As the van came to the end of the trees, an orange glow flickered across an expanse of water. A bonfire burned on the opposite side of a good-sized pond. The van turned and crossed the earthen dam. Once they arrived on the other side of the dam, the land opened into another vast field. Christian saw lines of trees on all three sides of the open ground, and water formed the boundary of the fourth side.

Other cars had filed into parking spots along the edge of the bonfire. Christian counted eleven vehicles as they pulled into an open area. As he got out, Christian saw two sets of headlights winding through the trees on the other side of the pond.

The group made its way through the cars to the fire. A couple of coolers sat to one side, and some girls perched themselves on a log that was pulled close to the flames. Christian recognized one of them as a cheerleader, but her name escaped him.

Two pickups crossed the dam, and Christian heard hoots and shouting coming from that direction over the roar of stereo speakers and the engines. Football players piled out of the back of the trucks, as a couple of carloads of cheerleaders and other high school girls invaded from the trail through the trees. Beer cans were tossed to waiting hands, and Christian decided to take a walk to the water. He sat down on a rock near the edge and grabbed a handful of pebbles.

"I shouldn't be here," he thought.

Christian figured out that the location of Sam's house had to be toward the inlet of the pond, to the east. He guessed that a little creek ran from near the Banner house to here. The dam they drove across had to be west. Christian could hear a couple of players shouting, and he realized that Eaton and Strat both had arrived. They performed a reenactment of the argument in the locker room at half time, and Ricky Downs did an impersonation of Coach Cozad. The impersonation impressed Christian, so he walked back to the fire.

It didn't take long for the beer to take its effect on everyone. Eaton started getting foul-mouthed, and Strat made different freshmen get beers for him from his cooler. Things got heated when Emily Thompson showed up. Eaton gave her a few choice words in a tirade about the level of her intelligence and sexual orientation, but Emily didn't back down an inch.

Christian tried to stay at the periphery of the party because he had no desire to draw unneeded attention to himself. He failed to locate Brad anywhere, so he sat down on a log with Jesse and Omar.

"Hey, Omar," Christian interrupted their conversation. "Did you drive out here?"

"Yeah," Omar responded.

"Any way I can hitch a ride back when you guys leave?" Christian asked, wanting to be sure he had a ride back to town.

"No problem," Omar answered. "I'll come find you when we're ready to leave. I'm not drinking, so I'll remember."

He smiled, and Christian relaxed at knowing he had secured a safer way home.

"Thanks, man," Christian said.

Calvin Robinson was completely hammered when he staggered up with his arms around Ruby James. Cal slurred his words, and Ruby tried to keep him from tipping over. Christian wished deep down that she would let Calvin fall, but his wish did not come true. As Christian stood up to move away, Calvin put his arm around him. Cal reeked of stale beer.

"Christian," Robinson slurred, "you made one heck of a play to save that game."

"It was a team effort," Christian replied, trying to move out from under Calvin's arm.

"Nah, I mean it," Cal explained. "I have been kind of hard on you, and I shouldn't."

Cal was blasted, but at least he was a happy drunk.

"Someone give this guy a beer," Cal said.

"Nope, no thanks," Christian said, lifting Cal's arm over his head.

The limp arm fell to Calvin's side, almost tipping him over.

"What? Don't you drink?" Calvin asked puzzled.

"Not tonight," Christian said.

"Hey, get this," Cal turned to the group. "Christina here doesn't drink."

No one paid much attention with the noise, so Christian walked away. He chose to go back to the edge of the water, but as he neared the rock he had been sitting on earlier, he noticed the seat was occupied by a girl. He decided to find another place to sit.

"Did I take your spot?" a familiar voice asked.

"Uh, no, I just didn't expect to find someone out here," Christian responded.

"At least you weren't thrown out here like you were thrown into my locker," she said.

Emily Thompson motioned for Christian to sit down by her.

"Why aren't you boozin' it up with the rest of them?" Emily asked.

"I don't drink," he muttered. "I've seen people do too many stupid things while drinking."

Emily laughed, and Christian thought she had a pretty laugh.

The two outcasts sat for a while in silence, when all of a sudden Christian felt the presence of someone large standing over him. Johnny Stratton and a small group of people had moved to his spot near the water, and they formed a semicircle around Emily and Christian.

"Drink!" Strat demanded, as he pushed a beer into Christian's face.

Christian stood up.

"Drink!" Strat repeated in a booming voice.

"No thanks," Christian answered.

"Maybe, you don't fully understand the situation. I said DRINK!" Strat bellowed.

"I don't drink," Christian stammered.

"Well, I'll be. Cal was right. He bet me that you didn't drink, and I took him up on it," Strat explained.

"You win, Cal!" Strat shouted over his shoulder.

"Then do it!" Calvin hollered from the fire.

"Do what?" Christian asked, as Strat shoved him hard.

Christian flew backwards into the water, and the small entourage began to laugh as Christian got back to his feet.

"Back off, Strat!" Emily roared, as she stood to face Johnny Stratton.

"What? Is Christina your new boyfriend?" Strat hooted.

"I said leave him alone!" Emily shouted.

"Hey, Jeff!" Strat hollered. "I guess Christian is moving in on your ex-girlfriend."

Eaton was swearing, as he walked from the fire to the pond. Christian had no escape, but he thought maybe Jeff wouldn't come into the water, so Christian backed up until the water reached up to Christian's waist, and he could feel the bottom get deeper as he moved further away from shore.

"Get up here, Christina," Eaton shouted in rage.

Christian stayed put. More people joined the group of onlookers, and Jeff swore at Christian, as he entered the water. Soon, a crowd gathered at the edge of the pond.

"If you won't come up here," he growled, "then I'll drag you up here!"

Christian backed further into the pond as Jeff grabbed for him. He pushed Christian under the water and grabbed hold of his shirt collar. Christian heard Emily yelling for Jeff to stop, but others were shouting at Jeff to pound him as his head broke above the surface. He reached up and attempted to pry Jeff's hand loose, but Jeff tightened his grip as he dragged Christian closer to shore. Christian swung his feet around and kicked at Jeff's knees. Eaton tripped, and Christian freed himself from Eaton's hold. Christian got to his feet, but Jeff whipped around and caught Christian in the side of the head with one of his big paws. Christian fell backwards into the water. Eaton fell on top of him again, and Christian heard splashes, as other people came into the water. Christian flailed, and his knee caught Jeff Eaton in the one spot that can bring a man down in serious pain... the family jewels.

Loose from Eaton's grasp, Christian pushed out into the deeper water. Even though he was under water, Christian was close enough to hear muffled voices yelling. Christian felt along in the darkness, breathing easily as he stayed submerged. He found his footing and pushed up slowly until just his eyes breached the surface. Christian had moved off toward the east about twenty yards. The group searched the shoreline for him, thinking that Christian would have to swim back to the bank at some point. He continued to breathe, even though his nose and mouth remained under the water.

Compared to the chlorinated water of the pool in his back yard, this soup tasted nasty. Christian heard someone ask if he had drowned.

"He probably swam to the other side," Eaton said. "Let him walk home."

Eaton winced as he grabbed his crotch to make sure everything still remained in its proper place.

Someone pointed across the water, "There he is!"

A figure stood near the water opposite the side of the bonfire. The dark figure turned and jogged toward the trees, disappearing into the blackness of the night.

"Yeah, you better keep on running!" shouted Strat.

"Should we go after him?" asked Cal.

"Let him run," Strat shouted, "Now go get me a beer, froshy."

Christian moved off to the east, staying low enough in the water that he still saw where he was going. When he traveled far enough away, Christian lifted his head from the water and sucked in fresh air. Trying to stay quiet, he picked his way carefully, since he did not want to splash too much. Christian measured the distance between his position and the fire and figured no one heard him stagger from the pond dripping wet.

"Who was that?" Christian whispered to himself, thinking about the dark stranger that scurried into the trees from the lake. Had someone been watching the party, or had the night played tricks on all of their eyes?

Christian's jaw ached. Jeff caught him pretty good during the fight. Christian climbed up the bank and worked his way to a spot where he could see the bonfire. He had to figure out how to get home. Fortunately, the moon glowed in the sky, casting a dim light on his surroundings. His eyes adjusted to the darkness, so Christian navigated the terrain more easily. From where he hid, he only caught words and small phrases from the myriad of voices around the fire.

"Now what?" he said to himself in a whisper.

Christian sat for a while in the darkness, contemplating the possible paths from here to his house. Following the creek to J Avenue would be difficult at night. Circling the pond to find the road that wound through the trees meant going in the wrong direction. He thought about trying to head north to Bluegrass Road, but he had no idea what lay between here and there.

Christian whispered each possibility to himself, and he did not expect to hear a voice respond.

"Or you could follow me to my house," a voice whispered from the shadows behind him.

Christian whirled around in surprise.

"Who said that?" he whispered.

"It's me, Alexis," the voice answered.

Slowly, a shadow appeared from behind a tree. Alexis wore blue jeans and a black hooded sweat shirt, and Christian stared at her in disbelief.

"They think you've run off toward the road," Alexis said, pointing to the south.

"How do you know?" Christian asked. "I can't hear a word they're saying."

"Trust me," Alexis said. "They're talking about one of the teachers at the high school right now, and they aren't concerned about you anymore. We can head out this way."

She turned to walk away.

"Come on," Alexis urged. "Let's get you to my house. We'll get you some dry clothes."

Alexis did not seem concerned with revealing their location to the drunks around the bonfire, so Christian rose to his feet and followed her.

"Was that you across the lake?" he asked.

"Yes," she said. "I figured you needed a way out. Man, that big guy really let you have it."

"Which one?" Christian asked rubbing a possible bruise on his face.

"The one who chased you into the water," Alexis said.

They traveled far enough away that he only heard the occasional shout from the bonfire party, so Christian's voice relaxed a bit.

"How long have you been here?" he asked.

"Oh, I was sitting out here well before you asked Omar for a ride, since you couldn't find Brad," Alexis responded.

"I didn't see you at the party," Christian said.

"Oh, I wasn't at the party. I was sitting near the trees on the opposite side," she stated.

"Then how did you know about Omar?" he asked.

"Well, I heard you talking," Alexis said, irritably.

Christian could tell Alexis rolled her eyes even though her face looked in the opposite direction.

Christian grabbed Alexis' shoulder.

"Wait," he said.

Alexis turned to face him.

"So, you were sitting on the other side of the pond, up in the trees, but you heard the conversation I had with Omar?" Christian said puzzled.

"Yes," Alexis answered.

"From over three-hundred yards away," he said, estimating the distance. "That's almost three football fields in length."

"Wow, you really are a math whiz," Alexis said, sarcastically.

"Whatever," Christian said. "Really, where were you, up in a tree?"

"If I was up in a tree near the fire, how would I have made it to the other side of the lake to make them think I was you, genius," Alexis said with a growing frustration in her voice.

"No way," Christian scoffed.

Alexis stopped walking. They had left the edge of the trees and stood three rows into a bean field.

Alexis explained, "Here's the deal. I will do this once. I am going to walk ahead of you. I will go about a hundred yards. That's the length of one football field, so don't get scared."

She mocked Christian with her sarcasm.

"I will holler back at you to say a word, I don't care what the word is, just pick one word. Whisper that one word, as if you are whispering while a teacher is talking in class. After you whisper the word, come to me. I will tell you what you whispered. You got it?"

Christian nodded, "You walk away, I whisper one word, and you tell me what it was. Sounds easy enough."

"Let's hope so," Alexis said in irritation.

She walked away from Christian, and he stood and watched her pass down a row of beans. Finally, she stopped and turned toward Christian after she had traveled about a hundred yards.

Alexis hollered, "Go ahead!"

Christian whispered, "Football."
"Football!" she yelled.
"Holy crap," he whispered in response to her feat.
"Holy crap is two words!" she yelled to Christian.

CHAPTER
10

Christian stood with his mouth gaping in the middle of a field of soybeans. The sun had set a long time ago, but the glow of the moon allowed him to see his surroundings quite clearly. Alexis stayed put about one-hundred yards ahead of him, down the same row in which he stood. The stifling, humid air took a brief rest as a cool breeze reached Christian's wet clothes and refreshed him. The wind rustled the rows of soybeans giving them the appearance of gentle waves on an open sea.

As quickly as the breeze appeared, it disappeared. Locusts droned from the trees at his back, buzzing the air. Christian walked toward Alexis, slowly at first. Even though he could see fairly well in the dark, he wanted to tread carefully. The hot, humid summer was perfect growing weather, and the crop of soybeans stood well above his waist, so the leaves of each plant tugged at his legs with each step. As he became more comfortable with the terrain, his pace quickened. By no means did Christian plan to run. He was too tired, but he strode much faster than before as he approached Alexis.

"Do all three of you possess a gift?" Christian asked as he neared Alexis.

"Not the same gift," she stated.

"How did you know about mine?" he said.

"Sam," she answered. "I know you have a million questions racing through your mind, but let's get to the house."

"You're afraid someone might hear?" Christian questioned.

"No," Alexis responded, "the bugs are eating me alive. Can you move faster?"

Alexis jogged lightly up the row. Christian stumbled twice before they reached the end of the field. Neither Christian nor Alexis breathed very hard. The football conditioning paid off for him, and volleyball players did a lot of conditioning as well.

"This way," Alexis said as she pointed toward an opening in the trees.

Christian followed as she turned up a deer path through the pines. They ducked around some branches before stepping into a clearing. He saw the lights of the house ahead of them. Alexis told him to wait on the back porch, while she entered through the door to the kitchen.

He heard muffled voices from the living room. The hallway light turned on, and Christian saw a tall, gray-haired man leading The Three to the kitchen. A light flashed on the back porch, blinding him as the door opened.

"Please come inside," a deep voice said from behind the light.

Christian stepped through the door and saw Ray and Sam standing on the other side of the kitchen counter. Alexis grabbed glasses from a cabinet near the sink.

Mr. Banner towered over Christian, who was at least half a foot shorter. Mr. Banner's gray moustache protruded from a lean face, hardened by the years. Weathered skin covered his bony jaw. Wrinkles punctuated Mr. Banner's cool green eyes at the corners, and his yellowed teeth shone in a wide smile as his hardened features melted into a grin.

"So, this is Christian," the man said. "I am Mr. Banner."

He extended a huge, bony hand toward Christian.

"Yes sir," Christian answered, as he placed his hand into Mr. Banner's enormous grasp.

Mr. Banner held firmly before releasing.

"I've been looking forward to meeting you," Mr. Banner said, "but I did not expect it to be so soon. Please, come this way," he said leading them. "Ray, take Christian to your room and let him change into some dry clothes. We'll wait for you boys in the living room."

Ray led Christian up the steps to his room.

"I don't have anything that doesn't have long sleeves," Ray said apologetically. "I do have a pair of jeans that we can cut the legs off. That way you won't roast."

"You don't have to ruin your clothes for me," Christian said.

"It's all right, I've been meaning to get rid of them. They're not my favorite," Ray said. "I think Sam has scissors in her desk drawer."

Ray disappeared down the hallway to retrieve the scissors, and Christian pulled off the soaked t-shirt. The air conditioning chilled his body.

"Could you grab a towel?" Christian called out.

Ray returned with scissors and a towel.

"I was thinking the same thing," Ray said. "I'll wait downstairs."

"I have a question for you," Christian said, seriously.

In the short time Christian knew Ray, this had been their longest conversation. Ray seemed a little uncomfortable at his request but shrugged and sat down on the bed as Christian closed the door.

Christian toweled off, and Ray went to work with the scissors on the old pair of jeans.

"Ray," Christian said, "I was on-line earlier today."

Christian stopped.

"Had it been today? Was it still Friday?" Christian thought.

"I think we should wait until we go downstairs," Ray said, interrupting his thoughts.

"Okay," Christian said. "It can wait."

"They're done," Ray said, tossing the jeans on the bed. "I left them long, so you can cut more off if you need to."

"I'm sure they'll be fine," Christian replied, grateful to have dry clothes.

"You'll have to wear wet underwear," Ray commented, "because men should not share underwear. I'm sure it's a law somewhere."

"If it isn't, it should be," Christian smiled, returning Ray's grin.

Ray left the room, closing the door behind him, and Christian changed hastily. He pulled the sleeves up on the shirt. Even though the air conditioner hummed, the long sleeves clamped down on the body heat trying to escape. The jean shorts fit loosely, but they worked. He used the belt from his wet clothes to keep the cut-offs from dropping to the floor. Fortunately, Christian left his wallet at home, but his watch had been on his wrist during the moonlight swim. He hoped it still worked, but it needed a good drying out before he would know for sure.

"Thank goodness I didn't get a new cell phone," Christian whispered to himself.

He searched a drawer for a pair of socks before gathering his wet clothes and shoes to walk downstairs. Sam waited at the bottom of the steps with a grocery bag.

"You can put your clothes in here and set them by the door with your shoes," Sam explained.

Christian hesitated at the bottom of the stairs.

"Don't worry about the floor, Christian, it's already wet," Mr. Banner said from the living room. "Come and sit down. I am sure you have questions."

Christian carefully laid the bag of wet clothes and his shoes on a mat by the front door and took a seat on the couch. Sam and Christian exchanged self-conscious glances as he sat next to her, and Alexis took a position on the floor opposite the couch, near the TV. Ray sat next to Alexis, and Mr. Banner occupied a chair on the other side of Sam.

"Alexis has brought me up to speed on the incident at the pond," Mr. Banner stated calmly, "so there is no need to rehash everything there. Alexis also informed me that she has shared her ability with you. Is that correct?"

Christian did not answer. He could not answer. A thousand questions raced through his mind, and he had absolutely no idea about where to begin. Christian stared at Mr. Banner, and Samantha reached her hand over and touched Christian's knee.

"It's okay, Christian," Sam said calmly.

"How did this happen?" Christian said quietly. "I mean, how did you know I had a secret?"

"Pardon me, Christian," Mr. Banner said, "I forget that you are not aware of everything like these three."

Mr. Banner motioned to Ray, Alexis, and Sam.

"But how did you know?" Christian said, turning to Sam. "How did you know I had a secret?"

Sam blushed, "I couldn't see you."

Sam read Christian's puzzled expression, so she continued to explain. "Christian, I have an ability to sense people's emotions. When I look at people, I catch glimpses of fuzzy colors on the periphery of my vision. The colors are slight in most instances. Sometimes, if an emotion is extremely strong, I will see much more visible, darker shades. On very rare occasions, I can't see any emotion at all. That only happens when I'm focusing on a phenomenon child, like you."

Mr. Banner explained further, "A very small percentage of children around the world experience what you are going through right now, Christian. They realize they have been given a gift, a special ability. The United States government calls these special children Phenomenon Children."

"So the government knows about me?" Christian interrupted with concern.

"No," Mr. Banner said in order to calm Christian's fears. "The government does know about the existence of Phenomenon Children, but they do not know about you, specifically. Not yet."

Mr. Banner took a drink of water. Christian grabbed the glass in front of him and gulped. Alexis rose from her spot and returned from the kitchen with a full pitcher of ice water, and she topped off Christian's glass.

"So, do they know about Sam, Alexis, and Ray?" Christian asked.

Mr. Banner hesitated briefly before he answered.

"They may know these three exist, but they do not know where they are," said Mr. Banner.

"Thank goodness for that," Alexis mumbled.

"So, what about you, Ray?" Christian said, turning away from Mr. Banner, wanting to ask about the article from the Montana newspaper.

"Let's not get too far ahead of ourselves," Mr. Banner said. "I am sure your head is swimming in questions. You possess a gift, and even though we do not know what that gift is, at this time, we are aware that you possess one."

Christian shifted uncomfortably, and Mr. Banner stopped and scrutinized Christian's face. Mr. Pearson always said Christian had a terrible poker face. Christian wondered if he could play like he had no idea what gift they were talking about, but they all seemed sure he was gifted in some way. His curiosity overpowered his desire to keep his secret.

"You don't know what my ability is?" Christian questioned.

"No," Mr. Banner stated. "And you can tell us when you are comfortable enough to share."

"We have all shared!" Alexis said in anger. "He can tell his secret before we go any further!"

"Alexis!" Mr. Banner chastised. "Christian will share when he is good and ready. We will not pressure him in any way."

Alexis huffed in disagreement, but she did not press the issue.

"I can share," Christian said.

The Three turned eagerly toward him.

"But first, I want to know Ray's ability," Christian added.

Ray said without hesitation, "My body is not affected by extreme temperatures."

"So, that *was* you I read about on the Internet," Christian marveled.

Ray's eyes flickered.

"Sam sent me an e-mail today," Christian explained. "She told me to look up phenomenon. After finding the definition, I decided to search the Internet for more information. I found an article from a Montana newspaper about a boy who had survived exposure to subzero temperatures."

"We will have to remedy that article floating on the web," Mr. Banner said coldly. "That should not be too difficult, though."

"So what is your ability?" Sam questioned.

"I am surprised you don't know," Christian said, "considering that Alexis witnessed it at the pond tonight."

"I have super hearing, but I can't see in the dark, genius," Alexis said.

"I can breathe underwater," Christian announced.

A wave of relief rushed through Christian. Finally, his secret no longer held him captive in fear. The weight slipped off his conscience, and he sighed in relief.

"How is that possible?" Ray asked.

"I don't know," Christian said.

Mr. Banner explained, "The government believes that a small percentage of the population is born with a phenomenal ability. They estimate it to be one in a million, but I think it's less than that."

"How do you know this?" Christian asked.

"I used to work for the government, in the field of human phenomena. Everything I was involved with was highly classified.

I was part of a unit that specialized in seeking out phenomenon children and making them disappear from society. The military had special uses for these children. We studied them, ran tests, and conducted experiments, but most of the children were put to use in military service when they were old enough. I was responsible for training phenomenal children to hone their special ability."

Mr. Banner's eyes took on a distant look as he recalled the events of the darker era in his personal history.

Mr. Banner continued, "But I realized not everything was positive. Some children were tested beyond their limits. Children were traumatized to the point of no return. Others were dissected like lab animals. Soon, I realized that none of it was positive. For two decades, I assisted with the kidnapping and experimentation of hundreds of phenomenon children from around the globe. Countless families were torn apart, and I could not handle it any longer."

Mr. Banner paused a moment.

"I disappeared," Mr. Banner said. "I went underground, and I decided to seek out phenomenon children and save them from the hands of our government. In my studies of these special children, I made a great discovery. It was something my colleagues failed to recognize in their quest for the ultimate military advantage. Their search for super humans and thirst for greater advancements made them lose sight of how these seemingly normal children came to be phenomenon children in the first place. Almost every single child who entered our facility had something in common, but my colleagues failed to see the connection."

Christian moved to the edge of his seat on the couch.

"They all experienced a severe emotional or physical trauma during the tail-end of puberty," Mr. Banner said. "That tornado story was what first led us down the path to finding to you."

Mr. Banner pointed directly at Christian.

"Once I met you," Sam added, "I knew you had a gift."

Christian asked the one question that nagged him, "But how is it that I have never heard of this? Even when I searched the Internet, there was no mention of the government secretly seeking out these phenomenon children. No conspiracy theorists shouted cover-up on the Internet."

"You have heard of it," Sam said. "It's in Roswell."

"New Mexico?" Christian asked.

"Yes," Sam said.

"I thought that was the U.F.O. place," Christian said.

"Typical government ploy," Mr. Banner huffed with a laugh. "They allow the world to think one outlandish possibility to cover up the real story, which happens to be another outlandish scenario."

Christian noticed a slight British accent in Mr. Banner's voice.

Mr. Banner continued, "The U.F.O. story took shape by accident in the '50s when a phenomenon child experiment went horribly wrong. They used the hysteria created by a local farmer to their advantage, covering up the truth with a flimsy U.F.O. story. Most of the people who work in the Roswell facility don't even know the true nature of it. In fact, the government flies prototype aircraft over it just to keep the rumor mill going. Even the President has no idea about what really goes on there. The entire facility is not strictly geared to phenomenon children. Other military endeavors are carried out there besides the phenomenon program. It's all highly classified."

Christian's head spun wildly. He filled his glass a third time and chugged it down.

"So what do I do now?" Christian asked. "I mean, what the hell do I do now? You're telling me that the government could kidnap me at any moment and whisk me away to Roswell, New Mexico, where I become part of some military experiment that is so top secret the government uses UFOs as a cover story?"

"You're safe, for now," Sam said, reassuringly.

"As long as no one else knows about this," Ray added.

"I haven't told a soul," Christian explained. "I don't have many friends to talk to anyway, and after tonight, I'm sure I will be alienated from the football team, too."

"You're one of us," Alexis said. "We watch out for each other."

"We won't be here long," Sam added. "We have to keep moving. If we stay in one place too long, suspicions arise. We can't risk people asking questions."

"I will have to miss volleyball the day of pictures," Alexis said, "and I will never play in a game, because I can't risk a photo."

Ray added, "That's why I don't play sports. Mr. Banner is positive there is a photo of me on file."

"They don't know about me," Sam said with enthusiasm, "so it isn't as dangerous for me to be seen."

"I will not lie to you," Mr. Banner stated, calmly. "Now that you have this ability, it is not safe for you to lead a normal life. Sooner or later, you will have to go into hiding. If you don't, you risk being abducted by the government. We will remain in Red Oak until Halloween before moving on. You will have until then to decide."

"Decide what?" Christian asked.

Sam answered, "Whether to join us or not."

Christian had not fully grasped his situation, until Sam uttered those words. In another two months, the Banners planned to leave, moving on to avoid the government and its search for more phenomenon children. Christian had not pieced it all together until now.

"You expect me to leave my family and come with you?" Christian said in disbelief.

"The choice will be yours," Mr. Banner said. "We will not force you to come with us. You will have to make that decision on your own. I have fostered over twenty phenomenon children over the years. You would get most of your education from me, even though you would attend school. I would also teach you how to cope with your special ability."

"But where are the rest?" Christian asked. "There are only three of you with Mr. Banner; where are the others?"

"In time," Alexis said, "after we are trained, we're sent out to live our lives. We will all have a chance to live out normal lives."

Alexis grabbed Ray's hand.

"Most of my children are sent out in pairs, to live as normal a life as possible," Mr. Banner stated. "It is better to go through life with someone who understands you, so I allow my children to stay with me until they're ready to continue life on their own, typically by the time they are eighteen. Alexis and Ray are almost ready to part ways with me and begin the next chapter of their lives."

"I was hoping you would be my partner in this," Sam said, as she moved her hand to Christian's.

"Wait a second," Christian said, standing up. "This sounds like an arranged marriage."

"In a way, it is," Mr. Banner answered.

"This is too much for one night," Christian said, as he moved to the stairs and sat down on the first step to put on his shoes.

"You are free to go," Mr. Banner said. "I will not hold you against your will. You are also free to come to this house at any time, day or night. Just remember, we will not be here forever, and you will have to make a decision, sooner or later."

Christian's shoes squished as he thrust each foot into them.

"Thanks for the clothes, Ray," Christian said as he reached for the door.

"At least, let me drive you," Alexis pleaded.

"I can find my way," Christian replied. "It's only a mile and a half up Bluegrass Road. I could use the time to think about all of this."

"Let him go," Mr. Banner said, as Christian turned the knob.

Sam followed Christian out the door and caught him before he started to jog up the drive.

"Can I walk you to the mailbox?" Sam asked.

"I guess," Christian shrugged.

They walked in silence for most of the way. As they approached the road, Sam stopped and turned toward him.

"I know what you are experiencing," she said as a tear rolled down her cheek. "A year ago, I went through the same ordeal. I had a wonderful family and a normal life. I had to leave it all behind. Most nights, I stay up late praying for someone to enter my life and bring me back to normalcy. That someone is you. I need you, Christian."

Sam hugged him.

"I need time," Christian whispered tenderly into her ear. "This is a lot to digest in one night. You know I have fallen for you, but I don't know if I can leave my family. I just don't know."

They hugged for a while longer, before Christian decided to begin his journey home.

"Be careful going home," Sam said. "I really wish you would let Alexis give you a ride."

"I'll be okay," Christian responded. "The moon is bright enough for me to see, and it isn't very far. It will give me some time to think."

Samantha brought her lips to his to give him a kiss goodnight. Passion flowed between them. For a minute, their bodies melted together. Then, they parted with neither of them saying another word.

He slung the bag of wet clothes over his shoulder and turned to walk up J Avenue toward Bluegrass Road. The gravel crunched beneath his feet as he left the Banner house and headed for home. Christian needed to think of an excuse for ending up home after midnight with a bag of wet clothes, and the journey gave him time to create a story. Christian approached the curve to the one-lane tunnel, wishing he had taken that ride from Alexis, when he heard the roar of an engine coming over the hill behind him. He moved over to the right-side of the road, on the inside part of the turn. Headlights cut through the blackness behind him, and he recognized the unmistakable growl of Johnny Stratton's pickup and the blaring sound of twanging country music.

CHAPTER 11

Christian moved into the ditch. He knew Strat was hammered, and the pickup truck weaved, as Strat cleared the top of the hill. The headlights jerked back to the center of the road, as the driver righted the pickup's course. The truck traveled slowly, not really in any hurry to get to its destination. The engine quieted as Strat took his foot off the gas, having finished the climb up the hill. The pickup coasted, as the truck weaved a bit more toward the far side of the road. Christian moved even further into the weeds.

"Where the whiskey drowns and the beer chases my blues away," Johnny Stratton sang as he neared Christian's position. Christian could hear Johnny bellowing the lyrics to the Garth Brooks song.

Strat pressed his foot down on the accelerator, and the engine roared to life again as the truck gained speed. Less than one-hundred yards away from Christian, Strat let off the gas again to make the turn toward the tunnel under the railroad tracks.

Christian thought about crouching for concealment, but decided against it. He wanted to be in a good position to jump out of the way if the drunk veered in his direction. Christian stood in what most coaches would call "a good athletic stance." The dangerous curve contained ten times the danger at night, especially with a pedestrian on the side of the road and a drunk football player behind the wheel of the pickup.

As the rusted hull of the three-quarter ton Chevy pulled even with Christian, Strat belted out another line of his awful country imitation.

"Well, I'm not big on social graces, take a slip on down to the oooasis," but Strat failed to finish the line.

The brakes squeaked as Johnny Stratton's eyes met Christian's gaze for a brief moment.

Christian hoped Strat would keep going and knew for certain that he would not ask if Christian needed a ride. Strat gunned the accelerator, and the engine revved to life again, as gravel peppered the road behind the truck. Christian flinched his body away from the churned up rocks and watched the pickup speed toward the tunnel. Strat did not stop to check if another vehicle occupied the tunnel. Instead, the truck roared like a movie monster about to attack New York City. The whine of squealing tires echoed through the concrete tunnel as Strat's truck met pavement on the other side.

Christian moved from the ditch to the edge of the gravel. He only had another two-hundred yards of ground to cover before he would have to negotiate the tunnel himself. Some clouds passed in front of the moon, and the night grew darker. Christian decided to move to the middle of the road since the sudden lack of moonlight hindered his vision. The streetlights of Red Oak waited for him on the other side of the tracks. He saw the soft glow over the top edge of the hill, and he quickened his pace.

Peeling tires chased away the buzzing of a locust, and headlights glinted off the concrete of the interior of the tunnel wall. Johnny Stratton's truck shot from the tunnel like a cannon ball. The headlights bounced as the pickup fishtailed to stay on the road. Having moved to the center of the gravel road, Christian stood out as an easy target, on the straightaway, just ahead of the curve.

The high beams bathed Christian in light. He moved right, and the truck mimicked him. He changed directions and dashed back to his left. Christian leapt from the road, not caring about where he landed. The truck swerved back toward him, missing by only a couple of feet. Christian heard the engine roaring in anger as dust from the gravel road fogged the scene in an eerie shroud of mist. Christian landed hard on his side, and a tree stump knocked the wind out of him as his head banged against the ground. He rolled over on his stomach, grimacing in pain.

As he struggled to catch his breath, he tried to get to his feet. His head pounded, and his lungs burned. Christian managed to crawl up the edge of the ditch on his knees. The incline on this side of the road seemed to be much steeper than where he stood only a minute before. Christian worried about Stratton turning his rig around and making a second attempt at killing him, but he no longer heard the engine. His lungs finally cooperated, so he staggered from the ditch to the road. Strat's truck was gone.

Christian waited like a rabbit searching for the predator it sensed but did not see. The cloud passing in front of the lantern of moonlight released the celestial orb from its prison. Christian saw a cloud of gravel dust floating on the roadway, but the dust did not continue around the curve and up the hill of Bluegrass Road. It just ended at the curve.

A throbbing pain pulsed in his right leg, as he followed the dust track of the truck. Christian had banged his knee on something when he dove from the road, so he limped with the pain. With each step, his leg function gradually returned.

"Walk it off, Christian," he muttered to himself.

The leg hurt, but the pain decreased by the second. As he closed the distance between himself and the curve of the road, a soft, red light caught his attention. The light appeared to be at least thirty yards from the road in the open space of a field. Strat had gone too far, and Christian was ready to threaten him with reporting his dangerous behavior. The drunk idiot had almost killed Christian. He reached the curve and noticed a steep drop off at the road's edge. He heard water lapping the shoreline. Stratton had driven into the pond. The tail light glowed above rippled water.

Without hesitation, Christian slid down the steep incline of the road's edge and barreled into the pond, soaking himself for a second time in the same night. He waded into the water until it covered his waist and plunged head first into the pond. Christian reached the back of the truck before realizing the pickup rested in an upside down position with the wheels pointed skyward. He held on to the undercarriage and put his feet down in an attempt to find the bottom. He could stand, but only his head remained out of the water.

"Strat!" Christian shouted. "Johnny Stratton, can you hear me?"

No one answered his calls.

Christian moved quickly to the front of the truck. Since the truck lay upside down, he ended up on the passenger's side. Precious seconds ticked away, as he dove under the water into the pitch black. He felt for the door handle, but it would not budge. He remembered Strat's windows had been open, so he moved to the other side of the overturned vehicle before going underwater a second time. Christian found the soft bottom with his hands and located the window. He reached into the cab in the underwater darkness. When he first put his hands into the truck, it appeared to be empty. As Christian swung his hands toward the front of the truck, his arm bumped against a leg. He tugged on the leg, but it did not move. Christian tried to visualize what happened.

He guessed Stratton had not been wearing a seatbelt. In fact, seatbelts probably did not come standard in the old truck. Stratton punched the gas as he approached Christian on the road, so Strat probably did not remember the dangerous curve. If Stratton did not have a seat belt, he definitely slammed into the windshield, if not through it.

Christian moved to the front of the truck. He attempted to squeeze under the front end of the pickup and failed, so he reached in from the side. He found Stratton outside of the windshield on the hood of the truck. Well, actually Stratton floated under the hood since the truck lay upside down. Christian pulled, but the tough angle compounded the problem of his slippery grip.

Christian felt along Strat's body, trying to estimate how much of Strat remained in the cab. Christian slid his hand past Strat's waist and brushed against the shattered glass of the windshield. He backed away, repositioning himself closer to the front of the truck and relocated an arm. Christian grabbed one of Strat's hands and pulled, but Strat refused to budge. Christian let go of the hand and crouched, placing his hands against the grill of the truck. His feet sank into the bottom, but the truck appeared to lift a couple inches. Christian located Strat's hand again. He pulled, and Stratton's body slid forward a little bit. Christian reached for Stratton's other arm, but failed to find it. Using the front end of the pickup as leverage, Christian created more pulling power, and Johnny Stratton's body moved a foot further. With one more heavy pull, the offensive lineman slipped from the clutches of the jagged windshield.

Christian had no idea how long he had been under the water working to free Stratton from the pickup as he struggled to get

Johnny's head to the surface. Christian could tell Stratton was not breathing, but he could not see anything or do anything for Johnny in the water, so he pulled him to shore. When they reached the shore, Christian examined Stratton more closely.

The teenager lying in the soft mud of the shore no longer looked like Johnny Stratton. His face had turned into a mangled mess, and it appeared to Christian that Stratton's jaw had been broken and then slashed by the force of his face smashing into the windshield. On the right side of Strat's face, the flesh was gone. Christian saw Johnny's teeth, even though Strat's mouth was clamped shut. A flap of Stratton's scalp was gone, and his nose had been shredded. Christian found no pulse. Johnny Stratton ceased living when that pickup hit the water.

Christian leaned away and puked onto the shore, and then he bawled. The events of the entire evening flooded out of Christian in a river of tears.

"What am I going to do now?" he thought.

Despite his exhaustion, he rose to his feet. Christian had to leave Stratton here. Maybe he would call the police when he got home.

"I can't call the police," Christian said out loud. "How will I explain all of this? I can't tell my parents. They will ask where I was coming from. It will draw attention to Alexis, Ray, and Sam."

Christian had to leave, and he had to get away before someone showed up at the scene of this horrible accident. No one knew Christian witnessed the event. Someone would see the truck in the daylight and report it. Stratton lay dead, and Christian had tried everything he could to save him.

A car door slammed behind Christian, and an engine sprang to life in the direction of the tunnel. Christian raced to the edge of the road, only to see the tail-lights of a car speed away.

His heart pounded in his chest. Someone had been on that road. How long had they been up there? Did they hear him talking to himself? What had he said aloud while lying on the bank? Christian instinctively crouched down. He had to get out, and he had to do it quickly!

He moved along the edge of the road until the shoreline turned into a ditch. He followed the ditch, staying as low as possible. Christian's senses piqued on full alert, and every sound tripped alarms in his head. As he worked his way closer to the tunnel, he continued to scan the road for traffic. A set of headlights illuminated the top of the hill from behind him. He lowered his body below the level of the road to watch the approaching vehicle. A pickup descended the hill. Christian recognized it from the party, and he dropped flat on the ground as the headlights rounded the curve. The truck slowed as it approached his position. He held his breath.

"Have they seen me?" Christian thought.

The truck cruised on the road very slowly. An engine growled from above as another car passed over the roadway from the opposite direction of the truck. Christian forgot how close he sat to the tunnel. The truck had stopped to wait for the other vehicle. The driver of the pickup gunned the engine, disappearing into the tunnel.

Christian scanned behind him on the road to see if the other car had stopped at the curve. The car slowed down before turning to the left and disappearing up Bluegrass Road. Stratton's pickup flew far enough off the road that it failed to draw the attention of the driver. Christian climbed from the ditch and peeked around the corner to look down the tunnel. A street light from the other side of the hill gave the tunnel an eerie glow. Christian tried to remember what the road looked like on the other side, so he knew what he had to contend with once he crossed through the tunnel.

A motor grumbled from the other end, and he retreated to the ditch to hide again.

"Is everyone going out for a late night drive?" he muttered to himself as the engine snarled in the tunnel. He wondered if the party was over.

Christian tried to focus his mind on the contours of the land beyond the tunnel as a car rolled by his hidden position. He remembered a streetlight on the left side, and another one was further down the hill. He knew darkness covered most of the street on the other side. The concrete of the tunnel extended a good twenty yards in both directions down the road from the entrance, so hiding near the tunnel posed a problem. In fact, the steep and rocky hill offered no concealment in either direction. If someone saw him coming out the other side, when word of the accident was public, he would be questioned for sure.

As the car passed the curve and disappeared over the hill, Christian remembered the backyard of a house sat directly across the street from the tunnel entrance. He heard the sound of a car pass by the tunnel. Christian noticed the hum of the engine had not entered the tunnel, so he crawled up to take another peek. His eyes strained to decipher the terrain on the other side. Even though the thin light made shadows of what lay beyond the road, he recognized the outline of a tree.

"That's right," Christian said excitedly. "There are pine trees along that road."

Christian gauged the distance of the tunnel. Thinking in terms of baseball, he calculated the distance through the tunnel to be roughly the same distance as a throw from the catcher to second base. That made it about one-hundred and twenty feet.

"If three feet equals a yard," he thought, *"the tunnel was forty yards long. Wow, a practical application for math."*

He could cover that ground in about five or six seconds. During football, every player ran a timed forty-yard dash at the beginning of the season. Christian figured he had about a ten-second window to get from his current location to the darkness of the pine trees.

Christian positioned himself for the sprint, but the noise of an engine rattled the tunnel. A car pulled to a stop at the opposite edge. Christian dropped back to the ditch and waited. He still heard the purr of the engine. The car continued to sit at the entrance, and Christian crept up to sneak a look.

Peeking around the edge of the concrete, Christian saw the front of a dark-colored sedan. Only the front tires stuck out from the concrete wall, so no one spotted him. He thought the car sat there for at least a minute. Christian heard the transmission shift, and the car moved away from the entrance.

Was that the same car from earlier? Christian thought to himself. *Had they seen me and decided to come back to the tunnel?*

He crouched in the stillness near the entrance and listened intently, searching for the sound of the car. A locust whirred in the distance behind him, then ceased. A deathly quiet hung in the air. In ten seconds, Christian would find out if his hearing proved correct.

He launched from his hidden position next to the tunnel, and his feet slipped a bit on the loose gravel before he reached full speed. The pounding of Christian's footfalls echoed down the tunnel disrupting the calm air, and Christian rocketed past the pledges of love in the graffiti covering the interior. He slowed at the tunnel's edge, checking for headlights before he bounded across the road and into the darkness of the trees. His heart pounded rapidly in his chest as he gasped for breath.

Christian stayed in the darkness of the trees for a minute to catch his wind, trying to decide whether to stay near the road or travel through backyards. He decided backyards would bring barking dogs, so he edged his way down the row of trees. Christian had a clear view of Highland Street from the pines, and nothing moved. He turned back to check for headlights from the other direction before making his way home.

An engine started from the other side of the trees.

Christian froze.

Did that engine come from the other side of the house or the road beyond the trees?

A sleek, black Monte Carlo crept into view. Christian slid behind a tree and examined the car from the darkness. The same dark car that waited at the edge of the tunnel slowly rolled by his concealed position. Christian moved deeper into the trees as the car passed and crossed the bridge over the creek by his house, slowing before it escaped up Highland Street. After a brief stop at Corning, two blocks further, the Monte Carlo slipped up the hill and disappeared into the canopy of trees.

The Monte Carlo had been waiting in the shadows. Whoever drove it must have seen him run out of the tunnel. Christian wondered if that exact same car had been sitting on the road after he pulled Stratton from the pickup truck.

He wasted no time getting home. Once Christian reached the bridge over the creek, he sprinted down the creek's edge before cutting through Calvin Robinson's backyard. He circled the Robinson's back deck, pushed through the hedge that separated

Calvin's yard from his own property, and jumped from the ledge into his driveway.

Christian knew about the key hidden near the back door, but he walked to the pool instead. Quietly, he unlatched the gate and pulled it open until the hinge squeaked. He slipped through the narrow opening and slid the gate shut. Christian pulled the shoes and socks off his feet before struggling to remove his wet shirt. He slid into the warm water of the pool and drifted to the bottom.

Christian had no idea of the time, but he wanted to wash off the smell of two ponds and the scent of death before going into the house. He replayed the Monte Carlo in his mind, trying to remember if he had seen it before tonight. Nothing registered, so he pushed it from his thoughts. The information from Mr. Banner made him feel better about his new ability, that he wasn't alone, but the thought of government agents possibly hunting for him some day sent a shiver through Christian. So much had happened in the last twelve hours. He should have been reveling in the big win in the football game, not worrying about if someone saw him coming out of the tunnel or if he would have to leave with the Banners in the near future. Christian's father always told him that a person is never tested with more than he can handle, but Christian wasn't sure if that was true. He had been assaulted, almost run over, attempted a rescue, witnessed a death, and told he may have to leave his family because he is a phenomenon child. On top of that, his parents wouldn't have a clue about any of this unless the driver of that Monte Carlo saw him. Brad would cover for Christian about last night. Brad's parents didn't have a curfew for him, and they thought Brad and Christian were going to the football party for only a short time. After making an appearance at the pond, they were going to someone's house to watch movies before walking home. Brad's parents would buy it.

Christian's parents expected him to be at Brad's, so he needed to remember to write a short note for his mother explaining that he came home during the night. He closed his eyes for a second, but exhaustion took a grip on him, and he drifted off to sleep.

He awoke from a nightmare of Johnny Stratton's face and found himself lying on the bottom of the pool. Christian rose from the water. Darkness surrounded him, but the faint hint of light bubbled from the horizon in the east. He grabbed a My Little Pony beach towel that had been left behind by his sisters.

He quietly unlocked the back door and slipped the key back into its secret spot. Christian closed the screen door carefully, before he shut and locked the back door. He quickly moved through the darkness down the stairs to his bedroom, thumping his head on the low ceiling. The blow rejuvenated the pains from the injuries he suffered the previous evening, and Christian cussed the makers of the house as he changed into boxer shorts and crawled into bed. Then he remembered he needed to leave a note. He found paper and a pen.

I wasn't feeling well, so I walked home. Please let me sleep late.

Another bump to the head welcomed him on the trip back to his room. Even though Christian's life had radically changed in the course of the night, he fell asleep in a matter of seconds.

CHAPTER 12

Christian awoke to a quiet house. Once his bleary eyes adjusted to the light coming through the windows, he read "12:00" on the clock. He rarely ever slept past nine o'clock on a Saturday, but his body needed the rest. After a football game, Christian ached, and compound that soreness with the blows he took from Strat and Eaton at the party, then add in his dive out of the way of Johnny Stratton's pickup truck before he pulled the 300-pound offensive lineman from the submerged vehicle, and this equaled one battered and bruised teenager.

He found some leftovers in the fridge and used the microwave to warm his lunch, then he noticed a note on the counter.

Christian,

Sorry to hear you weren't feeling well last night. Too much excitement from last night's game? There are leftovers in the fridge if your stomach is up to it. The girls and I are at the city pool, and your father went fishing. I will be home around 5:00, and who knows when your father will return.

Love, Mom.

Christian chuckled at the thought of paying money to go to the city pool when a pool sat in the back yard, but his sisters loved the diving boards.

The phone rang.

"Dude, what happened to you last night?" Brad asked.

"I ended up walking home from the party," Christian said. "Where did you disappear to?"

"Molly and I spent part of the night in the back seat of the van," Brad said, and Christian sensed Brad's smile on the other end of the line.

"Well, while you were playing, I was getting drowned in the pond," Christian said, a little irritated.

"What?" Brad said surprised. "What are you talking about? All I heard was that you left. Omar said there was a fight, and you ran off. He said something about you and Emily Thompson making out when Eaton wanted to fight you, and you swam the pond to get away."

"More like he tried to drown me," Christian said, "and I wasn't doing anything with Emily Thompson."

"Why not?" Brad said disappointedly. "She's hot!"

"We were just talking when Stratton pushed me into the water because I didn't want a beer," Christian said as his mind flashed to the grotesque face he pulled from the water less than twelve hours ago.

Christian continued, "Then he yelled to Eaton that I was putting the moves on his ex-girlfriend, so I had to swim away to avoid him tearing me apart."

"So you walked all the way home?" Brad asked.

"Yeah," Christian said, but he failed to mention to Brad anything about the Banners or his encounter with Stratton on the Bluegrass curve.

"Molly and I are going to go see a movie tonight," Brad said. "You are welcome to join us, but I think Calvin and Ruby are going to tag along. I know you don't like him, but I hung out with him a little at the party. He ain't that bad, and Ruby and Molly are inseparable, so..."

"I think I'll pass," Christian answered. "I don't want to be anywhere near Calvin. He is part of the reason Stratton pushed me into the water."

"I didn't think you'd wanna join us, but I didn't want to leave you out," Brad said.

"I gotta go," Christian lied.

"I'll see ya later," Brad said, before he hung up the phone.

Christian polished off his lunch in the kitchen, just as someone pounded on the back door. He pulled open the door and found Alexis on the back stoop.

"What are you doing here?" Christian asked, as Alexis pushed past him into the house.

"Anyone home?" Alexis asked.

She had a strange look in her eyes.

"Nope," Christian replied.

"Good," she said anxiously. "Get some clothes on. We need to go!"

His mind flashed to government agents in black suits and sunglasses.

Christian realized he had no shirt on, and he turned to go into the basement when Alexis grabbed his shoulder.

"What happened to you?" Alexis said, pointing to his side and back.

"Huh?" he said, as he lifted up his arm.

Christian noticed a huge bruise along his ribs. He could not see his own back, so he rushed into his room to open the closet door and looked in the mirror hanging inside his closet. A series of scratches ran along his back from the bruise to the middle of his waist.

"What happened to you last night?" Alexis asked. "You didn't get that from the fight with Eaton, did you?"

"No," Christian said trying to hide his face from her. "I didn't get those from Eaton."

"What happened to you after you left our house?" she asked.

Christian turned to Alexis.

"Johnny Stratton tried to run me over with his truck," he said. "I had to dive into the ditch to avoid becoming roadkill."

"So you pulled him from the truck," Alexis said.

"How did you know that?" Christian asked in shock.

Alexis explained, "After volleyball practice, I decided to grab a drink of water from the fountain outside the gym. I heard people talking in the office, so I decided to listen in. I could see a sheriff's deputy cruiser parked in front of the school. The deputy told Mr. Matthews that Johnny Stratton was killed in a single-car accident early this morning, but the deputy also said they suspected Johnny had been pulled from the vehicle. They found vomit by the body, and shoe prints littered the mud of the shoreline."

"Crap," Christian sighed.

"The sheriff's office knows about the party, and they are questioning Jeff Eaton about who was there. They're guessing that someone else was involved in the wreck and survived. I guess you would be a person of interest to the sheriff. Get dressed! We need to get you to our house. Mr. Banner will know what to do."

Christian threw on a shirt and grabbed some shorts while Alexis went upstairs. He grabbed dry shoes from his closet. The shoes reminded him about the clothes he left at the pool.

He rushed to the pool and grabbed Ray's shirt and jean shorts.

"I should return these to your brother," Christian said, thinking that dirty, wet clothes would not be a good thing for his mother to find when news of the party and Stratton's death got out, especially when those clothes did not belong to Christian.

"Let's go!" Alexis said impatiently.

"Wait," Christian pleaded.

"What now?" Alexis cried in irritation.

"I need to leave a note," he said.

Christian scribbled a note to his parents, saying that he went out with friends, and he would be back after supper. While he wrote the note, Alexis turned the car around in the driveway. He locked the back door and jumped into her car. The quickest way to the Banner house meant taking Bluegrass Road, but Alexis turned north and went out to old Highway 34. Christian thanked her for not driving past the scene of last night's tragedy. Alexis probably did not do it for his benefit, but he was grateful anyway.

Even though his life had been turned upside down at the Banner house, he relaxed when the car turned up the drive. Alexis parked in the garage and Christian ran to keep pace with her sprint to the back porch.

"Mr. Banner!" Alexis hollered as the two of them entered the house.

"I already heard on the police scanner," Mr. Banner said from the living room. "Don't worry, they will probably come ask a couple of questions and then be on their way."

"We have a bigger problem," Alexis said.

Christian rounded the corner to the living room just behind her.

"Christian was there," Alexis stated, and she appeared to be pretty upset about it.

Christian heard footsteps from upstairs as Sam and Ray descended to the living room.

"What?" Mr. Banner uttered in disbelief.

"I knew Alexis should have taken him home!" Sam blurted from the base of the stairs.

"Everyone, calm down," Mr. Banner demanded in a quiet but assertive tone.

Christian sat down in the Banner living room and relived the events of the previous night. Mr. Banner showed no concern until Christian told him about the Monte Carlo.

"Do you have any idea who it was?" Mr. Banner asked.

"No," Christian said.

"This poses a greater threat than I initially thought," Mr. Banner said as he leaned back in his chair.

"What are we going to do?" Ray asked.

"Let's see what comes of the investigation by the sheriff," Mr. Banner stated calmly, surprising all of them. "I have learned that the police move slowly. Christian, you must not admit to anyone that you were there, not even to your parents or closest friends. You can say you were at the party but nothing about the accident. Try not to mention our house, unless it is impossible to avoid it. If you notice anything unusual, you must notify me, immediately. That goes for all of you, too. Let's keep a look out for this black Monte Carlo. I will see if I can get into a DMV database, but you keep watching for that car."

Christian spent the afternoon getting more of his questions answered. Sam explained what she knew of Mr. Banner's work for the government, and Mr. Banner corrected the flaws in her telling of the tale. Most of it seemed like a strange, science fiction novel. Mr. Banner decided to disappear into his room when Christian asked Sam about her life before the Banners.

"I think I'll do some searching for that Monte Carlo," Mr. Banner explained as he rose from his chair.

"Thanks," Sam said. Mr. Banner got up to leave them.

"I was born in Morinville, Alberta, Canada, not far from Edmonton," Sam started. "My parents moved to the United States when I was two. I did not get my ability through some tragic event, like most phenomenon children. Instead, I can remember my ability from when I was very young. My mother used to joke about how I would see colors when I was three years old. I started to gain a better understanding of what the colors meant when I went to grade school in Tacoma, Washington. My father was in construction. He managed large construction jobs, so we would pick up and move every couple of years. New jobs took us to new places, so it was exciting. However, as I moved into new schools each year, it became more and more difficult to make friends. I yearned for relationships, but I knew I would be saying goodbye by the end of every school year. Instead, I used my gift to find people who were green."

"Green?" Christian asked.

"Yes," she said, "green is the color I see when people are happy. I used my gift to keep myself insulated from negative people. Knowing the relationships would not last very long, I figured it would be easier to survive my life with people who enjoyed life as much as I do. I avoided people who spent their lives in anger and continual sadness."

"Wow, that must be nice to avoid people who are in a bad mood for your entire life," Christian said.

"Well, it didn't work with Alexis," Sam joked.

"I heard that," shot a voice from upstairs.

"Anyway," Sam continued, "I ended up in Phoenix, Arizona for my eighth grade year of school, and I met a boy. Let's call him Charlie. Charlie was a lot like you, Christian."

Sam smiled.

"You mean he was cute and heroic," Christian grinned.

"Oh, brother!" Alexis yelled from her upstairs bedroom, as she slammed her door and turned up her music.

"Nope," Sam said. "I couldn't see his emotions. He was a mystery to me, a lot like you were when I first met you, Christian. I began to hang out with him at school, trying to figure him out. As hard as I tried, I could not solve the riddle. About two weeks after school started, Charlie began hanging out with this new kid who moved into our school. He was a big kid for an eighth grader, kind of intimidating. The new kid joined the football team that Charlie played for. When I was introduced to the new kid, I noticed he had the same strange ability to cloak his emotions from me. When I met the new kid's sister, she too had the same colorless shroud."

"Who were these other two kids?" Christian asked, but he already knew the answer.

Sam merely pointed towards the upstairs.

"Alexis and Ray were somewhat unwelcoming," Sam said. "When I would come near, they would whisper or stop talking, so I knew something was up. I was watching the three of them talking at lunch, when I whispered to myself, 'Why can't I see the emotions of all three of you?'

Alexis immediately turned her cold stare on me. It was unnerving having Alexis's black eyes glaring at me, so I took my lunch outside. Later in the day, Alexis approached me in the bathroom when no one else was around."

"Was she going to beat you up?" Christian joked.

"Hardly," Alexis said, as she entered the living room. "I needed to find out more about her."

"She cornered me in the bathroom," Sam said. "Then she asked me point-blank if I could see emotions. I told her yes, before explaining that I could not see her emotions, her brother's, or Charlie's, so she told me to meet her after school."

"Later I met with Sam, and we walked to Mr. Banner's house," Alexis said, taking over the story. "I wanted her to explain that unique ability to Mr. Banner. Instead of stumbling onto one phenomenon child, we managed to find two of them in the same school."

Sam interrupted, "The Banners had already explained it to Charlie, but I was hearing it for the first time. Of course, I refused to leave my family to go with Mr. Banner and the phenomenon children, but I thanked them for everything. Charlie pleaded with me to join the group, but he was from a broken home. Charlie didn't understand, and he had no idea what it would be like for me to leave my loving family."

Christian sympathized with Sam in that regard.

"So what happened?" Christian asked.

"Later that week, Charlie asked me to meet with him one more time, but I never got the chance to see him after that."

"What happened to Charlie?" Christian asked.

Alexis looked at Sam, and Sam nodded.

"He was taken," Alexis stated, coldly. "Government agents nabbed Charlie while he was buying a coke at a convenience store. Ray and I were going to meet him there, but we left the house late because Mr. Banner had some concerns about the rendezvous. We persuaded Mr. Banner to allow us to go see Charlie, and we arrived at the convenience store just in time to see him loaded into a black van with no windows."

"I was there that night, too," Sam said. "Charlie was explaining how dangerous it was to be a phenomenon child. He was selling the idea of joining them, and he gave me more insight to the danger that existed for me if I chose to stay with my family. Charlie told me, 'Would you want to spend a lifetime imprisoned or three years in exile?' I spilled some of my drink on my shirt, so I ran to the restroom to rinse it, and Charlie told me he would wait outside. As I exited the restroom, a commotion outside the convenience store drew the attention of the customers. I pushed to the window and witnessed two men in black suits and sunglasses shoot Charlie with a taser. He fell to the ground, and the men worked quickly, lifting him into the black van Alexis mentioned earlier."

"Basically, Charlie disappeared from the face of the planet," Alexis said. "Police arrived at the scene, but a government agent stayed behind to explain what happened. I'm sure no report was filed, and Charlie became a missing person to his family and the police."

"The event made me rethink my situation," Sam said. "Out of fear, I chose to join Mr. Banner. In essence, I disappeared along with Charlie that night. I wrote a letter to my parents, and without giving much detail, I explained that I feared for my safety and the safety of my family. I asked them not to contact the authorities or hire a private investigator because this would draw unneeded attention to the situation. I told them I was safe for now, but it would be a couple of years before I could contact them further. I needed to disappear for awhile to let things blow over. I made the decision that a couple years were better than a lifetime as a lab rat."

"And they were okay with it?" Christian asked.

"Not really," Sam responded, "but I called them the next morning. That was the hardest phone call I ever had to make. I told my parents there was something special about me, but I didn't tell them what it was. I also explained that the government was to blame for me being on the run. I reassured them that I would keep in touch, but if they contacted anyone about this, it could mean my life. My mom bawled for most of the call."

"What happened since?" Christian asked, thinking about the decision he was going to make.

"I send them a letter on occasion," Sam said. "I have not spoken with them on the phone, but I know they still reside in the same house in Phoenix. My father quit his job. He works for a company based out of Phoenix now. I'm assuming they're staying put so it will be easier for me to find them. I plan to seek them out when Mr. Banner thinks I am ready to leave him."

"How long have you been in hiding?" Christian asked.

"A year," Sam answered. "Ray has been hiding for three years."

"Two for me," Alexis said.

"Mr. Banner says that Ray and Alexis will be leaving us soon," Sam stated. "That is why I need you, Christian. Losing my own family was tough, but I know I'll be reunited with them in the future. When Ray and Alexis leave, I'll never be able to see them again. They are my brother and sister, but contact is forbidden between phenomenon children after they pair off on their own."

"Why is contact forbidden between phenomenon children?" Christian asked.

"According to Mr. Banner, it puts us in danger," Alexis explained. "If we continue to maintain contact after we leave, we may lead other phenomenon children into capture. Mr. Banner has ways of keeping tabs on those seeking us, but he can't tell us how. If we are caught while out on our own, we might give up information that would lead agents to others. Phone numbers, addresses."

Christian knew exactly how Sam felt, and he could relate to the difficulty of Sam's decision to leave her family. The choice could not have been an easy one, but Christian saw the reasoning behind it. The idea of a few years in exile instead of a lifetime as a science experiment made more sense, and he pondered on his own predicament. Mr. Banner came back down the stairs.

"I found out who the Monte Carlo belongs to," Mr. Banner stated seriously. "Is there a last name James at the high school?"

"No, but Ruby James is a freshman at the junior high," Christian answered.

"The car is registered to an Ellen James," Mr. Banner said. "As far as I can tell, it is the only black Monte Carlo in the county."

"How did you find that information so quickly?" Christian asked.

"The Internet is a powerful tool, and I have some special talents in that arena," Mr. Banner said. "Now, who is this Ruby James?"

"Well, she was at the party," Christian said, "but that doesn't make any sense. She isn't old enough to drive, unless…"

Christian trailed off in thought.

"Unless what?" Alexis said, quite irritated that Christian failed to finish his sentence.

"Unless she has a school permit," he said. "Her stepbrother lives on the farm where the party was held, and if she uses that farm as her home address…"

"She can get a school permit," Sam said finishing Christian's sentence.

Christian grabbed the phone and dialed.

"Brad, yeah, it's Christian," he said. "How did you get back into town?"

"I got a ride with Molly's sister," Brad said.

"How did Ruby get back into town?" Christian asked.

"She drove into town with Calvin," Brad explained, "but Calvin told his parents he was spending the night with Miles. Cal told me that him and Ruby were going to park when they left the party. Then Ruby said her parents weren't going to be home last night, so I guess they shacked up together. Why? Are you still interested in Ruby, because…"

Christian cut him off, "No, I'm not interested. Hey, I gotta go."

He hung up on Brad before Brad said another word and turned to the group.

"Calvin and Ruby were in that car," Christian said.

"How do you know?" Sam questioned.

"Because he called Brad," Alexis said, "and Brad told Christian that Ruby and Calvin were going to go park."

"Does she always do that?" Christian asked.

"All the time," mumbled Ray, as he strolled leisurely into the living room.

"It gets annoying," Sam laughed.

Alexis grinned.

"Sam," Alexis said, "Christian is not interested in Ruby."

"Thanks," Christian said, sarcastically.

"No problem," Alexis replied, as she walked into the kitchen for a glass of water.

"Can we assume the car was parked there because Cal and Ruby were making out?" Ray asked.

"Let's hope," Mr. Banner said. "I still think we need to keep an eye on this Ruby and Calvin couple to make sure they aren't on to you, Christian."

"Wait a second," Christian said, excitedly. "Calvin and Ruby are going to be at the movies tonight."

Christian shot a look at Alexis, and a wry smile crept onto Alexis' face.

"I am always up for a little surveillance," Alexis said. "You wanna see a movie?"

Alexis hugged Ray.

"Do I get to smack Cal around a little bit if he pops off?" Ray asked.

Christian cut Alexis off before she could answer.

"Why don't all of you come to my house for a little swim party?" Christian said. "Then you two can go to the movie, and Sam and I can hang out at my house."

"Aren't you four a bunch of schemers," Mr. Banner said with a smile. "I would say you make a pretty good team."

The events of the past evening melted away as Christian called home to see if anyone was around. His father did not have much luck fishing, so he answered the phone. Mr. Pearson liked the idea of Christian hanging at the house with some friends, but his father really liked the idea of greasy burgers the most. The girls changed into swimsuits while Ray grabbed a pair of shorts.

"I'll change at your house," Ray explained.

"In a different room," Christian joked.

Ray actually laughed, and Christian sensed their friendship turning a corner.

Mr. Banner waved as they backed the car out of the garage, and Alexis rolled down the driver's window.

"It appears that The Three is now four," Mr. Banner said with a smile.

Christian's mind was not made up yet, but his spirits rose as they left the Banners's house. They drove with the windows down and enjoyed the summer air. Alexis avoided Bluegrass Road which Christian again appreciated. Sam snuggled up next to Christian. She wore a t-shirt and shorts, but Christian looked forward to seeing Sam in a bathing suit.

CHAPTER 13

Alexis parked the car in the Pearson's back yard under the canopy of branches supplied by an ancient oak. The former owners of the Pearson home sprinkled some gravel in that area to make it a parking spot. The four teens jumped out of the car, and Christian heard his father in the garage, so he led The Three over to make formal introductions to his father.

"Dad, thanks for letting me have the Banners over tonight," Christian said. "I know it was short notice."

"Anything to get some red meat for supper," Christian's father said with a smile. Mr. Pearson already knew each of them, but Christian introduced them anyway.

"What were you fishing for?" Ray asked.

"Well, I was trying for crappie," Christian's father said.

"Isn't it a little tough to get them from shore this late in the summer?" Ray said.

"Yes, I think they were suspended in deeper water," Mr. Pearson responded, delighted that Ray had some fishing knowledge. "I caught some nice bluegills, but I didn't feel like cleaning three fish, so I threw them back."

"Likely story," Christian said with a smile.

"Christian, didn't you tell them?" his father responded.

"Tell them what?" Christian asked in puzzlement.

"You didn't tell them that I have forgotten more than you will ever know about fishing?" his dad said, his face opening into a wide grin.

"Yeah, yeah," Christian said, "we'll be in the pool. Do you need help with anything before Ray and I change into our swim trunks?"

"Nope," his father said. "I'm going to check the messages and then head to the store. Your mother won't be home until five o'clock. I don't know why that woman needs to take the girls to the pool, when we have a perfectly good pool here."

Mr. Pearson grabbed an empty five-gallon bucket from the back of the car, and Christian escorted the Banners to the pool.

"Ray and I will go change," Christian said. "You guys can dive in whenever you want."

Christian led Ray into the house by way of the back door, so they walked through the kitchen and living room.

"The bathroom is the first door on the right," Christian said, pointing up the steps near the front door. "I will change downstairs and meet you outside."

Ray nodded, and Christian headed back to his room. He changed into swim trunks and grabbed towels that were stacked on the dryer in the laundry room, then he headed out to the pool. Christian managed to get a couple of steps from the pool gate when his father hollered from the back door.

Christian turned and noticed a serious look on his father's face.

"Did you listen to the messages?" Mr. Pearson asked, as he walked toward Christian.

"No. Why?" Christian asked.

"There was a message from Mr. Matthews," his father said, seriously.

"What about?" Christian said, trying to keep a reign on his emotions, because he already had an idea about the topic of the message.

"There was an accident last night," his father said solemnly. "Johnny Stratton was killed."

"Do they know what happened?" Christian said, trying to look like he had been taken off guard.

"The message said it was a single-car accident," Mr. Pearson said, "and no one else was with him. Did you see Johnny last night?"

"Yeah, but Brad and I didn't stay very late at the football party," Christian said.

"I walked him up to our place," Alexis said from behind Christian.

Alexis leaned over the wooden fence surrounding the deck of the pool, as she pulled wet, black hair from her face. It clung to the olive skin of her right shoulder, and her black eyes looked dark, but innocent as she continued to speak.

"We weren't enjoying the *nature* of the party, so I invited Christian back to our place for a Dr. Pepper. We all watched a movie, and then I drove him into town around midnight. I hope that was okay."

"Yes, that's fine," Mr. Pearson said, as he turned away and walked back into the house.

His father seemed to buy the story. Soon, Christian heard the car fire up in the garage. Mr. Pearson hollered out the window that he would buy some burgers and buns, and his car disappeared around the side of the house.

Ray lounged in a lawn chair that he moved into the shade of the oak tree. He asked for a towel, so Christian threw one to him. Ray still wore a long-sleeved shirt.

"Don't you get hot wearing those long sleeves?" Christian asked.

"Nope," Ray said, smugly.

"With that pasty, white skin," Alexis said, "you would think he would burn like crazy."

"You don't burn?" Christian said.

Ray shook his head, as he adjusted the chair.

"Actually, if I get too much sun, my skin gets whiter. That is why I wear long sleeves, to avoid losing all pigment. When the pool is in more shade, I'll get in the water."

"That shouldn't take long," Christian said. "Usually, the pool is in total shade by five, maybe a little sooner."

While Christian's attention focused on Ray, Sam climbed out of the pool and wrapped a towel around her body. Sam looked like she had nothing on underneath the towel. She caught Christian gawking at her. After a quick shove, the cool water embraced him as he fell backwards into the pool. Instead of giving Sam the satisfaction of quickly coming to the surface and going after her, Christian decided to sit and wait on the bottom. As the surface of the water calmed, Christian saw Sam standing on the edge of the deck. Christian waved, but he continued to stay seated on the bottom of the pool.

Sam dropped her towel and dove into the water, staying above Christian. He clearly saw the red one-piece as Sam glided over him. He turned to follow her, but he continued to stay under the water. Sam stopped her swim and stood facing Christian. Sam's chest dipped just below the water line. Her light copper legs looked more muscular than he first thought as she stood with her hands on her hips. When she remembered Christian did not need to come up for air, Sam held her right hand out in front of her, just below the water. She motioned with her pointer finger for him to come closer.

Christian rose from below and broke the surface of the water. Sam started to chastise him for sneaking a peek under the water, but he planted a kiss on her lips before she said another word. Instead of trying to speak, Sam wrapped her arms around Christian and kissed him back.

"You're cute under the water, too," Christian whispered, ending the brief kiss.

"You two make me sick," Alexis complained.

Alexis pulled her lawn chair into the sunny spot next to Ray's shaded position.

"You're just jealous that you can't be open about it like we can," Sam said to Alexis in rebuttal.

"Not until it's dark out," Alexis grinned, as she reached over to put a hand on Ray's leg.

Christian swam over to the edge of the pool by Alexis and Ray.

"Now remember," Christian cautioned Alexis. "Cal Robinson lives in the house next door."

Alexis removed her hand from Ray's lap, like she had touched something hot.

"That's good to know," Alexis said, as she leaned her head back and glanced at the two-story house from an upside down viewpoint. "If the air-conditioner wasn't running, I would be able to tell who is home."

"That is so cool," Christian whispered.

"It has its drawbacks," Sam said.

"Like what?" Christian asked.

Alexis began to explain, "Well, have you ever been in a classroom when everyone is talking?"

Christian nodded.

"That is what it's like for me everywhere I go," Alexis explained. "It makes it difficult to focus when everyone's whisper comes through loud and clear. Take for instance the movies the other night. Every time someone whispered something, I heard it. Not to mention the orders from the concession area and the discussions in the bathroom. Anything outside the theater itself was more like static, but everything inside the theater was clear, like I was sitting in between the two people having the conversation. School can be difficult when the door to the classroom is open, then every conversation in the hallway makes its way to my ears. I have found that focusing my eyes on someone allows me to hear that conversation more clearly."

"That explains the looks I got the first day you guys showed up at school," Christian said.

"I have been told that I make people feel uncomfortable when I do that," Alexis smiled.

"No kidding," Christian said, sarcastically.

They all swam a little bit longer before Christian's father returned home. Ray even ventured into the pool when shadows covered half of it. His fair skin was more than just pale. Christian had heard stories of albinos, and he guessed Ray had that comparison made more than once with blonde hair to match. With Alexis next to him in the water, Ray's skin looked ghostly. Alexis's brown skin took on an even deeper tone in the fluorescent green bathing suit she wore.

As Christian's father unloaded the groceries, the teens toweled off in the shade. Alexis hushed the rest of the group and motioned for them to sit down, as she sat facing Cal's house.

"Someone's on the phone," Alexis said in a whisper.

Alexis's eyes focused on the upstairs, as she sat motionless at first. Slowly, she moved the towel up and down her legs, but her eyes stared over Christian's shoulder toward the Robinson home.

"Don't turn and look," Alexis said, seriously. "Calvin is peeking at us from behind the shades. I can hear the bending of the metal blinds behind the window. He must be talking to Ruby on the phone. They are still planning to go to the movie, but they're going at seven instead of the late show."

The group continued to dry off, but all eyes zeroed in on Alexis.

"He is talking about Stratton now," Alexis said.

"What is he saying?" Christian asked.

"Crap," Alexis said angrily, "Would you shut up so I can hear? I heard your name, but then you interrupted it."

They sat like marble statues, waiting to hear what else Alexis found out. The seconds crawled by them slowly, and Alexis leaned back and closed her eyes.

"What else did you hear?" Ray asked in a whisper.

"Something about seeing Christian near the tunnel last night," Alexis said, solemnly.

They all sat in silence, and Christian felt the color draining from his cheeks as he put his head in his hands. He wanted to throw up.

"Now what?" Sam asked. "Do you guys still go to the movie or what?"

"Of course we do," Alexis said, a little too chipper considering the bomb she just dropped on Christian. "How else will we find out if Cal or Ruby saw Christian last night?"

"Huh?" Christian said, as he lifted his head to meet Alexis's eyes.

"Kidding," Alexis laughed.

"You... No... but...," Christian struggled to make a coherent sentence. "You mean..."

"They didn't mention you," Alexis said. "Got you!"

"Ohhhhh, that is not funny," Christian yelled. "That is not cool."

They gathered the towels, and Alexis grabbed a duffel bag from her car. Christian led the girls to the bathroom, and Ray and Christian changed downstairs in the laundry room. First Ray, then Christian. Christian commented to Ray about how easily girls changed together, but guys just did not work that way.

"I'm glad we're on the same wavelength," Ray said from the laundry room.

The two boys hung their wet trunks on hangers above the dryer and walked upstairs. Christian grabbed the suits from Sam and Alexis and took them downstairs before giving them a tour of the house. Christian's father was preparing burgers as they came back into the kitchen.

"Can we help you with that Mr. Pearson?" Sam asked.

"Nah, you guys just hang out while I prepare some of the best burgers you will ever taste," Mr. Pearson announced.

Christian's dad made good burgers. His father had some special seasonings that he added to them. Mr. Pearson always told Christian that someday he would be ready to receive his father's secret recipe. A sickening pang gnawed at Christian as the tour finished in the basement.

"Your father is a happy man," Sam said. "I can see that."

"Yeah, he's a good man," Christian replied. "That's what makes all of this so hard."

Ray looked at the shelves above Christian's bed.

"Are all of these yours?" Ray asked, pointing to the trophies and medals that lined the wall.

"Yes," Christian said proudly.

"I used to have trophies like this," Ray commented.

Ray's eyes turned distant as he remembered the past.

Alexis walked over and put a hand on Ray's shoulder, and he reached up and took her hand but continued to scan the shelves.

"Mine were all football and wrestling," Ray said, as he turned to face Christian. "I played baseball and basketball, but I was more suited for the power sports."

"Do you miss it?" Christian asked as he probed Ray for more information.

Christian wanted to have all the details before he made his own decision.

"I miss the nature of a team," Ray said. "I miss the camaraderie of belonging to a team. I think it will be hard for Alexis and me to leave when we do."

Ray hugged Alexis and kissed the nape of her neck.

"Then we will be a team of two," Alexis said, softly.

"We may have to stick around a while if Christian joins us," Ray said flashing a rare smile. "Look how exciting he has made things already. We get to do surveillance tonight."

They heard voices from the garage, and Christian announced to The Three that the rest of the Pearson clan had arrived from their trip to the pool. Kat entered through the door first and stopped cold in her tracks when she saw more than just Christian standing in the basement in front of her.

"Mom!" she yelled. "Christian has girls in his room."

Ann burst through the door, and Christian's mother came in behind her.

"Well, hello," Mrs. Pearson said. "I wasn't expecting this."

Christian's mother seemed a little frazzled after spending most of the day at the pool with her daughters.

Kat skipped up to Sam and said, "I'm Kat. Are you Christian's girlfriend?"

Sam blushed, and Christian's mother tugged at Kat to go upstairs.

"Leave your brother alone," his mother said.

"Christian's got a girlfriend," sang Ann as she skipped to the stairs behind Kat.

They both chorused it in perfect unison as their mother shooed the two up the steps. Christian led The Three up to the kitchen and introduced them to his mother.

"Will you be staying for supper?" Mrs. Pearson asked.

"The burgers are already on the grill!" Mr. Pearson hollered cheerfully from the back porch.

The idea of burgers bugged his mother, since Christian's dad had eaten a lot of red meat this week. However, this meant she would not have to cook, and that tipped the scales in Mr. Pearson's favor. Christian's mother ushered his sisters to the shower.

"You'll get green hair if you don't wash the chlorine out," she said to Ann and Kat.

"I want green hair," Kat whined to no avail.

Christian and his friends decided to eat their supper on the deck of the pool. Christian's mother sensed his irritation with a repeat performance of the song about his girlfriend serenaded from Kat and Ann, so she did not put up a fight. Ray and Christian cleaned up the kitchen after supper while the girls prettied themselves in the bathroom.

At 6:30, Ray and Alexis left for the movies. Christian told his parents that Sam planned to hang out with him until the movie ended.

"Sam will catch a ride with them after the show," Christian said. "I thought we would watch a movie here."

Christian's mother seemed delighted that Sam and her son planned to be in the house tonight. Christian hoped his mother would not embarrass him by pulling out the photo album. The photo album experience entered every boy's nightmare. For Christian it was because in one of his mother's photo albums, a picture of him in a bathtub at eight months lurked.

Since the family had church the next day and Christian had a girl over, his mother decided to put his sisters to bed early. Kat complained about the lack of darkness, and Ann argued about being old enough to stay up later. Their mother compromised and let Ann read books to Kat. Kat definitely got the better end of the deal.

Mr. and Mrs. Pearson decided to sit out on the back porch once the girls quieted down in their bedrooms. Christian realized his parents entered new territory. In the past, they dropped him off at the movies or the mall with no worries, but this time Christian brought a girl home. Of course, his mother and father made a point of walking through the living room every five minutes to ensure that Sam and Christian were not up to something inappropriate.

"They really want to make sure we don't make out," Sam whispered, when Christian's dad walked through for the tenth time.

"I have never had a girlfriend in the house," Christian whispered back. "I don't mind it. At least I get to hang out with you. Hey, do you want to go for a walk?"

"Sure," Sam said.

Christian walked out to the back porch as soon as his dad returned through the living room.

"We're going to go for a walk," Christian said. "You guys can have the TV."

"Good," his father said, jumping at the chance. "I want to see the weather. They're calling for more storms tomorrow."

"They'll be wrong," Christian said, laughing.

"How long will you be gone?" his mother asked.

Christian sensed some nervousness in her voice.

"Lynette, would you let the poor boy go for a walk!" Mr. Pearson hollered from the living room.

Christian's father had already turned the channel to the "all-weather, all-the-time" station.

"They'll be fine," Mr. Pearson added.

"Well, I just worry sometimes," his mother said, as she walked into the living room.

"They mean well," Christian commented, as he led Sam back through the living room and out the front door.

The setting sun cast shadows of a different kind through the canopy of tree branches. The orange glowed softer than the midday sunshine. Out of habit, Christian opened the mailbox, guessing the mail had already been checked today. The lid creaked, and Christian noticed a white envelope.

"I already checked it," his father hollered from the living room. "You didn't get any mail."

Christian flipped the envelope over in his hands. His name appeared in the address spot, but it had no return address and no stamp affixed to it. Christian hesitated to open it near the house, so he carried it while they walked. Sam and Christian strolled, hand-in-hand, toward the creek on the other side of Cal Robinson's house.

"Who is this from?" Sam said, as she grabbed for the envelope.

"Not sure," Christian said, holding it away from Sam before moving the envelope up to the light of the setting sun to see if it contained some clue to its contents before he opened it.

"Someone sent me a letter, I guess, but they must have dropped it off, because there's no stamp," he explained.

Christian shuddered as he remembered crossing this bridge the previous evening.

"Are you cold?" Sam asked, putting an arm around his waist.

"No," he said, "I was just remembering the ordeal of last night. I hid in those trees up there."

Christian pointed to the curve in the road outside the tunnel before opening the envelope.

"I hid in the pines while that Monte Carlo sat up the road a ways," he said. "When that car started its engine, it scared the crap out of me."

"Don't worry," Sam said, trying to calm him. "Alexis will find out what Cal knows."

"I hope it's nothing," he said.

Christian tore the edge of the plain, white envelope carefully, not knowing what it contained. He pulled a single sheet folded in thirds from the envelope and opened it.

Christian,

I know you were there. If you do not turn yourself in by Monday, I'll go to Mr. Matthews and tell him that you were involved.

Sam and Christian heard a car coming down the hill on Coolbaugh Street. Instinctively, they turned to look at it as it raced toward them. Alexis' car veered in their direction and skidded to a halt on the bridge.

"Get in!" Alexis yelled.

Sam jumped into the back seat, and Christian followed after her. Alexis gunned the accelerator, and they sped up the hill toward the tunnel.

"What is going on?" Christian asked.

"He knows!" Alexis yelled at the top of her lungs.

"Hold on a second," Christian demanded. "Stop the car! Who knows?"

Alexis slammed on the brakes, and the car idled at the entrance to the Bluegrass Tunnel.

Alexis explained, "We hung out in the lobby until we were sure they were at the movie. We sat toward the back of the theater, and they didn't know we were there. About ten minutes ago, Cal and Brad went to the bathroom. I followed them out, so I could hear their conversation more clearly. Cal told Brad that while he was making out with Ruby by this tunnel, he saw someone come out of the tunnel soaking wet. He didn't think much of it until he heard about the accident this afternoon."

"Holy crap," Christian said in disbelief.

"There's more," Alexis said.

"There's more?" Christian responded.

"Yes," Alexis continued, "Calvin asked Brad if his father knew about anyone else being involved. Brad told him that they found shoe prints of someone else at the scene of the accident, but they had no idea who it was or what they were doing there. Calvin told Brad that he thinks he knows who the other person is."

"This is not good," Sam said. "Show Alexis the letter."

Christian handed the letter to Alexis while asking, "Did Cal tell Brad it was me?"

"No, but we need to get to our house," Alexis said.

"Take me home," Christian demanded.

"No way," Alexis refused.

"Trust me," Christian said.

Even though he reeled from the news, Christian thought clearly. It felt like the final minute of a basketball game. The intensity sometimes sharpened a player's senses in situations like this one, and Christian's mind moved at warp speed, but his thoughts remained logic-based.

"Trust me," Christian repeated.

Alexis cranked the steering wheel and whipped the car around.

"Just wait in the driveway," Christian ordered as he jumped out when Alexis pulled up to the house. "Just wait, I won't be long."

Christian raced into the house and found his mother and father resting on the couch.

"Can I spend the night with Ray?" Christian asked. "Mr. Banner will be home, and they want to rent some movies. I will go to church with them tomorrow."

"I don't know about that," his mother fussed.

"Please?" Christian pleaded with his mother. "I'll even pack clean underwear."

"How will you get out there?" his mom asked.

"They're waiting in the car," Christian said. "I finally have some friends, please be cool with this."

Christian really pressed his luck, but he had no time to debate this with his mother. Christian banked on support from his father, and he got it.

"Didn't you hear him say he'll go to church with them tomorrow?" his father said. "He's a good kid. Then, we only have to fight two in the morning for church."

Christian looked with puppy dog eyes at his mother, and he sensed her caving in.

"Do you have homework?" she asked.

"No," Christian said quickly, before darting downstairs. "No homework on Friday because of the big football game."

Christian hastily filled a duffel bag with as many clothes as possible. Just in case the stay became extended, he wanted to be prepared.

"I am packing clean underwear, Mom!" he hollered up to his mother.

Christian grabbed the wet bathing suits, threw them in a plastic grocery bag, and rushed up the stairs.

"I love you," Christian said as he kissed his mother's forehead. "Thanks for being wonderful parents. If it's alright, Ray said I could stay for lunch and supper, but I will call you."

He raced out the door.

"We cool?" Christian asked as he looked at Alexis, knowing she had listened in on the entire episode.

"Yes, your dad has settled your mom's nerves. In fact, your father said he hopes you stay at our place all day. He said you have been much happier since meeting the Banner children."

"I hate being called children," Ray snapped from the front seat.

"Me, too," Christian said.

"Impressive display of quick thinking," Alexis added as she backed out of the drive way.

"Now, let's find Calvin," Christian said.

"What?" Sam said in surprise. "Why would you want to do that?"

"We need to know exactly what is going on," Christian stated.

Alexis looked at Christian in the rearview mirror, and Ray turned around in the front seat.

"What are you talking about?" Ray asked.

"They will be walking home," Christian explained. "Cal and Brad will drop the girls off at Ruby's house before they walk back to their own houses. They will probably talk more about it then. Alexis can walk behind them, far enough that she isn't seen. Hopefully, she can get some more information."

"Maybe we should go talk to Mr. Banner first," Sam said.

"No time," Christian responded.

Alexis agreed with Christian.

"At least we may have a better idea about what we are dealing with," Alexis said from the front seat.

She parked a block from the theater just as the crowd exited. Cal and Brad walked with their girlfriends. She moved the car a block from Ruby's house, and soon Calvin and Brad appeared on the front porch with Ruby and Molly. After some lengthy goodbye kisses, Calvin and Brad left for home.

Alexis exited the car and waited in the shadows. Christian explained to Alexis that the car would be waiting down the street from Brad's house. Alexis just had to follow Corning Street, and they would pick her up a block up from Brad's house.

Alexis leaned over and kissed Ray.

"Wish me luck," Alexis said, as she slipped out the door and into the shadows of some bushes. The last rays of sunlight disappeared over the horizon.

Ray slid into the driver's seat. He turned up Corning Street and passed Cal and Brad. Ray parked the car on a side street a couple houses up from Brad's home. The minutes passed slowly as they waited in shadowy silence.

Ray whispered, "At least he didn't mention your name to Brad. Maybe Cal doesn't really know who was out there."

"That doesn't explain the letter," Sam grunted. "He knows. I just hope he doesn't tell anyone."

"My guess is that Cal doesn't want to tell anyone," Christian said.

"Why is that?" Ray asked.

"Well," Christian explained, "if you did not have a license to drive a car, and you had been driving that car after drinking heavily at a party, and the car belonged to your girlfriend's mother, and you had been making out with that daughter in that same car, would you want to explain it to anyone?"

"Good point," Ray admitted.

They waited a little longer, and no one said a word. Christian rethought his strategy, wondering if the hasty plan was worth the risk.

Would this really work? Christian thought.

Two figures appeared on the corner in front of the car, and Christian recognized them immediately. All three of the occupants of the car slid down in the seats.

After a minute passed, Alexis crept out from behind a tree. She moved to the car, and Sam rolled down the window.

"Wait here," Alexis said in a whisper. "I'll be right back."

Alexis crossed the road and disappeared behind a hedge in front of the house on the corner. A few moments later, she reappeared from the hedge and jogged to the passenger side.

"Let's go," Alexis said. "I can fill you in on the way."

Ray turned the key, and the engine came alive. He turned on the lights before putting the car in gear. The car turned onto Corning and drove past Brad's house. As they came to a stop at the intersection of Corning and Highland, Christian saw the lean outline of Calvin Robinson cross the road as Cal made his way back to his house. Ray turned the opposite direction, and soon the car left the blacktop of old Highway 34 and headed toward the Banner house.

Alexis refused to release any details as they drove. She explained that she did not want to tell the story a second time, and she planned on waiting until they joined Mr. Banner. As the car neared the house, the front porch light flipped on.

"Don't turn in," Alexis said as the car neared the drive.

Alexis rolled her window down and leaned out.

"Just drive slowly," Alexis said. "I think someone is at the house."

The car cruised past the driveway.

"Pull over up the road a ways," Alexis said, "but don't turn the car off."

Alexis grabbed the edge of the car door, leaned out of the vehicle, and tried to listen. She focused on the house. Christian saw the outline of a car in front of the house. Actually, he only saw the top portion over the field of soybeans. The light of the front porch glinted off what appeared to be an empty bicycle rack.

"What is it?" Sam asked.

"Mr. Banner is talking to a man on the front porch," Alexis explained.

"Any idea who it is?" Ray asked.

"No, I really can't see him very well," Alexis said, "but Mr. Banner is standing on the porch, while the man is down next to his car."

They sat quietly, waiting for Alexis to share more information. Christian heard only the sway of the soybeans in the light breeze over the purr of the engine. The bike rack Christian spied on the top of the car had a familiar look to it. Then it registered. The rack looked similar to the lights on top of the trooper's cruiser he saw at Lake Albert.

"Those are police lights," Christian whispered.

Alexis slid back into the car.

"Go," Alexis said. "We need to go."

Ray pressed the accelerator, and the car shot from the edge of the road, churning up gravel in its wake.

"Turn here," Alexis ordered. "We need to get to the highway."

"What is going on?" Ray asked.

Alexis turned in her seat and said, "That was a deputy who was asking about the accident, checking to see if anyone had turned up at the house last night. They think a second person was on foot and may have been injured. Mr. Banner said that he was not home last night. The officer asked to speak with his kids, but Mr. Banner said we were not around, and we would not be back for awhile. The deputy said he would stop by later to question us at the end of his shift. Mr. Banner said that he did not think we would be home until late. The deputy said someone would be by tonight, and if we weren't there, they would come by early tomorrow to question us."

"So, why don't we circle around and go back to the house?" Sam asked.

Alexis responded quickly, "Because after the deputy got into his car, Mr. Banner said something else."

"What did he say?" Ray asked.

Alexis answered coldly, "Alexis, if you can hear me, you need to leave town."

"Can't you just call him?" Christian asked.

"How? We don't carry cell phones," Alexis said.

"Why not?" Christian asked.

"Mr. Banner's rule," Sam said, "and I'm not sure why."

Ray leaned back in his seat, and Sam put her forehead on the seat in front of her. Alexis turned back around and stared out the windshield. Ray banged the steering wheel with his hand.

"Just great," Ray said. "Not even two weeks in this town, and we're going to be on the move again."

"We need a place to hide," Alexis said. "We can call Mr. Banner on the road from a pay phone, but for now, we need a place to stay."

"We can't stay around here," Ray stated. "Where the hell are we supposed to go?"

"I know," Christian said, "but it's about three hours from here."

"Just point me in the right direction," Ray said. "We have three-quarters of a tank, so we won't need to gas up anywhere around here."

"Head toward Omaha," Christian explained.

"Drive the speed limit," Sam added. "You guys only have your school permits with you."

"By the way," Alexis said, "Calvin plans on leaving an anonymous letter at the high school on Monday before football practice, and he never told Brad that it was you."

"That's a relief," Ray said.

"Some relief," Christian added, sarcastically.

"Hey, at least you have until Monday to make up your mind," Ray said.

"About what?" Christian asked.

"Whether or not you want to join us," Ray stated.

Christian forgot about that, and he did have a way out of this new development. He did not want to spend his life in hiding, but that appeared to be his only option. He leaned back in his seat, and Sam moved next to him, resting her head on Christian's chest.

"I can feel your heart pounding," Sam whispered to him.

"Can you sense it breaking?" Christian asked.

She looked up into his face. In the darkness, Christian could not see into her eyes, but he knew Sam felt his pain.

"So, do you have a friend in Omaha?" Ray asked, as the car slowed and turned onto the main highway on the edge of Red Oak.

Christian did not answer. He sat in silence, as they passed through town. Ray did not ask again, sensing the moment. In fact, they all sat in silence, and Christian felt they all thought the same thing he thought.

"This may be the last time any of us see this place."

"We aren't going to Omaha," Christian explained, as the car passed the football field on the north side of town. "We're just passing through it."

Ray turned left, and the lights of Red Oak disappeared behind them.

"What is our final destination, then?" Alexis asked.

"A farm," Christian said. "My grandpa owns a farm about an hour-and-a-half past Omaha, so we'll go there."

Sam mumbled groggily, "I like farms," and then she snuggled in closer to Christian.

"That girl could sleep through fireworks," Alexis said.

The exhaustion caught up to Christian, too. He heard Alexis and Ray talking in the front seat, as he closed his eyes.

"Those two were made for each other," Alexis commented, as Christian drifted off to sleep.

Christian wanted to argue with Alexis, but his exhaustion urged him to avoid a debate. Besides, Alexis just stated the obvious. Sam and Christian were made for each other, and Christian knew it.

CHAPTER 14

Christian awoke to a slamming car door. Ray had pulled into a gas station to top off the tank and stretch his legs. Sam had curled up against Christian, and he eased her off and gently laid Sam's head down on the seat then climbed out of the car.

"Where are we?" Christian asked as he rubbed the sleep from his eyes.

"84th Street Exit," Ray responded.

Christian looked at his surroundings, recognizing them immediately. The Interstate ran to the south of them, and Christian saw the light poles of a baseball complex on the other side. He played in a baseball tournament on those fields midway through the summer before moving to Red Oak.

"What time is it?" Christian asked as he rubbed his eyes some more.

"It's about midnight," Ray said.

Christian decided to go inside and use the restroom. Alexis was filling up 32-ounce cups as he walked over to her.

"What can I get you?" she asked, cheerfully. "They're only 47 cents."

"Dr. Pepper," Christian said.

After using the bathroom, Christian cleaned himself up in the sink. He smelled the chlorine on his skin from the afternoon dip in the pool. He splashed cool water on his face and then wiped it off with some paper towels.

When he returned to the car, Alexis occupied the driver's seat. Ray took a spot in the back and leaned his head against the window on the driver's side. Sam still slept, but Ray had repositioned her against the passenger side window. Sam's check pressed against the glass, and her hair covered part of her face.

"She really could sleep through about anything," Christian thought.

Having washed off the chlorine from his face and the sleep from his eyes, Christian actually felt refreshed. He plopped into the front passenger seat and buckled up. Alexis handed him a Dr. Pepper.

"Where to now?" Alexis asked as she started the car.

"Get back on the Interstate and head the same direction," Christian explained. "We will take 680, north to Dodge Street, and that will take us out of town."

Christian knew this part of town because his family moved here when he started preschool, so he spent the better part of a decade in the city of Omaha. As they drove down Dodge Street, Christian pointed out the neighborhood where he grew up.

"When we moved to Omaha, 156th Street was the end of civilization," Christian explained. "Now the city extends out another five miles before giving way to farmland."

Christian pointed to an apartment complex on the left side of the road.

"I used to live in a house on the other side of this complex," Christian said. "When we moved in, there was nothing but trees and grass where those apartments are."

"Do you miss it?" Alexis asked.

"Yeah," Christian answered, "just because it's where I grew up."

"Do you like Red Oak?" she asked.

"I thought I would," he responded. "I was excited about moving to a smaller town, but I'm not sure Red Oak is the right small town."

"I know what you mean," Alexis replied.

"Moving into a small town your freshman year is not easy, anyway," he said. "Couple that with the way they treat outsiders…"

"And it makes it tough," Alexis said, finishing his thoughts.

"Where did you grow up?" Christian asked.

"A small town," she said. "In fact, it's about the size of Red Oak. I spent most of my whole life in that town."

"Did you like it?" he asked.

"Sometimes," Alexis answered. "The problem with a small town is that everyone knows your business. Everyone knows you, so it isn't easy to blend in when you live in a small town."

"Yeah, blending in was a problem for me from the start in Red Oak," Christian said.

"You can't blend in because you play sports," she replied. "But if you don't play sports, you wouldn't be able to blend in because you were the one who wasn't playing sports. In a small town, everyone notices you. No matter what you do, you can't blend in."

"That was the nice thing about Omaha," Christian said. "There were so many kids. It was easy to find someone to hang out with. We never knew who the new kids were, and in Omaha, there were no Calvin Robinsons."

"That's where you are wrong," Ray said from the back.

Christian assumed Ray sawed logs like Samantha, but Ray had been eavesdropping on the conversation.

Ray continued, "There are Calvin Robinsons in almost every school. You just don't have to interact with them as much in a big school."

What Ray said made sense to Christian, as he mentally listed a handful of guys he did not care for last year, but with so many people in Christian's former school, he did not have to deal with them as often as he did in Red Oak. Last year, Christian hung out with his core group of friends, and he didn't know half of the people in his classes. In Red Oak, only ninety-two students comprised the freshmen class. They all knew him, and they all knew he moved into town over the summer, and they all knew his dad was the principal of their school.

"Yeah," Christian said in agreement, "but I just don't understand how everyone else follows Calvin's lead. Why do they all bow to him?"

"Fear," Ray answered. "In a small town, you have to spend every day with your classmates. It's like one giant dysfunctional family. When you go to the store, you see them. When you go to the high school game, you see them. When you go to church, you see them. A big city is different. You aren't always running into people you know. In a small town, you can't get away from them."

"It's much easier for us to start school in a big city," Alexis added. "We can blend in easier. We can disappear when the school day is over. Most of the students in a large school don't know that we are new to the building. In fact, most of them don't care who we are. It's easier to go unnoticed."

"So, where will you go next?" Christian asked Ray and Alexis. "When you leave Red Oak, where will you go?"

"We don't know," Alexis said. "I'm guessing we'll go back to Arizona."

"Why Arizona?" Christian asked.

"Mr. Banner has a home in the mountains," Ray said. "You could say it's sort of a home base for phenomenon children if there is trouble."

Alexis added, "Mr. Banner is a wealthy man. None of us knows where the money comes from, but he provides for us, so no one asks questions. We can pretty much get whatever we need through him."

"So, he doesn't work for the Department of Roads or some construction company?" Christian said.

"No, he doesn't," Ray responded with a chuckle. "In fact, he spends all of his time searching for phenomenon children."

"Tell me more about this home base," Christian said.

"We spend our summers there once school is out," Alexis explained, "and we go there when Mr. Banner doesn't have a lead on another phenomenon child. It sits up in the mountains. The house isn't that far from Flagstaff. It's a huge house, but you wouldn't find it unless you knew where you were going. If things ever go bad, I mean end-of-the-world bad, we are supposed to make our way back to the house in Arizona."

"Every phenomenon child Mr. Banner has found knows about this place," Ray added. "Mr. Banner says it is the safe house."

"Have you ever seen any other phenomenon children besides the three of you?" Christian asked.

"Just Charlie," Sam said.

At some point during the conversation, Samantha awakened in the back seat.

"But the government got Charlie," Sam continued.

Christian asked, "But you haven't met other phenomenon children at this house in Arizona?"

"No, we only go there during a down time in Mr. Banner's searching for phenomenon children or if there is an emergency."

"Did you go to the safe house when Charlie was taken?" asked Christian.

"No, we didn't," Alexis said. "Why would we have?"

"I thought maybe the three of you would be fearful for your own safety," Christian said.

Christian told Alexis that she neared the turn onto a new highway, and the disruption effectively put an end to the discussion. They drove the rest of the way to his grandparents' farm listening to the radio. A little before 1:30 in the morning, the car turned off the main highway onto a gravel road. Christian tried to remember the turns in the black of night. Twice, Alexis had to backtrack, but finally they came to the corner that signaled Grandpa and Grandma Pearson's farm. They drove east on a gravel road.

When they came over a hill marked by a twenty mile-per-hour road sign, Christian said, "Slow down. A lot of people don't make this turn."

The road veered sharply to the south. If a driver failed to heed the sign, a ten-foot drop off the road into a field of alfalfa greeted the car. About twenty yards after the curve, a little dirt path led into the farm.

"This is the back road into the farm," Christian explained. "There is a main driveway that comes in on the south side, but that would take us right by the house."

"That is a nasty curve," Ray commented.

"Yes it is," Christian responded. "I have heard stories about cars that have missed the turn."

"I can see why," Alexis said. "It comes out of nowhere right after you come over the top of that hill."

The car quieted once it left the gravel. The back way into the farm wound along a dirt road, and Alexis drove past three grain bins on the right before the headlights reflected off the metal of a huge building.

"That's the A-barn," Christian said. "Turn off the headlights."

Alexis doused the lights, and Christian told her to park in front of the A-barn, explaining that he would get out to open the door. She would park the car inside, and then they could pull the door closed to hide it.

"Won't it be locked?" Sam whispered.

Christian laughed. "My grandparents never lock anything up around here. Not only is the garage unlocked, they keep the keys to each car in the ignition."

Christian jumped out and ran into the giant steel structure through a door on the side. After flipping on the lights, Christian unlatched the doors. His grandfather parked some big equipment in this building, so he had to move two massive rolling doors. The rollers groaned as Christian pulled on the door closest to him. The door shuddered loudly as it opened.

Alexis pulled her car through the opening, and Christian pushed with all of his strength to close the door as quickly as he could. Once the door was shut, Christian turned off the main lights, so only a small section of the back of the barn stayed illuminated.

"No need to attract too much attention," Christian said.

"Those doors were loud enough to wake up anyone close," Ray commented.

"My grandparents are asleep, so they didn't hear a thing," Christian replied.

"This place is huge," Sam said, marveling at the size of the building.

"This A-barn was built a couple of years ago," Christian explained. "There used to be a giant wooden barn here, but it was old and falling apart, and Grandpa replaced it with this."

Inside the A-barn, Christian's grandfather stored the combine, his fishing boat, the planter, and the camper. He led them back to the tiny camper that rested on steel beams that looked like giant sawhorses. The camper could fit into the back of a pickup and contained a bed above where the cab of the pickup would sit. It had a small sink and a table that resembled a booth in a restaurant. The small table doubled as a bed, if needed.

"I don't want to wake them up," Christian said, "so we will stay in here tonight. It's pretty comfortable, but it's small. There are only two beds, so we'll have to figure out the sleeping arrangements."

Christian looked uncomfortably at Ray. He really had not wanted to spend the night with another guy.

"Great," Alexis said. "Ray and I in one, and you two can sleep in the other one."

Christian opened the door to the camper.

"You have got to be kidding me," Ray chuckled. "This is tiny."

Christian jumped into the camper and showed them the bed on the top. He lowered the table before pulling the spare mattress off the top bed and placing it on the table.

"There you go," Christian said, "sleeps four uncomfortably."

Ray and Alexis climbed into the top bunk, and Alexis pulled the little curtain shut.

"We would like some privacy," Alexis giggled.

Sam said, "We need to call Mr. Banner."

"It will have to wait until tomorrow," Christian said. "I can't wake my grandparents now. He might shoot us, thinking we're prowlers."

Christian sat on the kitchen bed and unlaced his shoes. Sam sat next to him and giggled. He opened his mouth to say something cute to Sam, when Alexis shushed them from the top bunk. Christian saw a beam of light flash along the wall outside the camper window. Someone had entered the A-barn.

Christian heard a familiar click outside the camper.

"What was that?" Sam whispered.

"Someone pumped a shot gun," Alexis replied.

"I hope it's my grandpa," Christian said anxiously.

"Who's in there?" the gruff voice of an old man shouted. "I'm armed, so choose your next move carefully."

"Grandpa?" Christian said meekly. "It's me, Christian. I'm going to come out, so don't shoot me."

Christian turned the knob of the door and opened it slowly.

"I didn't mean to scare you," Christian said as he peeked around the corner, "but I didn't have any other place to go."

The beam of his grandfather's flashlight blinded Christian.

"Christian, what in the world are you doing in the A-barn at this hour?" the old man said rather surprised to see his grandson.

"It's a long story," Christian sighed.

"Well, let's get you into a better bed in the house," his grandfather said. "You can tell me about what is going on when we get inside."

"Grandpa, I'm not alone," Christian replied.

"I figured that much," his grandfather said. "Someone had to drive this car all the way here. You guys can explain what the heck yer doin' here when we get inside."

Christian's grandpa walked off toward the front of the barn. He lumbered away with the shotgun resting on his shoulder, and Christian laughed to himself. His Grandpa Pearson, a former Marine from World War II, wore his wife's robe and his work boots. The old man must have dressed in a hurry.

"I forgot to take my hearing aids out when I went to bed," his grandfather hollered, "otherwise, I wouldn't have heard you open that door. I could've gotten a good night's sleep."

Christian helped The Three out of the camper while his grandpa stood at the door. As they walked toward Grandpa Pearson, he shut off the lights to the back of the barn.

"Four of you show up in my A-barn like raccoons around the corn crib," Grandpa Pearson said as they paraded past him. "You're lucky I didn't shoot you."

"I felt pretty safe with you at the trigger," Christian said with a grin. "I haven't seen you hit anything with that shotgun in years."

His grandpa closed the door to the barn and said, "Well, we weren't expecting company, but I suppose Grandma will start breakfast. Once she's up, she won't be goin' back to sleep."

They trudged past the long gray shed that housed the tractors before coming to the two-story farmhouse. The lights illuminated the kitchen and the living room, and Christian spotted his grandma looking through the screen door. Grandma pushed open the door, as they climbed the concrete steps and walked into the house.

"Christian, what are you doing here?" his grandmother asked surprised.

"It's a long story," Christian told her as he gave Grandma Pearson a hug.

"Do your parents know where you are?" his grandmother asked.

"No, but please don't call them," Christian pleaded.

"Are you in some sort of trouble?" Grandma Pearson asked.

"Yes," Christian said, "I don't think I could explain everything in one night."

"Are you hungry?" she continued.

"No, we're all right," Christian said, "just tired."

"Well, you four sit at the table, and I'll put some coffee on since we're up," Grandma Pearson said, motioning them to sit at the kitchen table.

Green linoleum covered the living room floor with dark wood paneling on the walls. With the outdated couch and recliner, the room appeared to be stuck in the 1970s. An old console TV sat on the floor with large, outdated rabbit-ear antennae protruding upwards. An antique China hutch stood against one wall, and a small wooden table sat beneath the window of another wall with pictures. Kitchen cabinets hung from the ceiling above a counter that marked the beginning of the kitchen. A round wooden table sat to the left.

Christian introduced his grandparents to Alexis, Sam, and Ray as they seated themselves at the table. Alexis asked to use the bathroom, and Christian knew Alexis would listen in on every part of the conversation from there. Christian pointed Alexis to the door off the living room.

"Now, what in the world are you four doing on my farm in the middle of the night?" Grandpa Pearson asked, returning from placing the shotgun back in its rack near the back door of the house.

Christian responded, "We're hiding."

"From what?" his grandpa asked.

Grandpa Pearson's cool, blue-green eyes studied Christian carefully.

"You're going to think I'm crazy," Christian said, not wanting to tell his grandfather anything.

Grandpa Pearson reached over and grabbed hold of Christian's shoulder. His grandfather's face grew stern, and his eyes stared coolly into Christian's eyes. His grip was strong but not in a painful way. He squeezed as his eyes scrutinized Christian's face. Christian sat quietly, and his body relaxed in Grandpa Pearson's firm hold. Christian had seen this look from his grandpa before. Grandpa Pearson's eyes flickered, as Christian sat motionless. Christian wanted to speak, but his words failed to come out. Then, his grandfather let go.

"Christian," Sam said. "Is there another bathroom?"

Her words echoed in Christian's ears, like Sam spoke to Christian in a tunnel.

"Yeah," Christian said. "There's one in the basement."

"Can you show me where it is?" Sam said, as Christian's hearing cleared.

Sam's eyes pleaded for Christian to go with her, so he took her down the steps from the kitchen into the basement. Christian flipped on the light when they reached the small landing near the gun rack by the back door. From there, they continued downstairs. He led her from the stairs to the bathroom, and Sam stopped. Christian turned around.

"I can't see your grandpa," Sam whispered.

"Huh," Christian asked, confused, not understanding what she meant.

"I can't see your grandpa's emotions," Sam said.

"You mean you think he's a phenomenon," Christian asked, skeptically.

"Yes," Sam responded. "I can see vibrant colors around your grandma, but your grandpa has the same lack of color that you possess, the same as Alexis and Ray."

"Are you sure?" Christian whispered.

"I thought it was just because of the darkness outside," Sam said, "but once we were in the house, I focused on him more."

"You didn't see anything?" Christian said in disbelief.

"No, Christian. Your grandfather is a Phenomenon."

Sam and Christian waited downstairs for a couple of minutes, and Christian had no idea what to do about this new information. Sam confidently claimed his grandpa was a Phenomenon, and Christian trusted her.

"We can't just go up there and tell him that we know he has a secret," Christian said to Sam.

"Why not?" Sam fired back. "We don't have time to hint at this. Monday, Calvin is going to tell all. Maybe your grandpa can help."

"He doesn't even know what's going on," Christian whispered, harshly. "It will take all day to explain everything, and like you said, we don't have time."

"You're going to have to tell him everything," Sam said calmly, "including your secret."

Christian drew in a deep breath.

"I know," Christian responded dejectedly.

They slowly climbed the stairs. Following Sam into the kitchen, Christian took his place in an empty seat at the table. Ray sat quietly across the table from Christian with his arms crossed in front of his chest. Ray looked toward the kitchen window behind Christian with distant eyes. His grandfather sat next to Ray. Grandpa Pearson's rough paws held Alexis's slender hands. Christian could not see Alexis's face, but he saw his grandfather's eyes flicker.

Christian opened his mouth to say something, but Grandma Pearson placed a hand on his shoulder and put a finger to her lips.

Christian remained quiet, and no one spoke. Ray shook his head slowly from side to side and blinked hard before rubbing his eyes. Then, he leaned back in his chair and rolled his head around trying to loosen his neck. Christian had seen his father do that same series of movements after staring at a computer screen too long.

Grandpa Pearson released his grip on Alexis's hands and sat back in his chair.

"You okay, Alexis?" Christian's grandfather asked in a soft, gentle voice.

Christian leaned over the table to look at Alexis. Her eyes had the same distant look in them that Christian had seen in Ray's eyes when he first entered the kitchen.

"Yeah," Alexis responded, as she slowly turned to Christian.

Alexis rubbed her eyes.

"Grandpa," Grandma said in a low voice, "I think you should explain."

"I know what you have all gone through," Grandpa Pearson said matter-of-factly. "Well, almost all of you."

Grandpa Pearson's eyes moved to Sam.

"I think I have a pretty good idea about why you are all here, and I think I can help," Grandpa Pearson said.

"How is that possible?" Sam asked. "How could you have any idea about why we are here?"

"I can see things," Grandpa Pearson replied. "Let's move to some softer seats first. These old bones can't sit in these hard wooden chairs for long before I feel like I got splinters in my rear end."

Christian's grandfather rose from his seat and walked through the living room. The group followed him past an old eight-track stereo before entering a second living room. This room had a large window that faced the other buildings on the farm. Grandpa Pearson turned the switch on a lamp, and the room was bathed in a soft, orange glow. A couch with an outdated floral pattern sat below more wood paneling. A large brass frame contained a faded picture of the entire Pearson family. Christian was two years old when someone snapped that picture. His mother and father looked to be in their twenties at the time, and his grandparents looked young, as well.

A black and white photo hung to the right of the family portrait. Marines from Grandpa Pearson's unit flashed toothy smiles, while flexing their right arms to show off the unit's tattoo.

Above the World War II photo, another black and white picture had been placed in a similar brass frame. This contained a picture of Christian's grandparents on their wedding day.

The other side of the wall contained more recent pictures, one for each of Grandpa and Grandma Pearson's children, three in all. Since his father sat second in the birthing order, Christian's family picture was the second one down. Kat still had all of her front teeth in the picture.

"Christian, I knew about you in South Dakota," his grandfather said.

Christian turned his attention away from the photographs on the wall.

"I knew what you'd gone through that night. Even after all these years, I find it difficult to explain. I have a secret like all of you. Well, not the same secret, but an ability that I've hidden for about fifty years. Your grandmother is the only other person aware of what I'm about to share with you.

"While fighting in the Pacific, my unit was sent to a little island called Iwo Jima. During a nighttime firefight with the Japanese, a grenade exploded in our foxhole. A friend a mine threw himself on the grenade, savin' me and four other men. If he hadn't done that, I would not be here today. The blast propelled us from the foxhole, and I woke up as the sun was comin' up.

"After spendin' some time at an aid station, I was cleared to return to the line. That afternoon, I came across a wounded Japanese soldier. It was rare to come across one who was wounded, since they always fought to the death or committed suicide rather than be captured. Having lost a close friend the night before, I fell on that wounded soldier like a wild animal. I had a hold of him, screaming as I stared into his terrified eyes.

"In an instant, a flash of images flooded my mind. In seconds, I saw how he'd been wounded and how he tried to commit suicide, but didn't have the strength to use his own saber to achieve his goal of death. That was the first time I used my ability.

"As the war continued, I used my ability to read the images of my friends and my superiors. I got better at it, and by the time I returned home, I mastered my gift, but I never told a soul."

Christian's grandma interrupted him, "You didn't have to tell me. I knew there was something different about you the day you got home. You were changed."

"Of course, I told your grandmother," Grandpa Pearson said. "You can't marry someone and keep somethin' like that from 'em."

"So you can read thoughts," Alexis inferred.

"Not thoughts," Grandpa Pearson answered. "I can't tell what you're thinkin'. I can only see pictures of the past, things that you have seen or events from your viewpoint. With Christian, I saw his memory of a truck veering across the road. When I put my hand on Alexis, I saw Christian soaking wet in a house and a man standing on a porch talkin' to a county sheriff. It's like readin' a book with no words, just pictures. I can flip through the pictures to get most of the story."

"I feel kind of violated," Alexis muttered.

"I am sorry for that," Grandpa Pearson said, gently. "I knew it was the only way to get the whole story from four scared teenagers."

"So you can see images stored in our minds," Ray stated, incredulously.

Grandma Pearson stood up and said, "Anyone hungry? I'll make some breakfast."

Christian's grandmother hurried out of the room.

Grandpa Pearson shared some more of the images he saw in their minds. Soon, the smell of bacon made Christian's stomach growl.

"Now that I've shared with you," Grandpa Pearson said, "I need you to fill in some of the missing pieces. Since I only have pictures, I need the four of you to give me the full story."

They moved into the kitchen to help Grandma Pearson set the table. Grandpa Pearson asked questions, and they answered them the best they could. Christian found it fascinating as his grandfather asked about the pictures he had seen. His grandpa acted shocked when they shared details to explain the images.

Breakfast hit the spot. Even though the clock displayed 3:30 in the morning, they ate more than they thought they would.

"You kids eat up," his grandfather said. "You have a long trip to make before the sun comes up."

They all stopped eating.

"What are you talking about?" Christian questioned.

"You need to finish up your breakfast and get home," Christian's grandpa replied.

Grandpa Pearson laughed, when he saw the puzzled expression on Christian's face.

"Well, we can't all show up at your parents' house together," Grandpa Pearson said. "That would really draw suspicion. Grandma and I will leave after church."

"If we don't show up at church," Christian's grandmother said, "well, those ladies in my Sunday morning Bible study will think we've been kidnapped. We didn't tell anyone we were gonna be out of town."

"You're coming to Red Oak?" Christian questioned in puzzlement.

"Sam, call Mr. Banner and tell him you're comin' home," Grandpa Pearson said. "No need to go into details. Just tell him that you'll be there before seven, and don't tell him about me. The less he knows, the better off you are. The phone is by the front door."

"But he's going to wonder where we are," Sam said nervously.

"Just tell him you're safe," Grandpa Pearson said. "If I'm gonna to help you, I don't want anyone else to know I'm involved."

"Well, maybe I shouldn't call him," Sam said. "Maybe we're better off if we just show up."

"No, we should call," Alexis said. "We don't want to show up if Mr. Banner thinks there is any danger. I'll call him."

Alexis walked over to the phone near the front door and dialed the number. The clicking of the old, rotary-dial phone echoed through the house as she turned the dial for each number. She concisely explained to Mr. Banner that they were safe, and she reiterated the lack of time to go into details.

"Everything is okay," Alexis said, returning from the call. "Mr. Banner didn't mean for us to leave the state. He wanted us to leave town for a while, stay off the roads until the trooper was out of the area. He thought the sheriff would be looking for kids driving around with alcohol in their cars, and he didn't want us to get pulled over late at night and asked a bunch of questions without him being there. He just wanted us to leave the area. I guess I jumped the gun. Sorry."

"I would rather we were extra cautious than caught," Sam said.

Grandpa Pearson still insisted that they leave right away. Christian was not sure why his grandfather felt like he needed to come to Red Oak, but arguing with him would not change his grandfather's mind. If Grandma and Grandpa Pearson wanted to come see Christian's family, Christian had no power to stop them. Besides, Christian liked having them around.

Grandma Pearson sent a box of crackers, in case they got hungry, and his grandfather grabbed some cold sodas from the basement refrigerator.

"You won't need to stop for anything on the way home," he said.

They all took a turn in the restroom before leaving. Grandpa Pearson slipped Christian a piece of paper before his turn in the bathroom.

When Christian walked into the bathroom, he opened the piece of paper and read it. His grandpa had scrawled the note hastily, making it tough to read.

Don't tell anyone about me. Be sure the other three don't say anything about me to Mr. Banner. No one needs to know.

Christian crumpled up the paper and threw it in the trash can. His grandfather had not met Mr. Banner, but Christian sensed his grandpa was concerned about the man. Christian guessed his grandpa wanted to protect his grandson, but he sensed something had tickled the worry button in the back of his grandfather's brain. Christian planned to ask Grandpa Pearson if he had seen something inside any of them that had him nervous, but the question had to wait until Red Oak since Alexis' ears seemed to be everywhere.

Christian washed his hands and headed out of the bathroom. They walked to the A-barn, and Grandpa pushed open the door. His grandfather made it look easier than when Christian had tried to pry those doors open upon their late night arrival.

Grandpa Pearson asked them to pull the car up to the gas tank in front of the garage. His grandpa had gas delivered to the farm every month, and even though it was illegal to utilize the gas for highway use, Grandpa Pearson topped off their tank before they headed home.

They spent most of the trip discussing Grandpa Pearson's amazing ability. Christian reminded The Three about his grandfather's request to remain anonymous.

"He doesn't want us to mention this to Mr. Banner or anyone else for that matter," Christian said, seriously.

"Relax," Alexis replied. "Our lives are full of secrets."

"Even from Mr. Banner?" Christian questioned.

"We keep things from Mr. Banner all the time," Alexis said. "It's the nature of the Phenomenon Child."

"I am sure there are things he keeps from us," Sam said.

"How do you know?" Christian asked.

"I can read his emotions," Sam replied. "There have been a number of times when I could tell something was bothering him, and he acted as if it was nothing."

"So, he isn't a phenomenon," Christian said, realizing he had never asked that question.

"Nope," Alexis said smugly from the front seat.

"Sometimes," Sam added, "I think it bothers him that he isn't like us."

Christian expected Mr. Banner to be relieved upon their arrival, but he greeted the teenagers with a harsh tone and looked like he had not slept all night. If Christian's parents had waited for him all night long, hugs and kisses would have gushed from his mother. Christian's father would have hugged him so hard his eyes may have popped out. Instead, Mr. Banner sat impatiently in the living room, when the four weary teens dragged in through the back door.

"Where the hell have you been?" Mr. Banner growled as Alexis, Ray, Sam, and Christian walked in exhausted from their trip.

"Hey, we erred on the side of caution," Alexis said, as she plopped onto the couch. "Isn't that what you have always taught us? We didn't know what to do."

"I just wanted you off the roads," Mr. Banner said, calming his tone. "I didn't want you to leave the state. I guess I should have been more specific. Where did you go?"

"My family owns a farm outside of Omaha," Christian said. "We figured it would be the best place to stay undetected, until we could contact you and find out what was going on."

"Things are getting too close for comfort around here," Mr. Banner said. "The sheriff stopped by last night, and I was assuming that was you guys I saw on the road when he was leaving. It's a good thing the soybeans have had an excellent growing season this summer. I received a phone call from the police this morning about the accident. They would like to come out and speak to Samantha, Alexis, and Ray about the party at the pond. I told them you guys had gone to visit friends, and they could stop by this evening. I was already uncomfortable with what was going on around here, and then you guys disappear all night."

"We're okay, for now," Alexis said.

"But we found out that someone can place Christian at the scene of the accident," Ray added. "Calvin plans to tell Mr. Matthews, the athletic director, about seeing Christian come out of the tunnel on the night of the accident."

"He didn't actually see Christian at the scene of the accident," Samantha said.

"But just the mention of seeing Christian at the tunnel will be enough," Ray added.

"To draw the attention of the police and the sheriff," Mr. Banner finished the sentence. "We will be leaving tonight. Christian, you must decide by this evening whether to join us or not."

"By tonight?" Christian asked. "That isn't enough time."

"If you don't come with us, you may be facing prosecution," Mr. Banner stated coldly. "You may not be seeing your parents for a long time, anyway."

"This is ridiculous," Christian stammered. "I didn't do anything wrong. I tried to save Strat, and now I'm in trouble. Why can't I just go to the police and explain what happened?"

"Listen," Mr. Banner stated, "I can't let these three assist you in proving your innocence. The risk is too great that some government agency would run across this story, their pictures, or their personal information. Then everything I have worked for would go up in smoke. Either you come with us, or you face the consequences on your own. I don't know how anyone in their right mind could stay here when they have a ticket to freedom with us."

"Some ticket to freedom," Christian fired back. "Trapped and on the run with you or trapped with my family. Either way, I'm sunk."

"You can forget family," Mr. Banner said. "Once the government cross-references this accident with what happened at the lake in South Dakota, you can expect a visit from them. Your only option is to join us."

"No pressure, huh?" Christian huffed, reminding Mr. Banner of his statement to Christian during their first meeting. "You said the decision was mine, and you were not going to pressure me into coming with you."

"Well, things change," Mr. Banner said in a low growl. "Your whole world is about to be turned upside down. Whether you come with us or stay here, your life is over as you know it. You can face it on your own, or you can make the smart move and leave with us tonight."

"I can't make that kind of decision," Christian said. "I need more time."

"You are out of time!" Mr. Banner yelled.

Christian had never seen this side of Mr. Banner, but he had not known him that long. If Grandpa Pearson had not said anything about his distrust of Mr. Banner, Christian probably would not have questioned Mr. Banner's motives. Christian could tell by Alexis's and Sam's reaction that they were not accustomed to this angry side of Mr. Banner.

"I think we all need to get some sleep," Samantha said in a calm voice. "We have been going one hundred miles an hour for a day. Let's get a little rest and sleep a couple of hours so our brains are functioning properly."

"Sounds good to me," Ray said.

"I'll set the alarm for noon," Alexis stated. "That will give us some down time. Christian, you don't need to decide right this minute. You have until this evening, right?"

Alexis geared that question for Mr. Banner.

"Yes, get some rest," Mr. Banner said, quietly. "I need to run into town to pick up a couple of things before we leave. You guys can sleep here, and then you can take Christian home so he can see his family. I'll send Ray into town tonight to find out what Christian's final decision is."

"Sounds good," Alexis said. "Now, let's all get some rest."

CHAPTER
17

Christian awoke to the unnatural buzz of an alarm clock. Even though the sound emanated from Alexis's room, Christian heard it quite clearly from the living room. Ray yelled over the sound of the alarm, and finally, Alexis shut it off. Samantha came down the stairs first.

"I know this is a difficult decision for you to make," Sam said.

"I just can't believe that this is my life," Christian replied. "I was hoping I would wake up, and the world would be normal again. I want to be in my own house with my family, and I want things to be the way they were."

"I know you do," Sam said, "but Mr. Banner is right. When Calvin Robinson saw you come out from that tunnel, all hope of going unnoticed went away. You stand to lose everything if you decide to stay."

"I know," Christian said, "but I can't leave my family and just disappear into thin air. They will spend a lifetime trying to find me, and I can't hurt them that way."

"Can you tell them?" Sam asked. "Can you tell them what happened?"

"Are you serious?" Christian responded. "Tell them that their son has the ability to breathe underwater, and because of that ability, the government could snatch me up and take me to Area 51 with the aliens?"

"So what are you going to do?" Sam asked.

"I don't know," Christian said.

Ray offered to give Christian a ride back into town. Soon Christian opened the front door to his own house. Church ended a long time ago, but his family had not come home yet. He figured they had gone out to eat for lunch, so he grabbed some clothes from his room and took a shower.

A shower had never felt so good. Christian realized a couple of days passed since brushing his teeth, so he scrubbed them twice to make sure they were clean. He decided to put his toothbrush and toothpaste in his duffel bag, just in case he decided to take off with the Banners. He double-checked the contents of the bag. Then he repacked it again, making sure he had enough clothes jammed in there for a week. Christian had no desire to leave, but he realized his options were limited. He had to decide whether or not to tell his parents. Maybe he would have Grandpa Pearson do it.

Grandpa and Grandma Pearson arrived as Christian finished his repacking. Christian heard Grandma Pearson checking to see if the house was occupied.

"I didn't expect you until later on this evening," Christian said as he climbed the stairs to the kitchen.

"Well, your grandpa insisted that we skip the Sunday school lesson after early church," Grandma Pearson said, "and you know how hard it is to change his mind."

"Glad you guys made it back okay," his grandfather said as he hugged Christian.

"Grandpa, Mr. Banner thinks this whole ordeal has drawn too much attention," Christian said. "He says they're going to be leaving tonight, and I need to go with them."

"He says you need to go with them?" Grandpa Pearson, said raising an eyebrow, "or you think you need to go with them?"

"I need to go with them," Christian said after a hesitation. "I don't know how I will explain it to my parents."

"Well, let's see if you actually need to leave with your friends first," Grandpa Pearson said with a smile. "You don't think I would drive all the way down here just to let you leave."

"What do you mean?" Christian said puzzled. "How can I stay?"

"Well, that boy you told me about, the one who saw you," his grandpa said.

"Yeah, what about him?" Christian replied.

"I may be able to change his mind about what he saw," Grandpa Pearson said, as his eyes flickered.

"How are you going to change his mind?" Christian asked.

"Your grandfather didn't tell you everything about his gift," his Grandmother answered.

"We just need to find him, and I will do the rest," Grandpa Pearson explained.

"You aren't going to hurt him, are you?" Christian asked, even though he hoped Calvin would experience a little pain.

"No," his grandpa said, flatly. "I just need a minute with him."

"Well, I could call Brad to find out if they're hanging out together today," Christian said, not believing anything could save him now.

"I don't want anyone else around," Grandpa Pearson said. "Just a minute with no one else near him."

"That will be tough," Christian replied. "I'll call Brad."

A quick call to Brad's house revealed that Brad had walked down to Ruby's house for the afternoon. Mrs. Matthews told Christian that Brad would be coming home for supper, and that Christian should try to call Brad then.

"If Brad's going to Ruby's house," Christian explained to his grandpa, "that means that Calvin will be there, too. Brad is dating Ruby's best friend, and Calvin is dating Ruby."

"So what does that mean?" Grandpa Pearson questioned.

"That means that Calvin will be walking home around suppertime," Christian answered.

"Do we know what time that will be?" his grandpa asked, raising an eyebrow.

"Yes, around five o'clock," Christian said.

Mrs. Matthews had given Christian a time to call Brad.

"Well, we have until five then," Grandpa Pearson said. "That means I have time for a nap. Christian, can you pull my pickup around to the back of your house?"

"You bet," Christian said as he grabbed the keys from his grandfather's hand and rocketed out the back door.

Grandpa and Grandma Pearson usually let Christian drive the truck around the farm. Christian learned how to drive at age eleven, and his grandfather considered him to be an experienced driver. Grandpa Pearson's new pickup dwarfed the one that was blown into the lake during the tornado. The extended cab added some length, but Christian knew he could handle it. He decided to back the truck into the spot under the tree. About the time Christian parked the truck, his mother and father came up the driveway. They honked when they saw the truck, and Christian could hear Kat and Ann cheering the arrival of Grandpa and Grandma Pearson. The Pearson family entered the kitchen about the same time Christian did.

Christian's mother showed a little concern with Grandpa Pearson giving Christian the keys to the pickup, but Grandma Pearson told Christian's mother that he had been practicing on the farm for a year now. Actually, it had been more than two years, but that fact would not have helped to put his mother's fears at ease. If only his mother knew what he had been dealing with for the last couple days.

The family spent the afternoon playing cards and board games in the dining room. Grandma Pearson spent some time reading books to Christian's sisters before she helped the girls bake cookies. For Christian's last afternoon with his family, life felt normal, but he still had no idea how to break the news to his mom and dad that he would be leaving. He didn't think Grandpa was going to be able to talk any sense into Calvin.

After winning three games of Rummy Tile, Christian's grandfather decided to let someone else win. Christian's father found a baseball game on TV, so the men moved into the living room. Grandma Pearson and Christian's mom went to the kitchen to get supper ready.

"Christian, let's go for a drive," Grandpa Pearson said, a few minutes later.

"You better not put him behind the wheel," Christian's mother grumbled from the kitchen.

"I'll do the driving," Grandpa Pearson responded with a laugh. "I just need a copilot to find the grocery store."

Christian looked at the clock and saw it was nearing five. He knew what Grandpa Pearson intended to do. His grandfather kissed his grandmother as the two of them passed through the kitchen, and they headed for the back door.

"We shouldn't be too long," Grandpa Pearson said.

"Supper will be ready by six," Grandma Pearson replied.

"How long do you plan to be gone?" his mother asked.

"Well, it may take a while to find the best ice cream in town," Grandpa Pearson answered.

Christian heard a chorus of cheers erupt from the other room. Kat and Ann were giving their approval for the decision to get ice cream. Even Christian's father cheered.

As Christian and his grandpa reached the truck, Grandpa Pearson sensed Christian had something on his mind.

"What's wrong?" Grandpa Pearson asked.

Christian climbed into the truck and closed the door, and his grandfather did the same.

"I don't know how I'm going to tell them," Christian said. "I don't know how I'm going to tell my family about my ability and about the danger I'm in."

Grandpa Pearson laughed as he started the truck and pulled out of the driveway.

"You may not be in any danger, if we can find Calvin," he said.

Christian wanted to know what his grandpa had planned, but he refused to go into any detail. Grandpa Pearson would let him know when the time came. They cruised past the Matthews's house and continued up Corning Street. As they neared the top of the hill, Christian saw Brad and Calvin walking in the opposite direction.

"There they are," Christian said, excitedly.

Grandpa Pearson took the next right and drove back down to Highland Street before turning again. He parked two houses up the street and waited. An eternity passed before Calvin appeared on the corner. Calvin crossed to the left side of the street, and Grandpa Pearson told Christian to jump into the back seat.

"Stay down," Grandpa said, as he put the pickup into gear.

The truck slowed as they reached Calvin, and Grandpa Pearson powered the window down.

"Excuse me," Grandpa Pearson said. "I can't seem to find where I'm going."

Christian's grandfather pulled his pickup to the curb on Calvin's side of the street, facing the wrong direction.

"What are you trying to find?" Calvin said from the sidewalk.

"Well, I'm from out a town, and my grandson lives around here," Grandpa Pearson said. "Let me see, what street am I lookin' for? I have that sheet somewhere in here."

Grandpa Pearson acted as if he searched for something in the seat. Christian peeked through the edge of the tinted window, as Calvin moved closer to the truck.

"Aw, I can't find that sheet," Grandpa Pearson said. "It's somethin' like Coolwater or Coolrock."

"Coolbaugh?" Calvin said, as he reached the open window.

Christian held his breath as he hugged the floor of the back seat. The carpet still had a new car smell to it. All conversation at the window ceased. Neither Grandpa Pearson nor Calvin Robinson said a word. The only sound Christian heard came from the cool breeze of the air conditioner and the purr of the engine.

"Well, thanks for your help," Grandpa Pearson said, pulling the pickup away from the curb.

Christian lifted himself off the floor of the back seat and glanced out the back window. He caught a glimpse of Calvin, who stood on the grass with a blank expression on his face. Cal just waited there, motionless, as Grandpa Pearson drove off. Calvin did not turn to watch the truck leave, and he did not start walking right away. Christian had seen that same expression on Ray and Alexis the night before.

"Now, let's go get some ice cream," Grandpa Pearson announced.

"What just happened?" Christian asked, completely puzzled by what had happened.

"I didn't tell you everything about my ability," his grandfather explained. "Not only can I look at the pictures in your mind, but I can erase them."

Christian sat in silence as he digested his grandfather's words.

Grandpa Pearson continued, "During the war, I found that if I focused on the images of those horrible events, I could destroy them, which came in handy when dealin' with the remnants of battle. There are some memories that should be forgotten. Unfortunately, I can't do it to myself."

"But you can do it to others?" Christian said as the puzzle pieces came together in his mind.

Grandpa Pearson had erased the image of Christian coming out of that tunnel.

"I promised myself to never do it again," his grandfather said, seriously, "but I realized the only way to help you was to do it one more time."

"So that's it?" Christian asked. "No more worries about being caught?"

"That's it," Grandpa Pearson said. "The picture of you comin' through that tunnel is gone forever."

Just like that, Christian's world righted itself again, and he leaned back and smiled. He would not have to leave with The Three and Mr. Banner after all, and he could live his life with no worries. Most importantly, Christian would not have to say goodbye to his family.

"What am I going to tell the Banners?" Christian wondered aloud.

"Tell them that Calvin is not going to tell anyone about what he saw," Grandpa Pearson replied. "Tell them that you are not going to go with them. Tell them you are stayin' put, but don't tell them about what I just did."

"I need to call them," Christian said.

"You can use my cell phone," Grandpa Pearson said.

"Since when did you get a cell phone?" Christian laughed, surprised at the thought of his grandfather moving into the technological age.

"Grandma said she doesn't want me to be without the ability to call her, like when we were in that tornado at the lake," his grandfather explained. "I think she just wants to make sure I'm not sneakin' off with some woman when I tell her I'm going fishin'."

Grandpa Pearson smiled.

Christian dialed the Banner house, and Sam answered.

"Sam, it's me, Christian," he said.

"Are you coming with us?" Sam whispered.

"No," Christian responded, "and you guys don't have to leave. I took care of the problem. Calvin won't be telling anyone about what he saw."

"That doesn't matter," Sam said. "Mr. Banner says we're leaving in one hour. He's been in a bad mood ever since he got back from town. Something is going on, and his colors are off the charts. Are you coming or not?"

"No," Christian said, again. "I'm not in danger anymore, and neither are you. We're safe. You guys don't have to leave."

"We leave in one hour," Sam said and hung up the phone.

"We have to go out there," Christian pleaded. "I need to tell Mr. Banner that they are not in danger anymore."

"We can't go out there," Grandpa Pearson said, coldly. "You are going to have to let your friends go."

Christian knew his grandfather was right. He would not be able to explain to the Banners what happened with Calvin. Christian's world had become normal again, but he stood to lose three friends in the process.

Grandpa Pearson pulled into the grocery store parking lot, but Christian waited in the pickup. Christian's elation of freedom had turned to sorrow. Grandpa Pearson quickly returned to the truck with two containers of ice cream, and Christian sat quietly as they drove home.

When the pickup turned onto his street, Christian noticed a black suburban parked in front of his house, and another black vehicle had positioned itself across the street.

"Turn here!" Christian yelled, pointing to the left.

Grandpa Pearson made a hard left onto a side street a couple houses up from Christian's home. Christian spied the white government plates on the suburban parked in front of his house.

"Who's at your house?" Grandpa Pearson asked.

Christian remembered the story about Charlie getting taken away in black vehicles.

"It's the government," Christian said. "They found me. But how?"

"What do you want me to do?" Grandpa Pearson asked.

"I can't go home," Christian answered. "You have to take me to the Banners's house."

Grandpa drove Christian into the country and stopped by a grove of trees on J Avenue.

"Take the phone," Grandpa Pearson said. "You wait here, and I'll call you. I'm gonna find out what's going on. Do NOT go to the Banner house until you hear from me."

Grandpa Pearson performed a U-turn and drove back to the highway. Christian sat in the safety of the trees with the phone gripped tightly in his hand. He could see the top of the Banner house from his position on the small hill. The sun slipped closer toward the horizon, and the hot day gave way to a cool breeze.

Christian found a spot to sit on the trunk of a fallen oak and peered up the road to the corner of J Avenue and Bluegrass Road. The minutes melted away as the sun continued to dip lower. Christian guessed that twenty minutes passed when the phone rang.

The words "Grandma's Phone" appeared on the screen.

"Christian, you need to get those kids out of that house," his grandfather's voice quivered. "You are all in danger."

"What's going on?" Christian said.

"No time for that right now," his grandpa responded. "You need to get those kids out of there, and Christian…"

"Yes?" Christian said.

His heart pounded in his chest, as he listened intently to Grandpa Pearson's words.

"You need to do it without Mr. Banner knowin'," his grandfather said. "Got that!"

"Without Mr. Banner knowing," Christian repeated. "Why?"

"No time! Just do it!" his grandfather said.

Grandpa Pearson hung up.

CHAPTER
18

Christian estimated the Banner's house to be less than a half a mile away from his hiding place. It would not take him long to cover the ground to get there. If he stayed in the rows of beans, he would easily get close without anyone seeing him. Christian decided to stay off the road as much as possible.

A corn field sprawled to the south from the grove of trees, so he decided to make his way to Bluegrass Road by walking three rows deep in the corn. This late in the year, the corn towered over him. By walking three rows into the field, Christian had the ability to keep an eye on J Avenue while staying concealed in the corn. When he arrived at the corner of Bluegrass Road and J Avenue, he knelt lower to the ground and moved to the edge of the field. He saw the windows of the Banner house to his left. Then he looked down Bluegrass Road straight out in front of him. He did not see any cars approaching from the right, down J Avenue, and he did not hear any car coming from his left. Christian hoped no one looked out the second story windows of the house as he slipped out of the field and into the ditch. Staying low to the ground, he crossed the intersection and leaped across the ditch on the opposite side of the road. Christian moved quickly on all fours like a gorilla and crouched in silence at the edge of the beans.

The bean rows ran parallel to the driveway which led to the house. This meant Christian would have to cross through the rows to get to the house, but it also meant he could not be seen from the driveway or the house. Christian crawled five rows into the field before making his way to the west. He wanted to get out of the line of sight of the bedroom windows overlooking the porch, and no windows faced him from the north side of the house, so it would be safer for him to take that path.

As Christian made his way across rows of beans, he peeked over the plants every couple of steps to keep his bearings. It did not take long for him to move out of the line of sight of those windows. From there, the pine trees created a wall of green. He moved across the rows, trying to make the plants move as little as possible. With no windows on the north side and thick pine trees to cover his movements, Christian decided to move faster. Soon, he crouched two rows from the end of the field, where he could see the open yard and the corner of the front porch. He moved further down the row until the pine trees shielded him completely. With the house blocked by the trees, he stood erect and darted along the tree line. Christian scanned the green wall for a space to look through to see what waited on the other side, but pine needles blocked every small opening.

Remembering the night at the pond, Christian worked his way around to the west side. Alexis had taken him through a narrow path in the trees that evening, and he hoped to find that opening. As he crept around to the west edge of the pines, he heard the back door on the house slam shut.

"Where are you going?" Alexis shouted.

Christian dropped to the ground. From this low angle, he saw through the dense underbrush into the back yard.

"I am going to make one last attempt to talk to Christian," called a voice as a car door opened.

Christian recognized Sam's voice. He could not let her go into town. He had to warn her of the danger.

"Sam, be reasonable," Alexis pleaded. "Mr. Banner said we need to leave tonight. Is Christian worth the risk?"

"Yes," Sam answered in tears. "He deserves one more try to talk him into it."

"You have to let him go," Alexis said. "It's his decision to make."

"He said on the phone that we didn't have to go, that it had been taken care of," Sam replied.

Tears dripped from Samantha's words.

"He said we weren't in danger anymore," Sam sobbed, "and Mr. Banner doesn't care. He just wants to leave him."

"I know, Sam," Alexis said, compassionately. "I heard your entire conversation."

"That's right!" Christian screamed in his thoughts.

Alexis heard the entire conversation.

Christian whispered, "Alexis."

"What?" Christian heard Alexis holler as she turned toward the door.

"Don't say a word," he whispered. "It's Christian. I am hiding in the bean field."

At his ground-level view, Christian saw Alexis turn her body toward his location.

"Do not tell Mr. Banner that I am here," Christian whispered. "Government agents came to my house. Do not let Sam go into town."

"Sam," Alexis commanded in a low voice. "Do not leave."

Sam must have recognized the change in Alexis's tone, because Sam walked away from the car.

"What is it Alexis?" Sam asked. "You look like you've seen a ghost."

The back door opened, and a deeper voice boomed from the back porch.

"I thought you were going into town," Mr. Banner called.

"I think I changed her mind," Alexis answered.

"Probably for the better," Mr. Banner said.

The back door slammed shut.

"How long before you leave?" Christian whispered to Alexis from his hidden spot behind the trees.

"We're leaving in half an hour," Alexis said loudly.

"I know Alexis," Sam said in irritation. "I'm standing right next to you."

Christian heard the phone ring inside the house. At the same time, the cell phone in his pocket vibrated, scaring the daylights out of him, and he almost yelled out loud.

Christian saw "1 text" flash on the screen. The message came from Grandma Pearson's phone.

Meet me at Johnson's pond in one hour. Dad

Moments later, Mr. Banner rushed out of the house.

"I have to run into town," Mr. Banner said, hastily. "I will be back in twenty minutes. Get all of the bags loaded in my vehicle and be ready to go when I return."

"Where are you going?" Sam asked.

"Alexis can tell you," Mr. Banner responded. "I am sure she heard it."

"The pizza is ready," Alexis said.

"Don't want to hit the road without something to eat," Mr. Banner shouted as he jumped into the door Sam left open on Alexis's car. "I'll be back in twenty. Then we can leave."

As soon as the car headed up the driveway, Alexis hollered, "Now, what is going on?"

"What are you talking about?" Sam questioned.

"Where is that stupid path?" Christian shouted.

"Christian!" Sam gleefully hollered. "What are you doing here?"

"Through here," Alexis called from twenty feet away.

"I would have found it sooner or later," Christian answered as he followed Alexis through the trees.

Sam greeted Christian with a huge hug.

"You did decide to come with us!" Sam said enthusiastically.

"Grab your bags," Christian ordered. "We need to get out of here."

"But Mr. Banner said we need to be ready to go when he gets back," Sam answered.

"I don't think you can trust Mr. Banner," Christian stated calmly as he entered the house.

Christian called for Ray to bring the bags down to the living room.

"What's going on?" Ray said, meeting Christian on the steps.

Alexis and Samantha followed close behind Christian.

"We need to go, now!" Christian shouted. "Agents just showed up at my house!"

"Government agents are here?" Ray gasped.

"Not yet, but they were ready to welcome me at my house," Christian said. "How could they possibly know about me? Did any of you call them?"

Alexis, Sam, and Ray shook their heads.

"No," Christian said, "so who is the only possible person who would do that?"

Alexis, Sam, and Ray just stared at Christian blankly.

"I'll tell you who," Christian said angrily. "Mr. Banner, that's who! Now, grab your bags and let's load that car of Mr. Banner's and get the H out of here!"

"But he is on our side," Sam said. "He looks out for us."

"Does he?" Christian asked. "Tell me who gets a call from a pizza place that the pizza is ready? Why wouldn't you pick it up on the way out of here? Sam, you told me that his colors were off the charts!"

Christian yelled and he sensed Sam's feelings had been hurt.

"Listen, I'm sorry I'm yelling," Christian said toning down his voice in a soft, but firm plea. "You told Mr. Banner that I had taken care of Calvin, and he still insisted on leaving. Not a half hour later, my grandfather drops me off out here because government agents are parked in front of my house. Then I get a phone call from Grandpa saying that I need to get you guys out of here without Mr. Banner knowing. For some strange reason, Mr. Banner needs to go pick up a pizza just before you're going to leave town. Doesn't this all seem a little strange to you?"

"How will we survive without Mr. Banner?" Sam asked.

Sam's fear appeared to grab hold of her firmly. All three of the Phenomenon Children in front of Christian seemed terrified by the changing circumstances, and Christian felt like he was the only one thinking clearly and objectively.

"In the auditorium, you took a gamble and shared with me that you knew I had a secret," Christian said calmly with his eyes focused on Samantha. "Ray asked you in the auditorium if you all could trust me. You took my head in your hands and told them that they could. Well, I need you to show that trust in me now. We need to grab your bags and get into that car and get out of here, and we need to do it now."

"But what if you're wrong?" Alexis asked.

"What if I'm right?" Christian replied.

A moment of silence passed between the four of them.

Ray moved past Christian quickly and raced up the stairs.

"I say we leave first and ask questions later," Ray hollered when he reached the top step.

They all rushed up the stairs behind him and grabbed their bags. Ray and Christian each heaved two duffle bags into the back of Mr. Banner's waiting SUV.

"Keys!" Alexis said.

"They're in the ignition," Ray called to her from the front seat.

"He never leaves the keys in the ignition," Alexis responded. The phone buzzed again.

They're coming!!!

Christian showed the message to Ray.

"Everybody in?" Ray asked as the engine started.

Christian handed the phone to Alexis.

"That is the second message I have gotten from my family," Christian said. "The first one was a meeting spot."

"Just point me in the right direction," Ray stated, as the vehicle flew up the driveway to J Avenue.

"Go right!" Christian shouted. "We can double back to the highway. It's the only way I know how to get there."

"Where?" shouted Sam.

"Johnson's pond," Alexis said as she showed the phone to Sam.

"It's a good spot to meet," Christian said as they turned left on a dirt road. "There is an old, abandoned farm house, and my father goes fishing there whenever he can. It's hidden from the road with a lot of trees around it."

The SUV roared at dangerous speeds across the narrow dirt track before slowing at a T-intersection.

"Go left," Christian said. "That will take us back to the highway. I'll have a better chance of finding the pond from there."

The gravel bounced against the bottom of the car as they raced toward the highway. Once they reached Highway 34, they turned right and drove three more miles. In the distance, the last remnants of the sun glinted off the white homes of a small town in front of them.

"Take the next right," Christian said. "You will have to pass through a narrow tunnel. The road curves back to the west, but there is a little tractor path into some trees."

The tunnel appeared ahead of them, and Christian breathed a sigh of relief. The vehicle passed through the tunnel, and Christian pointed out the left-hand turn to Johnson's pond.

"I would have missed it if you hadn't pointed it out," Ray said.

"That's why this is a perfect place to hide," Christian replied as he smiled. "We'll be safe here."

Ray followed the tractor path through the trees. The weeds climbed waist high across the entire road, except for the narrow set of tracks where fishermen's cars had reinforced an ancient, flattened path. The thistles scraped against the side of the SUV as they made their way to an open field on the other side of the trees.

"Back in over there," Christian said, pointing to an area of grass to the right.

Ray backed in so the car pointed toward the exit.

"Now what?" Ray asked.

"Now we wait," Christian answered. "We wait for my dad to show up."

"How long?" Sam asked.

"Until they come," Christian answered.

The sun set behind the trees, and slowly, the day faded to twilight. No one spoke. No words would calm their fears now. They escaped, not knowing whom to trust or what had happened.

"You know," Alexis said, "if you're right, this changes everything we know about Phenomenon Children. Everything Mr. Banner told us may turn out to be a lie. We will have nobody to trust and nobody to turn to."

"We have each other," Sam said, enthusiastically. "I trust all of you."

"Same here," Ray chimed in.

"Can we trust him?" Alexis asked, pointing an accusatory finger at Christian. "He led us out here. For all we know, he is leading government agents to us, right now."

"Alexis, that's unfair," Sam cried.

"She may be right," Ray said. "What if he cut a deal with them for his own freedom?"

Christian sat quietly because the headlights of a vehicle appeared through the trees on the road.

"If that is my father," Christian said, "will you trust me then?"

Christian turned in his seat toward Alexis. Even though he

could only make out the silhouette of her head, Christian could tell Alexis anticipated the worst.

"If that turns out to be your father, then I am with you," Alexis said, "but if it isn't, we are all screwed."

No one breathed.

The headlights turned off the road and onto the tractor path their SUV traveled down earlier. Ray started the engine.

"If it isn't someone we know, we're out of here," Ray said coolly, "and you can hitch a ride home, Christian."

Christian gasped when he saw the headlights did not belong to his father's car.

CHAPTER 19

"Easy Ray," Christian whispered, putting a hand on Ray's shoulder. "That's my grandfather's pickup."

The pickup pulled in next to the SUV, and the door opened. Christian's father rode in the passenger seat, and his grandfather drove. Grandpa Pearson quickly turned off the headlights and the dome light.

The four Phenomenon Children opened their doors and got out of Mr. Banner's SUV.

"Man, am I glad to see you," Christian's father said, as he squeezed Christian in a bear hug.

"We weren't sure if you were going to get here," his father said. "It took us a little longer than we thought."

"Dad," Christian said, as tears formed in the corners of his eyes, "I am so sorry."

"For what?" his father asked. "Your grandfather has filled me in on everything."

"He has?" Christian said in surprise.

"No, not everything," Grandpa Pearson hollered in a gravelly voice as he lumbered around the back of the pickup. "Just the important stuff. If your grandmother hadn't been there, your father probably wouldn't have believed a word of it. I guess I told too many fishin' stories to him when he was a kid."

"How's Mom handling it?" Christian asked.

"Well, she's ticked as all get out at the government," his father explained. "You know your mother."

Christian's father always reverted back to country slang when he hung around with Grandpa Pearson.

"You sound like a farmer," Christian said. "Ticked as all get out?"

"Well, shucks, I is jest tickled pink as a hog that you is all right," his father said with a smile.

"So all four of you made it," Grandpa Pearson said, relieved. "I was worried about you guys."

"What happened?" Alexis asked.

Grandpa Pearson decided to let Christian's father tell the story.

"Well, while Grandpa and you were out getting ice cream, a couple of guys show up in black suits, flashing government IDs. They were looking for you for questioning about the accident. While I'm explaining to them that you left with your Grandpa, they start tearing through things in the house. Christian, they found a duffel bag of yours downstairs. I was explaining to them that you stayed with friends the night before when your grandfather walks in through the front door with two containers of ice cream, telling me that some guy took his parking spot in the driveway. Your grandpa plays the senile old-man routine pretty good. They ask him about you, and Grandpa tells the agents that he left you at the square with some friends, that you were going to grab a bite to eat and then go see a movie. Well, they leave the house as quickly as they arrived, but they leave behind one agent to keep an eye on us.

"The next thing I know, Grandpa is talking to the agent real close, and the guy goes comatose. I mean, he just sits there and stares. Grandpa grabs the cell phone from Grandma and goes out back to make a call. Just as the guy is coming to, Grandpa hands me the phone and starts talking to the guy like he hadn't missed a beat. Grandpa decides that there is no need to wait for ice cream, and he starts scooping out heaping bowls of it. He even offered some to the agent. Kat and Ann are clamoring for a bowl, and your mother is chewing out this agent for harassing her family. Grandpa grabs the agents arm a third time and tells me to text you a meeting place. Grandpa sets bowls out for everyone, and I go to the bathroom to send you a text.

"When I come out of the bathroom, Grandpa is holding the agent's hand, and the girls are eating ice cream while watching a movie. Grandma explains what happened at their farm last night and starts talking about some secret that each of you possesses and that the government will stop at nothing to get this secret.

Grandpa fills in some other details while the agent sits at the dining room table with a bowl of melting ice cream.

"Those agents showed back up at the house, and they were not happy. I guess they turned that theater inside out trying to find you. You know, on Sunday, they show the movies earlier, and they stopped the whole movie searching for you.

"They are going crazy on the cell phones, calling all kinds of people. A car pulls up outside, and they all leave again, except that same agent they left behind the first time. Grandpa tells me to grab the duffel bag and my wallet just after he grabs the agent's shoulder. They have a van blocking the driveway, so we walk out to Grandpa's truck. I sent your mother, grandmother, and the girls up to the Matthews's house to hide until we got back, and we left."

"What about the agent?" Sam asked in the darkness.

"When we left the house, he was sitting in front of a soupy bowl of ice cream, just staring at the wall," Christian's father said in disbelief.

"Ken, why don't you wait in the pickup?" Grandpa Pearson said. "I need to talk to these guys alone."

"Okay," Christian's father replied, shaking his head in disbelief. "That was the darndest thing I have ever seen."

Christian's father climbed into the cab, and his grandfather led the four teens away from the truck.

"You four listen and listen good," Grandpa Pearson said sternly. "I don't like this Banner guy, and I suggest you stay clear of him. When I searched that agent's mind for images, I saw pictures of all four of you. From what I gather, these government guys know exactly who you are, and they're gonna be lookin' for you.

"You need to steer clear of main roads for a while. Go north 'til you reach the Interstate, but don't go into Omaha. They'll be lookin' for you there. Take the Interstate north toward Sioux City and find a highway to cut across northern Nebraska. Make your way back to the farm, but don't go *to* the farm. I'm guessin' that with us takin' off from your house, they'll come checkin' my place."

"Where should we go?" Christian asked.

"You remember your cousin David?" Grandpa Pearson said. Christian nodded, "Yes."

"I already called him," Grandpa Pearson continued. "He's building a house on my brother's farm. It sits back off the road in the trees. I called David, and he said you could stay there 'til we can find another place for you to hide out. You'll be able to hide that car out of sight, too. Blood is thick, so I didn't have to explain anything to David about what's goin' on."

Grandpa Pearson walked to the back of the pickup and grabbed a bag. He handed it to Christian.

"Your dad and I took all the cash we had and put it in that bag. Christian, I figured that's the bag you packed in case you had to take off with the Banners. I guess you're gonna have to leave after all."

Christian's emotions took over, and he hugged his grandfather and cried. Grandpa Pearson gave his grandson a tight squeeze before he let go of him.

"Whatever happens, you have to keep your wits about you," Grandpa Pearson said, and Christian sensed the tears welling up behind the Marine's façade.

"If you ain't got your wits, you got nothin'," Christian said, laughing through his tears.

"That goes for the rest of you, too," Grandpa Pearson said. "If you need anything, David will be checkin' in on you every day. Grandma said his number is programmed into the phone."

"What's going to happen to you?" Christian asked. "You guys are going to have to answer some questions when you get back."

"That's why I'm not tellin' your father anything," Grandpa Pearson responded. "He doesn't even know where you're goin'. I fought in World War II, so I can handle anything those government guys want to throw at me. I've lived a good life. They can't take anything away from me now. You just steer clear of the main roads and call David when you're close. He'll guide you the rest of the way."

Christian dropped the bag and gave his grandpa one last hug.

"Thanks," Christian whispered.

"Now, go hug your dad, and then get outta here. The sooner the better," Grandpa Pearson ordered.

Christian rushed over and opened the door to his grandpa's truck and his father got out.

"You all set?" his dad asked.

Christian hugged his father, and they both cried.

"Now, I'll see you when this whole mess is cleared up," Christian's father said through tears. "You four take care of each other. Look out for one another so I can see my son again."

"We'll follow you to the highway," Grandpa Pearson announced.

Christian's father kissed him on the forehead and told him to take care of himself again. Then his dad climbed into the pickup.

Christian picked up the bag and carried it to the car. The four Phenomenon Children climbed into the SUV, and Ray buckled his seatbelt.

Christian's dad rolled down the window, and Christian did the same.

"I love you, Christian," his father said.

"I love you too, Dad," Christian responded.

"Now get out of here," his father said as he rolled up the window.

The SUV followed the path to the road, and they passed through the narrow tunnel. The car quieted as they stopped at the highway. The SUV crossed the highway and headed north on the gravel.

Christian turned to see the headlights of Grandpa Pearson's pickup turn west. Christian could not help but think that he may never see his father or his grandfather again. The world changed so quickly sometimes and they all stood powerless to stop it. No matter how hard people wanted things to remain the same, they changed. In the span of one week, the world Christian knew had collapsed around him.

Christian bonded more with The Three who sat in the SUV with him than with any other friends he had known in his life. Even with each gift they possessed, they were unable to change what happened. Christian's father always said that life threw people a curveball every once in a while. Now he understood what his father meant. Things changed. Christian needed to adjust and move on.

The SUV slowed and rolled through an intersection of two gravel roads before continuing into the darkness. Alexis reached from the back seat and put her hand on Christian's shoulder.

"Thank you," Alexis whispered.

The SUV crested a hill before dropping down the other side. The drop reminded Christian of the effect a roller coaster had on his body when it climbed a steep incline before plummeting down the slope on a rickety wooden track. Alexis, Sam, Ray, and Christian had ridden a wild ride for the past couple days, and Christian knew the journey was not over.

They were Phenomenon Children, and they were on the run.

EXCERPT FROM BOOK TWO,
ON THE RUN

Christian wiped the water from his hands onto his shirt and pushed through the door to the fresh air. He could hear another shriek from behind the women's door, so he knew it might be awhile before the girls were done. Ray exited seconds behind him. Christian decided to walk over to the welcome center, even though Alexis had checked it when they arrived.

"Let's see if we can find a map," Christian said. "Maybe there is a stand on the other side."

Christian turned the corner, but he stopped cold next to the pop machine, and Ray bumped into him from behind.

Ray stammered, "Hey, why did you…" but quieted when he spied what had drawn Christian's attention. Another vehicle had pulled into the parking stall next to Mr. Banner's stolen SUV. Christian's feet suddenly became as heavy as cinder blocks, and an uneasy feeling nauseated his stomach.

The two boys stood wide-eyed as a man slowly moved toward them with his right hand reaching for something on his hip.

AUTHOR BIO

Chris Raabe is a graduate of Red Oak Community High School in Red Oak, Iowa. He received his Bachelor's Degree in Middle Grades Education from Peru State College and his Master's Degree in Educational Leadership from Doane College. Chris teaches seventh grade English and coaches high school softball in Omaha, Nebraska, where he currently resides with his wife and three daughters. *The New Phenomenon* is the first novel of *The Phenomenon Trilogy*.

ACKNOWLEDGMENTS

First, I would like to thank Lisa Pelto and the entire staff at Concierge Marketing. You showed me what real publishing is and put up with me through the process. Thanks to Julie Schram, a wonderful artist who is easy to work with.

I would not be the author I am without the honest input from my readers. A heartfelt thank you goes to Alecia Zauha and Brooke Scott for their young adult feedback on the second book of The Phenomenon Trilogy. I would also like to thank Megan Scott for a parent's perspective, Tiffiny and Brent Bradley for the encouraging reviews, and Lynette Dergan, a top notch middle school librarian who would tell me if this book stunk.

In addition, let me express my gratitude to Danielle and Courtney Kirgan and Dan and Vicki Koons for being who they are. These two wonderful couples were merged together to create Sam Banner's parents. These two couples have never met, and I find the irony of that to be quite funny.

And no thank you would be complete without acknowledging my wife and my daughters for putting up with me throughout the entire process of getting this book put together. They were extremely patient with me while I burnt the midnight oil to get this portion of the trilogy done.

Most importantly, I would like to thank my Lord and Savior, Jesus Christ. It is through Him that all things are possible.

THE PHENOMENON TRILOGY

SOLVE THE PHENOMENON MYSTERY.
PURCHASE ALL THREE AT
WWW.PHENOMENONTRILOGY.COM

Made in the USA
Charleston, SC
27 October 2013